THE
Flamboyant Fossil

Mike Cleary

Also by Mike Cleary

From the Banter Series:

Dick Clark Died Today
The White Dinner Jacket
The Heart of Everything
The Eloquence of Banter
The Grossly Unremarkable Ambrose Dowling

Non-Series:

Spiritual Mischief

For

FLAMBOYANT FOSSILS

EVERYWHERE

PROLOGUE

Dublin, Ireland

June, 1977

"Did I ever tell you I had the itchiest crush on you?"
Given the nature of this startling revelation, his tone was more matter-of-fact than fervent. He went on to explain: "I say itchy, my dear man, because my attraction for you was like one of those annoying itches you can never reach to scratch." He took a sip of his Campari and soda. "I say, you don't mind if I reminisce a little?"

"Reminisce away."

"We were in *Julius Caesar* together," he said. "Five years ago, I think."

"Aye, I remember. You were Murellus or Flavius. One of the two. You had lines and a toga. I was a Praetorian Guard. I had no lines and just stood there with little on."

"Oh, but you spoke volumes with your head erect and those shoulders... Oh my. I was really into big, burly, bearded blokes at the time and you fit into all three categories." Then he gave him a dismissive shrug. "But it turned out to be a phase. Hirsute no longer gets the water boiling."

Magnus Flaherty stared across the bar at his only customer. His name was PD Flanagan. Even though he was five-eleven, he insisted he was six feet. A slender man, he was fifteen pounds overweight which gave him a slight pudginess. It showed in his boyishly handsome face where his otherwise sharp masculine features were rounded out. All of this was wrapped in a faded Trinity College hooded sweat shirt, orange corduroys and a food-stained Burberry scarf. He called them his rehearsal clothes. HIs blue eyes were staring at his host while he patiently waited for a response.

"I thank you for picking such a discreet time to tell me this, PD. Another ten minutes and this pub will be overflowing and such a lovely reminiscence would have been lost in the happy drunken babble of my customers."

PD Flanagan spun around and noted the quietude. "What happens in ten minutes?" Realizing he knew the answer, he waved off his question. "No, no, don't tell me. The matinees are letting out. God, I *hate* matinees. I always have a harder time remembering lines in the afternoon. Man is meant to sleep between one and four."

The thirty-year-old publican brought him back to his opening statement. "So, PD, what prompted you to tell me all this now. We've known each other since when we were wee lads. We've been in a few plays together and you're a regular here. So, it's not like I don't see you."

"Settling accounts, I suppose," the young man murmured. He placed both hands on the bar, palms down; a sure sign an important pronouncement was coming. "Magnus, I am about to make a career change.

After this play I'm doing, I am giving up acting to pursue something that will be more financially rewarding."

Even at his young age, Magnus had heard more than his share of important pronouncements, gripping explanations of personal dilemmas and a litany of romantic oddities while standing behind the bar at the Sword and Parrot. The pub, which had been in the Flaherty family hands for generations, was located in the heart of Dublin's theater district, and prided itself as being the local for any number of noted actors, playwrights, directors and stagehands who all let their myriad eccentricities loose in the pub in one fashion or another.

"Why aren't you in rehearsals?" he asked his sole customer.

"I'm not in the first act," he replied. "Then I'm all over the place. I actually play a gay." PD found that terribly amusing.

"What's the play?"

"A new thing from Simon Towne. It's called *Little Things*. It's about this and that," he mumbled, indicating he still wasn't sure what it was about. "We open in a month at the Griffon."

"I read about it. Annie Doyle-Pearson has the lead."

"She of really bad breathe," PD said, making a face. "It's those godawful Russian cigarettes. At least, I don't have to kiss her. No wait, we do have two air-kiss scenes."

"I hate to bring this fascinating conversation to an end, but I've got to move along," Magnus told him, looking up at the clock. "So tell me succinctly what you're planning to do."

"I have always been good with numbers. I mean really good." he boasted. "To that end, I want to get into international finance. There's money to be made, Magnus."

The young publican pointed at him. "You're going to have to ditch the rehearsal clothes. This is a suit and tie world you're entering."

PD finished his Campari and soda and slid the glass toward Magnus. "I know. My plan is to have two bespoke suits made. Meantime, I'm scouring sales for shirts, ties, shoes and pocket-squares."

"Well, you'll certainly be one of the better dressed coming into this place," Magnus mused.

"Oh, my dear, I'm afraid I'll be frequenting other establishments that better fit the high-finance life-style. But I do promise to pop in on occasion. Meantime, you have my charming company while I'm in *Little Things*."

PD Flanagan paid up and left the Sword and Parrot. True to his word, he remained a regular through rehearsals and for the short time the play was in production. Alas, *Little Things* had been poorly received, cruelly reviewed and lasted only two weeks. The play's closing night was also the last time Magnus ever saw him.

Every once in awhile, a customer would inquire after the actor-turned-businessman. They would almost always ask if Magnus knew what the initials PD represented.

"I haven't the foggiest idea," he would tell them, wondering why after all those years together he never asked.

Chapter 1

"I've Got a Crush on You"

George Gershwin

"You look like a bearded turtle."

"Really? Well, I'll have you know, Ms Brand-new-on-the-job Executive Director, it was not the look I was going for when I dressed myself this morning."

"Come here and let me unturtle you."

Magnus Flaherty's wife, Maggie, for Christmas, had given him a beautiful purple and smokey-grey cashmere scarf. It was a lengthy thing, the kind that when worn became as much a fashion statement as a way of keeping warm. Magnus appreciated the wintry chill of January as he was most anxious to wear it as often as he could. So it was, because the third Thursday of the month served up a really brisk and shivery afternoon, he decided to bundle up in style and walk from the Midsummer Player's theater to Bar OSA where the Banter Foundation members would be gathering at four o'clock for their first meeting of 2019. Wrapping himself in the soft, plushy garment, he had poked his head into Sylvie Blanchard's office to tell her of his plan.

The pixieish, post-grad student, having playfully criticized his attire, rose from her desk to come around to where Magnus was standing.

"Actually, you look kinda cool," she said, retreating from her mischief.

"Thank you for that," he said gruffly.

"It's the way you have this scarf wound around you. It makes you look terrapinish," she said, giggling as she began to unwind his scarf.

Freeing him from it, she let the scarf unfurl. Her short height prevented her from letting it reach its full length, so she handed it to the the six-foot-three Irishman, instructing him to fold it in half and return it to her. She then put it around him, a task that required getting on her toes to reach his neck. Taking the two loose ends, she slipped them through the loop and tightened the scarf. She loved the cashmere feel and wanted to keep petting it, a gesture sure to be misinterpreted. Instead, she gave it an extra tug, adjusting the ends to show both the purple and the grey. That done, she looked up at Magnus and declared him fit to travel.

In an almost childlike voice, she added with a blush, "That's the first time I ever dressed a man."

"If there had to be a first time, I'm glad I'm the bloke. Technically, though, it was more of a wrapping than a dressing," Magnus said as he turned to look in the small mirror on the back of the door. "Aye, that's a much better look. Dashing, I'd venture to say. Thank you, Sylvie."

The new theater manager had one question to put to him before Magnus departed for Bar OSA. "I'm curious. What inspired you to pick the Shylock story? I thought we were committed to doing *Taming of the Shrew?*"

He took one of the two folding chairs that served as seats for guests in the tiny office. "I *could* tell you there's an emotional intensity, a gutsy and raw depth to *The Merchant of Venice* that appeals to me, but the truth is I never really liked *Taming of the Shrew* and I always wanted to direct the Shylock story as you called it." He shrugged his shoulders nonchalantly and added, "So I changed it. Besides, I think our crew can do more justice to it. One bonus is I can put a halt to the Banter Foundation's relentless campaign for me to cast The Redhead as Kate."

"Hey, what about me," she exclaimed while pointing to herself. "For the last two weeks I have been listening to my sister rant and rave as if *she* were the shrew. She even had me play Pistachio one night."

"Petruccio. It's Petruccio."

"I know. I just like calling him Pistachio."

"Well, tell your sister I'd like her to play Portia."

Sylvie clapped her hands. "That's great. She'd be ideal, Magnus. You know the Shylock play appeals to me because in the end, it's women to the rescue."

"They do, don't they? Come to the rescue, that is. One added note: Maggie thinks we ought to pick a different era. She suggested the late Thirties, early Forties. She admits her main reason is the fashions of that time. She loves the clothes both the men and women wore. As far as the story itself, it's relevant in any time period," he said, rising slowly with a barely audible groan from the small chair. "Anyway, I'm out of here. Off to hoof it to Bar OSA where a single malt whisky awaits."

Sylvie Blanchard watched as Magnus left, thinking he was much too big a person for the small office. She wondered if she should have told him to lock the front door as she was the only one in the theater. She decided she'd check it herself. Then she promptly forgot about it.

Sylvie Blanchard had come to her position in a most unusual manner. Seeking help in dealing with a professor known for inappropriate behavior, she had befriended a retired professor, Ambrose Dowling, who helped her get through a distinctly uncomfortable period of her life. Having lost a teacher's assistant position at Cal, she turned to Ambrose, who as a member of the Banter Foundation, got her a job as Magnus Flaherty's assistant at the theater. Her energy and enterprise caught everyone's attention and when the theater's founders, the Blumenthals, otherwise known as Oberon and Puck, decided to retire, despite having one semester left to earn her masters 'degree, she was hired to be the new executive director.

With Magnus on his way to Bar OSA, she dove straight away into the daily minutiae of operating a theater, even one that didn't currently have a play in production. Sylvie's total attention was given over to whatever was on her computer screen. The theater was eerily quiet which made the sound of the front door opening and closing so frightening to her. What followed were loud footsteps. Upon hearing them, Sylvie's eyes widened and her stomach tightened. What had concerned her were the street people who, battling myriad mental conditions, sometimes wandered the otherwise busy but tranquil neighborhood. This would not be the first time someone unbalanced or off their meds tried to enter the theater when it was, for all intents and purposes, closed.

"I don't know who you are, but I, uh, have a gun," she shouted tremulously, wondering whether she kept the fear out of her voice. "And I know how to use it."

The footsteps stopped. They didn't sound close to her office. Quiet had returned to the theater. Sylvie dared not move. She sat still, frozen in place behind her desk. "Oh shit, like that was totally stupid," she said, admonishing herself.

Then she remembered the footlocker in the far corner of her office. A week ago, the Blumenthals had purchased the locker full of various small stage props from a theater that had just closed in Yolo County. She sprang from her chair and headed toward it. Inside the large container were odd items like a dial phone, a man's beret, an oversized bra, a decorative dagger, two Renaissance women's wigs, a toaster, and a stage prop pistol. She grabbed the fake gun and returned to her chair,.

No sooner had she sat down than a male voice broke the silence. "Please, young lady. And I say young lady as there is a spring-like freshness to your voice. As regards this intrusion, I am here seeking information. Perhaps, we can chat. As regards your gun, I myself am unarmed except for a brolly, which in your language is an umbrella."

His voice was resonant. A joy to listen to, she thought. Whoever it was, he had to have been on the stage as his accent was what's called in Britain Received Pronunciation. There were, though, tiny traces of an

Irish brogue that could be detected, making it all the more charming.

Realizing she wasn't dealing with a malevolent intruder, Sylvie decided to invite him in. "My office is in the back of the theater. You are just steps away. And I am still armed," she reminded him.

He laughed lightly. "I'm much too charming to be shot."

The older man stopped in the doorway to her office holding his umbrella in a rakish manner. He stood there silent, almost as if he wanted Sylvie take him all in before introducing himself. A self-admitted old soul who loved the movies of the Forties and Fifties, Sylvie thought his pose and dress was that of a film star who had just stepped out of a movie poster. It was fitting because he enjoyed likening himself or parts of himself to famous actors. For example, his eyes were a dull blue and certainly not the mesmerizing, deep blue of the actor Peter O'Toole, although he drew a similarity to them. His hair was thinning and grey and looked much like Anthony Hopkins 'mane, so he would tell you. While good-looking, his face had aged and he had earned just enough wrinkles to let him think he resembled Ian McKellen. That comparison particularly delighted him. This unusual amalgam of features was suitably stuffed in a bespoke deep-blue pin-striped double-breasted suit. His pink shirt boasted white French cuffs and a starched white collar. A bright yellow bow-tie, worn carelessly, a silk pocket-square cascading out of the suit's pocket and his umbrella finished his outfit.

Sylvie, of course, just saw a dapper gent standing in her doorway. She did think he bore a slight resemblance to David Niven, but she decided not to tell him. Anxious to have him break his pose and silence, she waved him in with the pistol and pointed to a chair.

"I'll make you a deal," he began. "You put that prop gun back wherever you store it and I will let go my umbrella. While one would think they can't do much damage, they can be dangerous."

Sylvie opened the bottom drawer of her desk and placed the gun in it. "I don't even know if it has blanks in it," she laughed. "Sometimes we have questionable people in the neighborhood and they can be threatening."

"When I got out of the taxi, I saw a man talking to a parking meter in front of the theater," he said casually. "He was most agitated. I can't imagine what the meter did to offend him."

"There you are, you see," she said. "That's why I overreacted when I heard the door open and heard your footsteps."

She watched as he sat down, placing his brolly against her desk. He seemed so at ease. It had always been her impression that the more dressed up you were, the stiffer you acted. That certainly was the case for her. But there was no starchiness to the stranger in her office. He was so comfortable, she was convinced he came out of the womb dressed.

Looking about the tiny room and its spartan furnishings, her guest said, "You know, my dear, you really deserve an office more commensurate with your position. I am correct in thinking you run this fine establishment?" His smile was ingratiating.

"I am the executive director," she said proudly. She liked saying it, but had few opportunities to. "My name is Sylvie Blanchard." She extended her hand toward him. "And you are?"

They were close enough that he had no trouble shaking her hand. "And I, young lady, am Phineas Flanagan."

Sylvie faked a cough to cover up her laugh. "Excuse me," she said. "I'm getting over a cold. The cough lingers. What can i do for you, Mr. Flanagan?"

"I have come in search of a Magnus Flaherty." It was a sentence dripping in theatrical flair. Reaching inside his coat pocket, he pulled out a newspaper clipping. "This Magnus Flaherty, to be exact," he said, handing it to her.

She recognized it immediately. Two days earlier, the *San Francisco Chronicle* did a piece on Magnus and his wife, Maggie Leyton. It was a flattering article that gave the Midsummer Players and the theater much needed publicity.

"That's our Magnus," she said with a grin. "How do you know him?"

Phineas folded his arms and crossed his legs. "As you know, he owned the Sword and Parrot, a pub in Dublin's theater district..."

"Oh, he still owns it, His sister runs it for him," she interjected.

"I'm delighted to hear that," he replied, "When we were young, in between pouring pints of Guiness, he would snag a minor role in a play. Occasionally, we trod the boards together. While he dabbled in it, I was earning my keep as an actor and stayed quite busy." He paused and thought a moment. "I should also add that we were also school chums. So you might say we know each other well."

"Are you still acting?" she asked, appreciating his honesty.

"It was a passion of mine when I was young, but I gave it up decades ago and went into finance," he answered. "Pardon the pun, but It's an enriching occupation if you.... Dear me, I am blabbing on and I can see you are busy."

"Magnus isn't here right now," she told him. "I could try phoning him, but he often ignores calls on his cell. He's not a big fan of them especially when he's enjoying his single malt scotch. It's Tallisker, if you want to buy him one."

Phineas sat forward on his chair, "Ah, and that's what he's doing right now. I'd really like to surprise him. If you could tell me where he's imbibing, I can join him there." He sent a warm, trusting smile across the desk. "I assure you he won't object to our reunion, especially if I am buying."

Sylvie thought a moment. She liked the well-dressed man sitting across from her. He seemed harmless and certainly entertaining. Magnus might enjoy seeing him. She knew her patron well enough that if he didn't want anything to do with Phineas Flanagan, he would have no problem sending him on his way. Thus, she saw no reason not to tell him about Bar OSA. She also instructed him to lock the front door when he left.

***

The Banter Foundation members 'meeting at Bar OSA was scheduled to start at four-thirty. Magnus had a good twenty minutes to enjoy two fingers of Tallisker before they arrived, usually en masse. They reminded him of ducks, all falling in line and waddling in together, ready to quack loudly over cocktails. Their headquarters was the far end of the bar near the entrance.

The Banter members had Dick Clark to thank for funding their deep-pocketed foundation. On April 18th, 2012, the TV star died. The news of his passing reached Bar OSA in North Berkeley where a disparate but congenial group that included Walt Gillespie, a local plumber, George Crowder, a retired Oakland Raiders' offensive lineman, Ambrose Dowling, a professor emeritus from Cal and Mike Gearon, a recently retired radio personalty, was having a late afternoon drink. The owner, Duffy Hart, called them his Inbetweeners as they usually dropped in an hour or so before five when the place got busy. They were a talkative and humorous foursome and he enjoyed kibitzing with them. That afternoon, the main topic had been Dick Clark. They all had their own memories of the eternally youthful television star which they shared. It also happened that there was a nationwide lottery drawing that night that was closing in on half a billion dollars. The five of them decided it was only fitting to remember him by each tossing in a dollar and buying five tickets with numbers gleaned from the television personality's life. They entrusted Ambrose Dowling, the oldest of the group, to buy the lottery ticket. Because they all knew they hadn't the slightest chance of winning, they would have never known if Ambrose even purchased the tickets. There was some truth to that as the professor had invested their five dollars in the California lottery drawing by mistake. He was delighted to admit his faux pas, though, as the five of them ended up winning $188,000,000.

The men and their wives were a curious lot. First, they were all financially comfortable and either retired or nearing it. Second, they all had a keen and moral sense of what is enough. Although, it did take a bit of time to bring Walt Gillespie around to their way of thinking. They handled their winnings in a unique way; each taking an amount that enriched them personally and the remaining millions, of which there were many, went into the formation of the Banter Foundation, so named because it all started with barroom banter.

They soon earned a reputation as being an iconoclastic group. They were mavericks in not only the way they dispensed funds but to whom. There was no red tape, no administrative or management costs. Dollars from the Banter gang went directly to the charity. In six plus years, because money was involved, the Banter Foundation also found themselves in all manner of adventures, many of which dealt with righting moral or social wrongs. In that time, they'd brought to heel a sleazy financial advisor who was skimming money from the accounts of his elderly clients, an amoral and bullying property developer intent on denying Oakland affordable housing and a narcissistic, sex-obsessed university professor who preyed on his attractive female students.

They were particularly excited to be the major patrons of the Midsummer Players located in a church-turned-theater called Ashby-upon-Avon. It was there that Magnus Flaherty directed plays by the Bard. There was also something eerily odd about their relationship to the theater. It was much discussed among them. For whatever reason, after *As You Like It, Hamlet* and *King Lear* ran, they realized they had confronted situations that loosely paralleled the storyline of whatever Shakespeare play the Midsummer Players were doing at the time. Would it happen again with the theater's next production?

Magnus had the bar to himself as Duffy Hart had taken a phone call. It was just he and his single malt. Like he did whenever he and Mr. Tallisker had a quiet moment together, he first prayed before letting his mind wander. He often wondered how this all came to be, but it had and he'd been at it for years. When he prayed, he always began with a sincere declaration of gratitude. After that, his entreaty was all-encompassing. Prayers said, it was time just to muse. HIs sister. who was managing the pub in Dublin, had recently emailed him, sharing with him a funny childhood experience that involved Father O'Malley, their parish priest. It got Magnus thinking about his altar-boy days when the kindly father would always grab his hand when he poured the wine from the cruet to get more than Magnus thought reasonable. He remembered once, when he and his fellow altar boy were alone in the sacristy, they tried the communion wine. It was truly awful and the experience put him off wine for years. When he came of age and was working in the pub, Father O'Malley, a great fan of single malt, would always say to him, "Magnus, this is so much better than that foul-tasting wine you used to pour me when you were a wee lad."

Magnus got no further in his amusing reverie as someone had sneaked up behind him and in a rather pleasant voice began to sing, *"I've got a crush on you, sweetie pie..."*

Chapter 2

"With mirth and laughter, let old wrinkles come."

William Shakespeare

"And now don't you think the sainted Ella Fitzgerald is turning over in her grave," Magnus trumpeted, his brogue thickening. His back was to PD Flanagan and as if he were memorizing the labels, he continued to stare at the colorful mix of liquor bottles shelved behind the bar. He wasn't going to give the intruder of his private moment the pleasure of his being surprised by spinning around with a welcoming exclamation. "As for me, I thought your singing was respectable enough, but I was also of a mind that your infatuation for big bearded blokes like me ended decades ago."

"Oh, it did, it did," the stranger exclaimed cheerily. "The warbling was just I trying to be witty and wise in surprising you. By the by, I am no longer PD Flanagan. Years ago, I came to terms with my first name."

"So I finally get to know what P and D stands for?"

"For God's sake, turn around, Magnus," he snapped irritably. "This isn't some stodgy play where the director has staged a pivotal reunion."

Magnus inched his high chair away from the bar and turned slowly to face him.

Flanagan smiled at his old friend. "That's better. Now we come to the part where you say something like 'Oh, what a nice surprise.'But, of course, in your own words."

"Oh, what a nice surprise," Magnus said soberly, surveying a man who looked frighteningly like Noel Coward.

"Always the smartass publican, aren't you?" he said. "I know you're not the most emotional of men, but I thought I might have gotten a rise out of you after all these years."

Magnus 'smile stretched wide. "And indeed, you have, PD." He extended his hand and Flanagan shook it. Checking him out from top to bottom, Magnus observed, "You're certainly not the PD Flanagan I remember. Look at you. It's like you're the *Taoiseach* himself or one of those old, blustery farts in the *Seanad Eireann.*"

Flanagan leaned his umbrella against the bar. He pointed to the chair next to Magnus. "Mind?" he asked.

"Aye, not at all. Sit down and start explaining yourself."

"First, be assured I am not trying to emulate the Prime Minister or one of those fussy fossils in the Senate. However, I can see how my attire might suggest that." Pointing to Magnus 'drink, he said, "I was told by your charming theater manager that that is a Tallisker."

"Aha, that's how you found me," he replied, looking into the kitchen. Spotting Duffy, he signaled him to come out. "If PD is off the table, maybe you ought to start by telling me what I should call you."

Sitting ramrod straight and thrusting his shoulders back, he announced proudly, "I, sir, am Phineas Flanagan and I have been him since escaping the theater and entering the world of international high finance."

"Phineas," Magnus echoed. He shook his head in amazement. "I would have never guessed. What about the D?"

"Dermot. It's an old family name dating back to the Neanderthals," he answered. "When I was a wee lad, saddled with those titles, I was fair game in school. I was prey, Magnus. You know what sniveling little beasts children can be. So early on, I decided to just go with my initials. Now, gone are the initials and the middle name. I wear Phineas as proudly and confidently as I do these clothes."

"Your name reminds me of that Trollope novel," Magnus told him.

Surprised by his comment, Flanagan threw up his hands and grinned. "Phineas Finn. You know the novel?" he exclaimed. "Oh, I had a long-running crush on that wry, debonair Irish MP. He's the reason why I dropped the D and stretched the P in my name to Phineas."

"You called, sir." Duffy Hart broke in as Magnus was slow in responding to his friend's explanation.

"Ah, Duffy, I want you to meet someone I knew back in Dublin many years ago," Magnus said. "This is Phineas Flanagan." He turned to his bar mate. "Isn't there also a Roman numeral after your name?"

"I am Phineas Flanagan the Fourth," he told them both, not without a hint of pride. "Too alliterative and extremely difficult to say rapidly, so I ignore it."

That said, he extended his hand to shake. "Duffy, it is a distinct pleasure. I believe I'll have a Tallisker, too. And put Magnus 'drink on my tab, please."

Duffy placed his drink on the bar. "There's no tab. As a first-timer, Mr. Flanagan, the drink's on the house as I am the house. Have Magnus bring you in more and then I can charge you. Now, if you'll excuse me, I have phone calls to make."

Phineas nodded and waved him off. Turning to Magnus, he studied him for a long moment. "You know, considering our age, I must say we both look exceptional. While we have adopted different styles when it comes to what we drape ourselves in, we have what I would call *presence.* As for you, my dear, that scarf is positively luscious."

Magnus laughed heartily. "Thank you, Phineas. The truth of the matter is when I remove these clothes I'm wrapped in, my age becomes brutally apparent. My body is a wrinkly old thing in desperate need of ironing. And you might want to have some spot removers at the ready."

Phineas laughed at his friend's comment. Leaning back, he folded his arms. "'Let me play the fool. With mirth and laughter let old wrinkles come,'" he said, loud enough to catch the attention of others at the bar.

"'And let my liver heat with wine, rather than my heart cool with mortifying groans,'" Magnus added. "That's Graziano from the *Merchant of Venice.*"

"Indeed, and he's talking to Antonio who's complaining in much the same manner as you were, my dear friend." Phineas dipped his nose in his glass to catch the single malt's peaty, smokey fragrance.

Magnus was just about to tell him that the Midsummer Players were going to tackle that Shakespeare play when, after taking a healthy slug of his Tallisker, Phineas placed a hand on his knee.

"Look, old chum, I must run. I have a meeting in San Francisco and there's your traffic. I understand it is nightmarish," he said, checking his watch, a glittery gold Rolex. He pulled his smartphone from his inside coat pocket. "I'm sure there's an Uber somewhere nearby, one of the more luxurious ones, I hope."

"Can't you stay for awhile?" Magnus asked with a sincerity that surprised him. He found himself truly excited about Phineas Flanagan's sudden appearance. Perhaps, it's just plain old-fashioned curiosity, he thought. Nevertheless, he implored him to stay. "We have a lot to catch up on. Besides, there are some people coming here in just a few minutes and I think you'd enjoy meeting them."

A black SUV was eight minutes away. In that time, Phineas gave Magnus his mobile number, telling him that he was staying at the Four Seasons in San Francisco and would love to get together whenever Magnus could break free. Magnus also took advantage of the time, sharing with him a condensed, but colorful version of the Banter Foundation history. It so intrigued Phineas Flanagan, he decided to put off his meeting in San Francisco. In seconds, Uber was canceled and a text took care of his meeting.

"It's done, Magnus, I am free and clear," Phineas announced joyfully, putting his phone back in his coat pocket. "I am happy to report I am all yours until you're ready to send me packing."

Magnus stopped smoothing the sides of his beard, a habit he was trying to break. "All well and good," he said enthusiastically "But I do have two quick questions. I'll save the others for later."

"Fire away."

"What brings you to the Bay Area and how long do you plan on staying?"

Phineas pursed his lips and thought. They were two obvious questions. The first would take some explaining and certainly Magnus deserved to know the answer in detail. But not right now. "My reason for coming here is somewhat complicated. How long I stay depends on how long it takes me to uncomplicate things," he replied, his tone serious. Taking a quick sip of his drink, his lightheartedness returned, he added,"But I do have another answer to the second question on how long I plan on staying."

"I can't wait to hear the details of the first, but I'll take your next answer," Magnus laughed.

"Magnus, dear fellow, I promise full disclosure when the time's right. But know this, I am now retired and time is mine. So to answer the second question, I can stay here for as long as I wish."

Bar OSA was no longer the quiet, unpopulated place it was when Magnus first arrived. The Banter Foundation members all managed to be at the front end of the bar, their official clubhouse, by four-thirty. They were busy greeting each other with kisses and hugs and ordering a mix of standard and exotic cocktails. This January assembly was purely social. A month previous, they had discovered Zoom and the efficacy of video conferencing. Thus, all their business was now conducted virtually and not in a very public restaurant. They had noticed Magnus and an unidentified gentleman sitting at the other end of the bar. They were anxious to reconnect with Magnus but they were more excited to learn about the well-dressed stranger.

The rough-hewn Walt Gillespie with the messy, uneven crewcut spotted them first. The two men had slipped off their barstools and were making their way to the other end of the bar.

"Hey, Magnus, are you going to thrill us all and tell us The Redhead is going to be Kate in your next play?" the retired plumber asked.

As he neared the group, Magnus answered, "Walt, I'll buy your drinks for a month if you can tell me the name of the play?"

Walt's usual grimace disappeared. "No problem. It's the *Taming of the...*" He paused. "I know it begins with an S. It's something like *The Taming of Shrek,*" he said.

Mike Gearon laughed with the others. "Walt, you've been watching too many animated movies."

Sounding defeated, Walt uttered, "Well, it's something like that."

Magnus spoke up."It is *The Taming of the Shrew*. I'm glad you asked that question, though. I do have an announcement to make about it. But first, I want to introduce you to an acquaintance of mine from Dublin. We haven't seen each other in forty plus years. Back in the Seventies, we often found ourselves in the same play. And many an evening it was when Phineas was on the other end of the bar at the Sword and Parrot. I'd like you to meet Phineas Flanagan."

They were most welcoming with a battery of cheery hellos. Ambrose Dowling, the elder of the group, spoke up first. "Mr. Flanagan, you are indeed a 21st Century version of Phineas Finn, he of Anthony Trollope fame."

The dapper and glib Phineas Flanagan, who seemed to command the room by his sheer physical presence, responded. "Professor Dowling, he is one of my literary heroes."

Ambrose beamed. "You know who I am, Mr. Flanagan? I'm flattered."

Magnus responded this time. "No, professor, he'd not heard of you until I told him about you earlier. To save time, while we were at the other end of the bar, I pointed out to him each one of you by name and a brief biography. This way, you only had to meet him."

"But he had to remember all of us," Debbie Crowder commented

"Yes, I did, Mrs. Crowder," he replied. "I was told you were a former Oakland Raiderette. I'm not sure what a Raiderette is or does, but it certainly sounds naughty."

And so it was, like someone performing an enthralling parlor trick, Phineas Flanagan was quizzed by almost all of them as to their identity. Only Walt abstained as he was still smarting from his earlier faux pas.

Duffy and his wife were behind the bar. Both were anxious to hear about the Midsummer Players 'next production as they were eager to hear if their relentless campaign to convince Magnus that The Redhead should be the next Kate paid off. It had started out as a lark. Everyone knew Caitlin Hart, aka The Redhead, was hot-tempered and fiery, and the more they talked about her, the more convinced they were that she would excel as Katerina. Thus, the more they pestered Magnus.

Duffy waited patiently for that moment when there was a collective pause and then jumped in. "So, Magnus, Walt asked about your new play. We're looking forward to what you have to say."

The tall man stood apart from the rest that now crowded the bar. "This will come as good news to some and bad news to others. In a bit more than a week, we will go into rehearsals for another Shakespeare classic..." He laughed at his word choice. "Silly of me to call them classics. They all are. Anyway, we are trading one comedy for another. I have decided to shelve *The Taming of the Shrew* for a time."

"Let me guess," hollered Walt. "You're going to do the Odd Couple?"

"Close, Walt," he laughed. "Duffy, do you have a drink that would put him on mute?"

"Sorry, just fooling around," Walt said. "So, what are you planning to do?"

"The *Merchant of Venice*."

Their reaction was mixed. There were murmured groans and a couple of loud cheers, the loudest being from Ambrose Dowling who was a fan of the play. But no one was happier than The Redhead, who upon hearing the news, reached up and kissed her husband. Then she ran the length of the bar and came around to where Magnus was standing.

"You are an absolute doll," she shouted with glee." With that, she grabbed his scarf with one hand and kissed him on the cheek. "Thank you, thank you." Like Sylvie Blanchard earlier, she found the cashmere irresistible. Unlike Sylvie, though, she decided to keep stroking it, half expecting it to purr.

"And just what are you doing with my large Irishman, young lady?" asked an attractive woman who had suddenly appeared at Magnus 'side. She was five-feet-two, eyes of blue. Missing were a turned-up nose and turned-down hose. Instead, her nose was small, straight and symmetrical, and she rarely wore pantyhose. A well-known Hollywood screenwriter, Maggie Leyton was the wife of Magnus Flaherty. Expected back in Berkeley on Friday, she decided to surprise him by coming back early.

Recognizing who was asking the question, The Redhead continued to pet his scarf. "It reminds me of a furry snake," she said. Letting it go, she moved toward Maggie and gave her a warm hug. "Welcome back from hedonistic, hard-drugging and hard-drinking Hollywood, Maggie, and welcome back to genetically modified, gluten-free, organic Berkeley. Are you up for a Negroni?"

"Oh, am I," she said excitedly. "So what I have I missed? The scarf-fondling must have been inspired by something."

"Aye, and it couldn't be because The Redhead finds me irresistible?" Magnus asked.

Maggie slipped her hand into his. "The most important thing is I find you irresistible and that's why I came home early, " she said sweetly. Then she took some air out of the romance by adding. "It's not the only reason but I'll explain later. Now I'm curious. What have I missed?"

The Redhead spoke up, still beaming from the good news. "Your husband just announced that the

Midsummer Players are going to do *Merchant of Venice* and not *The Taming of the Shrew*. I, Maggie dear, am off the hook."

"I'm thrilled, too. I have always liked that comedy. You do know he never would have cast you as Kate," she said bluntly but affectionately.

"I know, Maggie. I'm happy because all the teasing, campaigning and talking about it from this crowd has now come to an end," she replied, pointing to the others who had surrounded Phineas Flanagan.

While they were talking, Phineas had decided to learn what he could about the Banter Foundation. That proved a challenge as they were more fascinated with him and were intent on finding out all they could. Phineas was adept at talking up a storm and not really revealing anything about himself. However, he was so entertaining, they were satisfied by what he told them.

Magnus and Maggie returned to the group and The Redhead went back behind the bar just in time to hear the tag end of a story Phineas was telling them about a play he and Magnus had been in.

When he had finished, Magnus jumped in. "Please, remember as the years continue to pile one upon the other, details of that story have changed dramatically."

George Crowder put his beer down. The big man in his lumbering fashion stepped off the bar chair and strode the few feet to where Magnus was standing.

"I was thinking, Magnus, and this may sound a little crazy, but if Phineas plans to stick around the Bay Area for awhile, maybe you can convince him to take a part in your next play," the former football player-turned-thespian suggested.

He was loud enough that the others chimed in. Walt spoke over their mumbling, "If we can't get The Redhead onto the stage, maybe you can consider George's idea. You'd have a bonafide Irish actor and that should generate some buzz."

Magnus cast a wary glance toward Phineas who was now standing by the bar. He wondered if Flanagan, always a cagey sort, had anything to do with their sudden enthusiasm for putting him to work. Phineas put his hands up and gave Magnus a smug smile.

"Aye, it seems you have an instant fan club," Magnus said. "You realize you'd have to stick around for awhile. Maybe a long while."

With the air of a bon vivant, he addressed Magnus. "My dear friend, time and money are two things I have plenty of. Scads, in fact. Your friends here are absolutely delightful and if seeing them means donning a costume and spouting 16th century English for a few months, so be it."

Magnus 'first thought was all this was so sudden. Just a few minutes earlier, Phineas Flanagan was hailing an Uber, ready to leave Magnus after a brief visit. Now, he's ready to take up residence for more than a quarter of the year. It was a puzzle to him.

Phineas 'thoughts were many. He was intrigued by the Banter Foundation members. It bothered him that he couldn't get a better fix on them right off. They seemed to him a genuinely selfless lot that rolled out the carpet for him and were less inclined to talk about themselves. His thinking was they could help him in more ways than one but it would take time. As for taking on the *Merchant of Venice,* the idea excited him. He was, he decided, an actor who had taken a forty year plus hiatus. Time to return the boards. Finally, he thought about the wisdom of setting up camp in Berkeley. Smiling to himself, he decided that the university city was as good as any other place to hide.

Chapter 3

"Modest doubt is called the Beacon of the Wise"

William Shakespeare

Friday morning was warm and welcoming, a pleasant respite from the unusual chill of the last few days. Maggie and Magnus sat huddled together at a small table outside Peet's Coffee. Their view, which they never tired of, was the grand old Claremont Hotel with the tree-studded Berkeley Hills in the distance. The one-block cluster of a coffee shop, cafe, bakery, restaurant and boutiques across from the Berkeley Tennis Club was full of people from the neighborhood.

Noticing Magnus 'sour expression, Maggie put her specially-constructed latte down and stared at her husband. "Either you don't like your coffee this morning or you're pouting because it's warm or you can't wear your scarf or it's something I said."

Magnus put his cappuccino down after taking a sip of the milky foam. It left a white mustache on his beard which Maggie quickly wiped off. "Come on, my Large Irishman, tell me." she urged him sweetly.

"The coffee is fine and I do like the weather and I love my scarf, thank you." Magnus stared at his wife. "Maggie, I know going to the premier of *Scepter II* is like a Holy Day of Obligation," he said. "But the truth is it's not something I look forward to. The red carpet stroll and the emphasis on what one is wearing is so artificial. I'd be out of place."

"Magnus darling, you and I are not strolling the red carpet and nobody cares what you're wearing. The crimson carpet and fancy dress is for the stars, the people in front of the camera, not behind it."

"*I* was in it," he said, pointing to himself.

"For all of four and a half minutes." she reminded him.

"I agree. It was not a large part and for that I'm grateful. You know, I only agreed to be a celluloid bad guy in a movie made in Bratislava by a brainy brat because you wanted me to. I'm a stage person through and through."

He had more he wanted to say, but Maggie had inched closer to him. In a low, breathy voice, she said, "Oh, but think about what an exciting time we had. We got married in Vienna. We went on a wonderful river cruise with friends. I finished work on the filming of *Scepter II.* And you got to be in a movie where you got shot forty-five times by a supersonically-altered Uzi. By the way, did I ever tell you I thought you died exceedingly well."

He laughed. "I did give Warren Beatty and Faye Dunaway a run for their money," he said, remembering their bloody death scene in *Bonny and Clyde.* He took a small bite of the croissant they were sharing. "Look, I am sorry for pouting, Maggie. Of course, I'll go with you and I promise I won't complain. Besides, I can't wait to see me writhing, twisting and jerking in excruciating mortal pain on a giant IMAX screen."

"I promise you a memorable time," she said, patting his leg. "Now tell me more about this old friend of yours who showed up out of the blue."

Magnus thought back to Thursday night at Bar OSA. After meeting the Banter gang, an ingratiating Phineas Flanagan, realizing he wasn't going to learn much about them that evening, had told Magnus he needed to get back to San Francisco. Before he left, someone had suggested he would be an excellent addition to the cast of *Merchant of Venice*. They left it with they'd think about it, even though both thought it a keen idea.

While considering how to respond to Maggie's inquiry, he made a fist of his right hand and checked his fingernails.

"Would you like me to give you a manicure," she asked.

Maggie already cut his hair. He had been uncomfortable at first, holding onto the naive belief that only a skilled professional should go anywhere near his face with a scissors. He now enjoyed his wife harvesting his mane every two weeks. "Is there no end to your talents, Maggie Leyton?" he asked.

"Better me than one off those tiny women with short black hair and an indeterminate age who are always in a bad mood, and while she is attacking your cuticles, she's arguing with the girl at the next table in a language you can't possibly understand and then she expects a whopping big tip. Or *I* can do them." Maggie said, exhaling what little air she had left in her lungs. She folded her arms and gave him a look that said she was happy with her answer.

Magnus shook his head, marveling at her "Let me guess, that's dialogue from a movie you wrote once upon a time," he said with a loving smile.

"Okay, a manicure this afternoon," she said. "Now tell me about Phineas Flanagan. He seems like quite a character."

"Aye, he is that, Maggie. And he was when I knew him forty years ago. Mind you, he was a damn fine actor. Probably still is. He's one of those who can lose themselves in a character. Because of that, he got a lot of work. But, he had one glaring fault. Because acting came so easy for him, he developed this almost reckless approach to the job. Directors both abided and abhorred him. Interestingly, about five years into his professional career, he called it quits. He told me he had always been good with numbers and was going to go into finance in some way or another." Magnus paused and took a sip of his now cooling cappuccino. "That's it. I never saw him again until yesterday afternoon looking like a cross between Noel Coward and Mr. Peanut."

"There are similar types in Hollywood," she remarked. Having grown up there as the daughter of a well-known screenwriter, she had known quite a few of them personally.

"The odd thing is you can't help but like Phineas, or PD as he was known then," he continued. "He was always in a chipper mood. Always charming as can be. A bit boastful but that comes with being in the theater." Magnus stopped and took a final sip. "But there was something about him that didn't sit well with me. It still doesn't."

Maggie was listening with keen interest. "The charm, I get. I also found him...," she paused to search for the right word. "Oh, I guess disingenuous might fit. Maybe conniving."

"Conniving?" Magnus thought about it a bit. "Yes, I agree. It is a crafty and wily creature that has dropped in on us unexpectedly," he laughed.

"He seems a sly one," she opined. "But you had a thought about him and I interrupted you."

"It slipped my mind," he said. "What I can say is I have my doubts about him."

"So, Mr. Flaherty, the question of the day is are you going to cast him in *Merchant of Venice?*"

"Absolutely."

***

He did not shake hands. Instead, he stood in the doorway of Phineas Flanagan's expansive suite at the Four Seasons with his hands behind his back. He bowed slightly when Phineas prepared to welcome him with a traditional handshake.

"Come in, come in," Phineas said with an exuberant cheeriness that brought a small smile to the man's face. "Please, make yourself comfortable. Coffee, juice and croissants are on their way up."

Phineas watched as the older gentleman strode confidently into the luxuriously appointed suite. He headed directly to a beige sofa. Because many of his clients preferred these kinds of glamorous surroundings, he was no stranger to the best the Four Seasons could offer.

Phineas Flanagan's guest was short, no more than five feet. He was well-proportioned for his height, thin-framed with an elfin face that was, like his hands, pale, soft and delicate. His hair was thin, light gray and parted on the left side. His clothes, while not stylish, were expensive. Phineas guessed he was in his mid-fifties.

"What should I call you?" he asked, entering the room and sitting opposite the small man.

The man thought a moment. "Horace," he said. "Yes, Horace will do nicely."

"Just Horace?"

"It worked well for a Roman poet." he said, placing a thin, tan leather briefcase on the cocktail table.

"I should say it did. When your parents christen you Quintus Horatius Flaccus, which hardly fits on a name tag, Horace becomes a welcome nickname," Phineas remarked with a quick laugh. "Did you know he was the man who gave us the phrase *carpe diem?*""

"I did," he replied. "Do you know the rest of the line?"

Phineas shrugged. "I'm afraid I don't. I always thought those two words said it all."

"No, indeed. It is *carpe diem quam minimum credula postero.*"

Phineas laughed heartily. "Sorry, my Latin is not what it used to be. Haven't used it since my altar boy days."

His guest sat forward. In a manner suggesting he was the teacher and Phineas the student, he translated the phrase. "It means, Mr. Flanagan, seize the day. Put very little trust in tomorrow."

Phineas had no opportunity to respond as room service had arrived. He jumped up and rushed to the door. His plan was to take the tray in himself as he didn't want anyone to see with whom he was dealing. As Phineas walked into the room with the coffee, juice snd croissants, he realized he was upset with himself. He was usually the glib, witty one in any social circumstance and here was this tiny man with a gentle manner who had taken charge. He didn't like being Aristotle to his Plato.

He placed the tray on the coffee table between them. "I'm afraid it's serve-yourself. I've given the butler the morning off," he joked. Reaching for a croissant, he said, "Horace is such a..."

With a look of frustration, his guest held up a hand to quiet him. "Please, enough about Mr. Flaccus and those two words from his ode that adorn a million throw pillows and tee-shirts. I should have told you my name was Clem."

'In other words, you'd like us to get down to business," a chastened Phineas stated.

"That would be a pleasure. First, I must say you come highly recommended. Jacob Asherman is a favorite client, and I always appreciate anyone he sends my way. To date, they all have without complaint paid well and are exceedingly discreet."

"You have my word, your record will stay in tact."

The man put his hands together as if in prayer. Putting them up to his face, he studied the Irishman sitting across from him. Well-dressed, he thought. Phineas 'clothes were also brand new. Horace glanced at his bed nearby where there were large bags and boxes from Brooks Brothers, Neiman-Marcus, The Hound and Nike.

Phineas saw his eyes wander toward the bedroom. He explained, "I came here expecting to stay no more than necessary to do what I had to do. Something's now come up and I plan on staying awhile longer. Thus, the new clothes."

"I see." He retrieved his briefcase and removed three manila files. "Look through these, please. They are samples of my work."

He would have sat back on the deep, over-sized sofa but, with his diminutive size, that would have required considerable effort. Instead, he sat forward and waited patiently for a reaction from his prospective client. It was short in coming.

"You are truly an artist, a very gifted one," he exclaimed after examining the contents of the three files. "These are all superb. No wonder you don't shake hands, Like a concert pianist, those are delicate and fragile instruments."

"The truth is I have never been a touchy-feely person," he confessed. Clapping his hands, he said with enthusiasm. "So, Mr. Flanagan, do you have your list? And are you prepared to be shocked at what this will cost you?"

"Jacob warned me," he said, rising from his chair and picking up two papers from an ornate desk nearby. He handed them to his guest. "Here you are. As complete as I could make it. If I am missing anything, please let me know."

Horace looked up and smiled at him. "One always misses something, my friend. It is just the way of these things." He then took the papers and with little noises, studied Phineas 'list of needs or wishes. With a final, nasal *hmm*, he put the list on top of the folders and put them all in his briefcase.

"Is that it?" an anxious Phineas asked.

"For now," he said, inching forward on the sofa to rise. "It's a slow process, so patience is required."

"As well as money," Phineas joked. Getting a subdued laugh from his guest, he added, "Please, stay and enjoy the coffee and croissants."

"Thank you, but no. I'll let you be. It will take you some time to remove all the wrappings and tags from those new clothes." His guest took hold of his briefcase and started for the door. "I will have an estimate in a few days."

Phineas, searching for a nifty goodby, said "*Quod Bellus.*"

The small man with the giant presence turned to look back at his new client. "You want me to be pretty?" he asked with a grin.

Phineas shook his head. "No, no, I wanted to say be gentle."

"Then it would be *quod lenis*," he said. "And I'll try to be, Mr. Flanagan."

Chapter 4

Pick a year. Any year.

Ambrose Dowling did not want to alarm Sylvie who was staring intently at her computer screen. Instead, he stood quietly to one side of the doorway to her office. He was enjoying watching her because whatever his young friend saw on the large monitor elicited any number of cute expressions and accompanying sounds. After a minute of this pleasurable snooping, he issued a polite *ahem*. She turned and upon seeing the retired professor, produced a warm, inviting smile. With a nod of her head, she invited him in.

"Greetings, Ms Blanchard," Ambrose said. The retired professor addressed everyone formally except for this late wife, Emily, to whom he talked often.

"Greetings to you, Professor" she echoed, her voice full of affection.

Three months previous, Sylvie Blanchard, a post-grad student studying economics, found herself sitting on Ambrose Dowling's doorstep waiting for him to return home. She had carried his name and address during her years at Cal. It had been given to her by her stepsister,

Ashley Porter, ten years her senior and a Cal alumna. She had told her younger sister if anything untoward occurred where she needed help, she was to call Professor Dowling, that he was one of the good ones. Her trouble was an economics professor named Kenneth Richter who was also a media celebrity thanks to newspaper columns, TV appearances and speeches. One of his goals was to seduce as many comely coeds as possible. Fortunately, he was lousy at it. However, he remained a menace and she was frightened. When Ambrose heard of her plight, he readily signed on to help. What followed was a sometimes comic and other times desperate adventure that involved an entire cast of characters. By the time all matters were resolved, there was a divorce pending for Professor Richter, an unexpected pregnancy for a Cal student and the beginning of a beautiful friendship for Ambrose and Sylvie.

"Isn't this exciting? The first day of rehearsals and I'm in it from beginning to end," she proclaimed. "Are you going to do some coaching?"

"Mr. Flaherty has asked me to help where I can," he said taking a seat directly across from her desk. "The *Merchant of Venice* is a play to my liking."

"Mine, too," she said with a youthful eagerness. "I'm so glad we're not doing *The Taming of the Shrew*. My sister brings her work home with her. Truthfully, Ambrose, Ashley as Kate would have been absolutely intolerable."

"How is Ashley?"

"She's busy, which is what she likes. I can never remember the lengthy Kafkaesque name of the department she works in. It's Berkeley, you know, and they don't keep things simple. But she likes the job, and, of course, she's thrilled to be playing Portia. Moving her computer to share the screen with Ambrose, she asked excitedly, "Can I show you what I've been doing?"

Ambrose leaned forward to get a better glimpse of the large screen.

"Magnus gave me the job of picking a year to set the play in," she explained. "It's up to me to find a year somewhere between 1935 to 1950. I wanted to avoid the hardcore war years, so I've been checking out 1946 on. I think I know which one I want. I'd like to know what you think, though." Her fingers danced across the keyboard and instantly an array of women's fashions appeared under a banner reading 1948.

With growing interest, Ambrose leaned further in. "Oh my goodness, these pictures remind of my mother. If Magnus were here he'd no doubt say his sainted mother. I'm not ready to canonize mine just yet, but that's another story. Notice, Ms Blanchard, not a pair of pants to be seen. All skirts and dresses."

"My mother told me that when I was little, dresses were the only thing I ever wanted to wear." She laughed at the memory. "I haven't worn a dress in years. In fact, I don't think I have one in my closet. Anyway, what do you think?"

"What do I think of the year? Well, 1948 or MC..."

"MCMXLVIII, Ambrose," she interjected. "I'm studying econ history, you know."

"I have always had a fondness for Roman numerals." he said playfully.

"So, I'll ask again. What do you think?"

"A sound choice. 1948 was quite a memorable twelve months. Israel became a nation. Gandhi was assassinated. WHO, the World Health Organization was founded," he said.

"I was also reading that President Truman ended racial segregation in the military and Margaret Sanger founded Planned Parenthood," she said, adding to the list of historical events.

"She did. And, ironically, in the same year, Alfred Kinsey wrote *Sexual Behavior in the Human Male*," he noted with a chuckle. "Nice of him to call us human, don't you think?"

"He obviously didn't take into account Professor Richter," she said with leftover anger.

"Ah, that name hasn't been tossed around in my presence for awhile. I assume he's leaving your sister alone?"

Sylvie turned from away from the computer. She wore a worried look. "Ashley thinks she's being followed. Personally, I'm not surprised. I mean, just look at her. She's a phenom when it comes to looking glamorous and sexy," she said without a hint of jealousy. "It's a wonder she doesn't have a platoon of men following her constantly."

"I hope she's being careful."

"She is. She suspects it might be Randy Richter," she noted.

Ambrose leaned back and thought a moment. "I wouldn't think that of him. However, he does seem obsessed with your sister, so I imagine he's capable of all sorts of bizarre behavior"

Sylvie put her hands on the desk and stared at the man she considered her unofficial uncle. "Well, now that we picked a year, let's join the others and tell them what we've decided."

"*You* decided, my young executive" he corrected her. "I simply prodded. Please tell them it was your idea and you might add that you know where to find the perfect clothes for the play." He rose from the chair as she popped up to come around the desk. "For now, just tell them your good friends, Amelia Palmer and Berra Hannigan, will handle it all. I'll give you the details later." He then put both his hands on her shoulders, much like a coach ready to send a player into the game. "Now, go out there and show them who runs things in this theater."

***

Magnus sat in the front row watching his cast reuniting on stage, He loved the hum and buzz of their conversations. He was looking forward to staging this particular play. He was personally happy with the casting and confident he did well giving the role of Antonio to Phineas. As for the others. they had not as yet met the former Irish actor. He knew much of the chatter going on amongst them had to do with that unusual casting. However, most, having been in earlier productions, knew unusual was par for the course. In *As You Like It*, Magnus cast a handyman with a Brooklyn accent as Hymen who then actually married two of the cast members in the final act. And in *King Lear*, he gave the role of the monomaniacal, rage-filled ruler to a former lineman from the Oakland Raiders. Why should *Merchant of Venice* be any different?

Nine days had passed since the suggestion of his old associate being part of the production was sprung on him at the Banter meeting. Since that evening, he had not seen Phineas. He had spoken to him twice and was given assurances that he'd be at the theater at noon sharp on Saturday, the twenty-sixth. Magnus remembered telling Maggie that directors both abided and abhorred him because of his devil-may-care manner. He knew he could not tolerate such mischief. What had he wrought, he asked himself with a quiet chuckle.

"Aye aye, Captain, Phineas Flanagan reporting for duty. I'm told I am to report to the stage for further instruction," he said, sneaking up on Magnus. He took a seat across the narrow aisle.

Magnus did a double take as Flanagan spun him back in time by wearing what Phineas called his rehearsal clothes. Instead of his bespoke suit, he was wearing ill-fitting, wrinkled khakis, a faded blue polo shirt that had seen better days and over it a dull russet-colored V-neck sweater beaten by age and wear. A pair of brand new dark grey Pikolinos shoes, which Sylvie deemed ultra cool, contrasted with what looked to be clothes he'd taken off one of Shattuck Avenue's street people.

Magnus looked his friend up and down. After a long gaze, he took a dollar and handed it to Phineas. "I don't know how you got in here, old man, but here's a dollar. Don't spend it on drugs. And, by the way, nice shoes."

Phineas didn't hand it back. Brushing an imaginary something off his hole-infested sweater, he expressed surprise and delight at receiving the dollar. Looking up at the stage, he addressed everyone in the small theater. "Will you look at this. I haven't been here ten seconds. I have not wielded a bodkin. I've not uttered an orison. I have not, with stentorian voice, bellowed, 'He is one whom I will beat into clamorous whining, if thou deniest the least syllable of thy addition. 'Nor have I delved into the jargon of Shakespeare to experience the joy of sounding out words like cockered, goatish and tardy-gaited. I have done none of these things and I'm already being paid." All this he said with a raised voice, waving the dollar bill about. "What an amazing theater group."

The entire cast heard every word and enjoyed it immensely. Magnus noticed them staring and thought this was as good a time as any to introduced them. Speaking up, he said, "I'd like you meet Phineas Flanagan. He and I were in several productions together back around the time Shakespeare was alive and thriving." He paused for a laugh. "Perhaps, not that long ago. As Phineas is going to be in the Bay Area for awhile, I thought it would be exciting to put him to work again. He and I once appeared in *Julius Caesar* at the Abbey Theatre. Phineas, or PD as he was known then, was Octavius. The play was well-received and Phineas was praised. I'm thrilled he's with us. Oh, and by the way, he will be playing Antonio. Interestingly, it was the one role left unfilled."

Franny Gaspar left his group and moved forward to the edge of the stage. "Magnus, what part did you have in Julius Caesar?" he asked.

"Um, I was a Praetorian Guard, 'he mumbled.

"And he didn't bungle a line," Phineas added, patting Magnus on the back.

"That's because I didn't have any," Magnus grumbled.

Phineas looked up at the young cast on the stage. "Oh, but let me tell you. In that skimpy guard outfit, he was positively yummy."

Magnus fiddled with his latest wardrobe addition. It was a bright yellow and blue silk pocket-square given him by Banter member, Michael Gearon. The retired radio personality was never seen without one. When Magnus told him he admired the look, Gearon pulled it from his pocket, instructed him on how to do the Hermes-fold which gave the square a flowery look and stuffed it into Magnus 'coat pocket. When Magnus protested, Michael's wife, Katherine, took another one from her purse and gave it to her husband, explaining he was always giving them away.

Phineas, realizing he now had a captive audience, marched on. "Did I ever tell you... Of course, I didn't. I just met all of you. Anyway, Magnus was also mentioned in that otherwise glowing review of *Julius Caesar* even though he had no lines. He'd forgotten to remove his wrist watch and it didn't go unnoticed. In 44BC, they might have tried wearing sun dials, but wrist watches wouldn't come on the scene for quite awhile."

When the laughter died down, Ambrose spoke up. "Mr. Flanagan, wrist watches appeared for the first time in 1868. Interestingly, it was the same year as the founding of the University of California. In the beginning, women wore them mainly for decoration."

Ambrose had come into the theater with Sylvie and was walking toward the stage. "Now that we have learned about the illustrious stage career or our director, I suggest we move on to the real reason we're here, namely to rehearse."

Phineas lifted a hand and gave himself a false slap. "Well, I have just been put in my place."

"Not at all," the professor replied. "It is just that time is of the essence. Am I right, Mr. Flaherty?"

"And I wonder which Shakespeare play gave us the phrase *time is of the essence,*" Phineas wondered aloud.

"It is an English term used in contract law, Mr. Flanagan," Ambrose said sharply, finding conversational fencing with Magnus 'friend boring.

And what of Magnus during all of this? When Ambrose and Sylvie joined the others, Sylvie had cornered Magnus to show him some promotional ideas she'd come up with and tell him which year she'd picked. While he tended to that, he kept an ear partially on the entertaining goings-on at his expense. When he decided enough was enough, he stepped in.

As he began to clap slowly and loudly, he encouraged everyone to join him. "That was a wonderful demonstration of how truly awful some drawing room comedy dialogue can be. I thank Ambrose and Phineas. If we're lucky, perhaps we can get them to give us a sample of Noel Coward's *Blithe Spirit* the next time. Meantime, let's get to work."

"Damn, I thought that applause was meant for me. I am on time, aren't I?" George Crowder asked..

"You just made it, Mr. Crowder," Ambrose said, checking his watch. "We have just the role for you."

"I heard I'm the Duke of Venice and that I preside over Shylock's trial. That means I sit down a lot," he announced happily.

With that he went up on stage to greet the friends he'd made during their recent run of King Lear when he played the ruler. Magnus and Sylvie were right behind him.

"Magnus, did Phineas trade clothes with a homeless guy? What's he playing at?" she asked, confused by his slovenly appearance.

"When he was making a living acting— if you want to call it that — Phineas had what he said where his rehearsal clothes. I think he might be superstitious."

When they reached the stage, everyone crowded around them, eager to hear more about the production. Magnus began by telling them that the play would be set in 1948. It was then that someone's smartphone began to ring. Interestingly, everyone went for their phone. It was Phineas 'mobile. He gave an apologetic wave to his director and moved to the rear of the stage.

"Mr. Flanagan, this is Horace."

"This is not a good time, Horace," Phineas whispered.

"I'll be quick. Everything seems to be in order. However, there's something that missing and it's a rather glaring omission. I need a birth date," he said. "Not your real one, of course."

"Uh, let me see," Phineas said. He looked at the calendar date on his phone. "January 26th. Yes, use January 26th."

"Now I need a year," Horace reminded him.

"I really don't know how old I want to be?"

"Pick a year, any year," Horace said, frustration in his voice.

Phineas smiled when he told him. "1948."

Chapter 5

Advice with a dash of admonishment

"I'd say you are suffering from a nasty case of unrequited love, Kenneth. It's that or you simply want to add this woman to your trophy case and she's proving to be immune to your many charms. Knowing you, I think it's the latter." Doctor Gretchen Sabranskey paused to sneeze suddenly. "Excuse me. It's way too soon to credit allergies for that kind of explosion," she said with a guttural laugh. "You know, duckling, when I talk to you, I feel like Lucy behind her sidewalk stand dishing out advice for one nickel."

"And what? I'm Charlie Brown?" Kenneth RIchter asked, his mood not affording him a chance to laugh.

"Good grief no," she huffed. "You don't identify with any of the Peanuts 'gang. Are you sure you even had a childhood? I'm guessing you reached puberty right out of the womb."

Dr. Gretchen Sabranskey was a professor of psychology at Cal. She was stout, square-jawed with a short, grey mannish hair-style. A no-nonsense woman in her sixties who was born in Munich, she had the appearance of someone who lived through too many Oktoberfests Her single best feature was a menacing and hypnotic glare. A glare so intimidating, a Marine drill sergeant would cower in her presence. Professor Kenneth Richter, who was on the other end of her Saturday morning phone call, was not officially her patient. He was her chew-toy. Such was her fascination with him. For Kenneth, this proponent of tough love was as close to a therapist as he would get. He thought of her more as a mother confessor.

While Professor Sabranskey was in the kitchen of her Craftsman home in the Elmwood District of Berkeley, Professor Kenneth RIchter was in his living room, sitting on the edge of his sofa, paying no attention to his knockout view of the Oakland Estuary and in the distance the San Francisco skyline. On the glass-topped coffee table were the remains of a Zachery's thin-crust pizza and two opened cans of Pabst Blue Ribbon. Nearby were notes for a speech he was to give that night to a convention-gathering in downtown Oakland. He'd been in his new high-rise, penthouse condo with it's floor-to-ceiling glass walls for just three nights which explained a notable lack of furniture. So far, his household inventory included a bed, the sofa, coffee table and one large-screen television. It would have to stay that way for awhile as RIchter had to deal with an event entirely unexpected.

The economist and media celebrity was in his early fifties. Through the years, he had paid careful attention to his appearance and health. It had paid off as he looked years younger. He was handsome in a TV anchorman sort of way. A well-rehearsed smile, whiter-than-white teeth and just enough hair dye gave him a look that satisfied him whenever he looked in a mirror which was often. A professor at Cal, he was recently divorced from his wife, Lauren Ainsworthy, an acclaimed and highly respected professor of Humanities. Her major failing, apart from being acclaimed and highly respected, was that of aging. His romantic urgings were fueled by youthful beauty. He'd been single for two months and was making up for not having sowed wild oats as a young man. However, the older professor was like a lot of younger men who didn't think through the myriad consequences of their bacchanalian activities. So it was that his perfect world began to crumble when he received a text from a Cal student he had been seeing. Her name was Mary Jo Walker, a brainy senior studying biochemistry whom he affectionately called The Lump because of the way she slept. She had sent him a sonogram of what she explained would in a few months time be their baby. The news had rattled him greatly, but, strangely, it didn't dominate his thinking. There was something else bothering him. These two issues were the reason for the phone call to Professor Sabranskey, a colleague and friend who had followed his escapades for years.

Gretchen had decided for herself one problem was far more important and that's what she wanted to talk about. "How do you know you're the pater?" she asked. "That's latin for..."

"I know what pater means," he snapped.

"Good. So how do you know?" she repeated.

"Uh, I just assumed I was," he stammered. "That's what she implied in her test."

"Okay, twinkle toes, follow my line of thinking. You have a brainy blonde whom I am assuming is big-breasted, small-waisted, long-legged and terrific in bed, terrific meaning experienced."

Stifling a laugh, he said, "You assume correct."

"And she's a Cal student, no doubt sworn to a party-throwing sorority, in her early twenties and says *like* a lot."

"You pretty much nailed her."

"You said you see each other on occasion."

"Saw is more like it," he replied soberly. "Maybe four or five times in October and early November mostly. We weren't intimate..."

He heard a loud guffaw. "I beg your pardon. What did you do? Play strip beer pong?" she barked.

"What I meant was we were mostly about sex. We didn't have much to talk about," he explained, his spirits sinking even lower. "Oh, I forgot to tell you that right after that text saying she was pregnant, she sent a second saying she wanted me to meet her mom and dad. For chrissakes, Gretchen, I'm probably older than her parents."

"Oh, I want to come to that wedding," she joked.

"There will be no wedding," he shot back.

"When did you get these texts?"

"They came in Wednesday afternoon. I didn't get them until this morning. Right before calling you," he said, still shaken by their impact.

"Why did you wait three days to see them?"

"I have three phones," he began to explain. "The number she has for me is a phone I use strictly for..." He paused to think of the best way to explain it. "Uh, its just for..."

"I get it, Casanova. It's your digital little black book, a must for the modern day lothario."

Frustrated, he groaned, "Give me a break, Gretchen."

"Professor, do you think you're the only man..." She suddenly raised her voice. "Wait, I take that back. You may have indeed been the only man she's slept with. Certainly, the only one in his fifties. However, there might have been a few boys..."

"I don't think so, Gretchen," he interjected. Why, he thought, am I defending her fealty if we didn't have a relationship.

"Kenneth, this is January, 2019. Need I say more. Dr. Gretchen suggests you get a paternity test. Meantime, sweat it out like all the men who previously found themselves in a similar situation. Now onto your other problem," she said tersely.

Kenneth stretched out on the couch. He felt like a teenager who grabs a close buddy's ear and talks endlessly about his soul-altering crush on someone because just talking about it feels weirdly satisfying. He wanted to tell Gretchen how he felt about Ashley but he found it difficult to put into words.

"She consumes me. She interrupts my thoughts. She's a constant distraction," he said finally. "She's like a really, really bad ear worm."

"I should have asked earlier. What is her name?"

"Ashley Porter. She works for the city of Berkeley and is an actress with the Midsummer Players."

Gretchen, a fan and supporter of local theater recognized her name right away. "She was Goneril in *King Lear.* Oh my, Mr. Smooth Moves, you've got your work cut out for you. That woman is major league," she told him.

"Are you in love with her, Kenneth?" she asked directly. "Don't answer that. My advice is clean up problem one before doing anything at all about problem two."

RIchter exhaled. "Yeah, you're right, I suppose. "

"And you might consider getting a vasectomy if you're still thinking of holding onto that sybaritic lifestyle of yours." There was a hard edge to the tone of her voice.

"Sometimes, Gretchen, I feel you don't like me. That I'm like some rat you study in your psych lab."

She laughed loudly. "Nonsense, Kenneth. I like you. You have promise. It may take some time but I do think you are redeemable."

Heavy with sarcasm, the professor said, "There's still hope, huh? Is that what you mean."

"Look at the bright side. You're very good at being an economist, and you're very good at being a teacher."

"Thank you."

"You're not very good at just being."

Chapter 6

"Young in limbs,
in judgement old."

William Shakespeare

A deflated Kenneth RIchter tidied up and headed out. The professor had no specific destination in mind. As a media celebrity as well as an academic, he enjoyed walking and counting the number or people who recognized him. He gave that up over time as the recognition count never got past zero. This particular Saturday, he just wanted to wander and think and, perhaps, shake the dark cloud that was following him. He had left his new condo feeling beaten up and he blamed it all on Doctor Sabranskey for her tough love approach to analysis. As he walked in the direction of Jack London Square, he reviewed in his mind the phone call with the salty professor of psychology. In the past, he had always benefited from their informal chats, but this time there was little he felt he could take away and put to good use.

He realized some of that may have been his fault. He'd let her think his attraction to Ashley Porter was akin to a school-boy crush when it was, in fact, far more complex.

He had conflicting thoughts and feelings when it came to Ms Porter. She had angered him when she had rejected his romantic advance. Actually, there had been two, ten years apart. Neither worked. Later, that anger grew when she, with the help of Ambrose Dowling, thwarted his nefarious plan to enrich himself off an idea he'd stolen from her.

What confounded him was the fact that he was still drawn to her. He'd never met anyone with such a powerful allure, unusual beauty and a whiz-kid brain. She was, as Gretchen described, major league. Well, damn it, so am I, the economist told himself, but with little conviction. The Porter woman had managed to get into his head to the point where the professor realized he was dealing with an obsession. It was a feeling he wanted to shake or satisfy.

In the fall of 2018, Richter and Ashely Porter met for drinks in a Carmel hotel. Business had brought them together but that didn't stop the then married professor from trying to get her up to his hotel room and not for a power-point presentation. She refused him flatly and firmly. Then in further conversation, she let him know of an ingenious plan she had conceived to mitigate the housing and transportation problems plaguing densely populated urban areas. With his eidetic memory, he had filed it all away with the intent of making it his own. He had stolen her idea and thought nothing of it. In fact, he felt the theft was justified. After all, he didn't hand out sexual invitations willy-nilly, so her refusing him was wrong on so many counts. However, thanks to the clever machination of friends in the Banter group, she was able to put a halt to his shameful scheme. The story became more clouded as RIchter added to his list of sins, both mortal and venial, by hiring a young man to accuse his wife of a drunken sexual assault. The reason was to sully her sterling reputation. In the end, cornered for his deceitful and criminal actions, he agreed to stay away from Professor Lauren Ainsworthy, his spouse, and Ashely Porter, his unrequited love. He had no problem keeping his distance from his soon-to-be ex-wife. As for the captivating Ms Porter, it was a different matter. She haunted his thoughts relentlessly and he had to do something about it.

RIchter walked into a restaurant on the waterfront. He found a table outside and ordered a Bloody Mary from an attractive server with a flirtatious manner. She was gypsy-like with large, dark eyes and black, curly hair, a trim figure and heavily tattooed arms and legs. He put on his best media smile for her, complimented her on her tats and wondered whether she recognized him.

To the right of his table was a young couple. The women was very pregnant, and that reminded him of his other problem. He knew he had to call The Lump and deal with her startling announcement of three days ago. He remembered Ambrose Dowling warning him of life's many life-altering consequences. This was certainly one of them. The more he thought about it, the more the economist felt himself losing his swagger, his confidence. He was perplexed by what to do and how to do it. While he pondered, he watched the young couple who were engaged in a happy conversation. Occasionally. she would rub her close-to-bursting tummy and sometimes he would lean in more closely to stare at the temporary home of their future child. I'm happy for them but that's not for me, he told himself. Never.

The Bloody Mary and The Lump's text arrived at the same time. He pulled his phone from his pocket, let his thumb print open the colorful display of apps and then he opened the one titled *Messages*. With a pounding heart and a churning stomach, he read:

OMG** I am like **SOOO** sorry. Those texts were meant for Cody and not you. What a complete screw up. I don't know where my head was. Anyway, professor, you're **not** going to be a **daddy**, so stop sweating if you think you were. And I'd never want you to meet my parents. Cody and I have been seeing each other and it's like the real deal. You and I had some fun though, huh? LOL **The Lump.

If Richter had been a flattened tire, he was now fully inflated. If he had been an off-key piano, he was now musically tuned. If he had been a smartphone low on power, he was one hundred percent. After reading and rereading The Lump's text, the swaggering, boasting, narcissistic and women-loving Professor Kenneth Richter was back. After he finished the Bloody Mary, he knew exactly where he wanted to go. First, though, he would find out just how available the overly-friendly server with all the body art was. He was certain he could get past the tattoos.

***

Magnus was satisfied with the cast's cold reading. It was too early to say with confidence but he felt the reading gave him a hint that the play would be a success. He was particularly impressed with his old friend, Phineas who, while seated and reading from the script, delivered up an inspiring Antonio, and to Magnus' amazement, he behaved himself throughout the afternoon. He remembered when they were acting together in the seventies, Phineas, or PD as he was known then, used to be a bit of a rehearsal trouble-maker. Not this time, though. When the reading was over, Flanagan asked Sylvie if he could use her office to get out of his grubby rehearsal clothes and into something more respectable. In minutes, the tall, thin gentleman was back on stage in dark jeans, a grey-blue Ralph Lauren sport coat, a pale pink shirt and new Pikolinos. A multi-colored silk pocket-square finished the fashionable look. He knew he cut a dashing figure but pooh-poohed it humbly when several cast members told him how sharp he looked.

"Mr. Flanagan, I'm looking forward to sharing the stage with a man of your repute and experience," Ashley Porter said, who as Portia saves Antonio's skin in the play.

She and the Irish actor were standing center stage, separate from the other clusters of actors and stagehands. She loved hearing Flanagan speak as he had kept his Queen's English stage accent from his acting days. He felt it suited him and he was right. She also admired his savoir faire.

The Irish actor was equally impressed with Ashley. "Please, dear girl, call me Phineas. I predict you and I will shine in our respective roles. With you as a sagacious

Portia and I as a scintillating Antonio we will be like Richard Burton as Marc Antony and Elizabeth Taylor as Cleopatra," he proclaimed grandiloquently. "After this run, you and I will join the pantheon of other great acting alliances. People will be talking about us for decades."

"Well, maybe not decades, but I'm glad *you* think so," she said, blushing at the mere thought of it.

Ashely Porter wondered if she had felt Kenneth RIchter's presence before spotting him standing in the center aisle halfway between the stage and the rear of the theater. The economics professor noticed her staring and, raising his arm, gave her a tentative, waist-high wave. She was not pleased to see him and chose not to respond in kind.

She was certain he was still intent on establishing a relationship. Why else would he be there? She could only guess at what kind of tack he would take. She grimaced thinking he would probably pull the standard *I've changed, I'm a new man* routine. Her prescience was frighteningly accurate.

Richter had, in fact, worked out what he was going to say to her on his way to the theater. He knew she would be there because he had been keeping tabs on her for the past two weeks. His Saturday had started out grimly, but by late afternoon, things had changed and, as a result, he was now full of himself. His new-found joy came from his learning The Lump's pregnancy was not of his doing and that she had slipped politely out of his life. Then, at the restaurant, the attractive server agreed to meet him for drinks. When he questioned her body art, she told him that if he was a good boy, she might show him the tattoos she had in what she called the adult section of her body. Yes, he thought, life was good.

While pondering just how to convince Ashley Porter that they would make an ideal couple, he remembered Dr. Gretchen Sabranskey's opinion that she thought him redeemable. That's it, he almost shouted to passersby as he walked to his car. It was all about redemption. He was convinced for no reason that women loved that word, particularly if they were instrumental in doing the saving. He decided that that was the card he would play when he saw her at the theater. He never gave a thought to simply apologizing.

Ashley did not want to confront him. Her Saturday was going swimmingly and she didn't want anything to happen to spoil it. She knew, though, that he would continue to stand there. She would have to go to him and send him away with as little drama as possible.

Phineas noticed her staring at the man in the center aisle. He nudged her and with a naughty grin asked, "Is that someone of interest or a pushy stage-door Johnny?

"No, that is a cretin of a man named Professor Kenneth Richter." she said angrily. "I really don't want to talk to him but I'm going to have to. By the way, he's supposed to keep his distance from me."

"Can I help?"

She tossed her hair back and looked up at him. "Do you Irish have a way of telling somebody to sod off. Maybe something a little more emphatic?" she asked. "Phineas, never mind. I am just going to go down there and tell him to leave."

As she began to move away from him, Phineas put his hand up to stop here. "How about you and I give him a good reason to leave. I have an idea, if you're up for it. "

"Phineas, you have a weird look in your eye," she said, wary of what he was planning.

"We'll approach him together," he started to explain. "I mean as a couple. That should unnerve him."

She stared at the tall, reasonably attractive man, her mouth agape. "Phineas, that idea is, uh, unnerving. You're old enough to be my father even if you married late in life. And on top of that, you're gay"

"Ashley, my lovely, I wholeheartedly agree with you on both counts. There is our obvious age difference. And I am gay which means while I find you an utterly charming and devastatingly beautiful woman, I find that man standing in the aisle far more appealing."

"I'm glad somebody does, because I sure as hell don't."

He looked out at the impatient man standing in the aisle. "But having said that, we are actors and I have had countless love scenes with women both young and old. Well, most of them old," he confessed, making a sour face.

Ashley Porter tossed her hair back and folded her arms. "Thank you for offering, but no."

"Might I remind you we are like Burton and Taylor. We can pull it off," he said with an actor's confidence. "There are all kinds of tricks to make it work. For example, when you and I look lovingly into each other's eyes, I will simply be thinking of him."

"You didn't have to tell me that" she said, stepping away from him. "Phineas, look, thanks for your help but I'll take care of this. I'm a big girl and I've already played this game with him. Give me a minute to tell the jerk to sod off and I'll be right back."

With a thumbs-up gesture, she stepped off the stage and walked toward Richter, who was growing impatient at the time it took her to greet him. Still he smiled warmly as she approached.

Phineas Flanagan watched her walk away. He was itching to participate but he would respect her wishes and remain in place.

"What's going on?" The question came from Franny Gaspar who had approached him after Ashley left.

Flanagan told him about her not wanting to confront the man and his ingenious idea of dealing with him.

Franny folded his arms and looked at the two people in the center aisle. "That's bad optics," he muttered.

"I beg your pardon, my fellow thespian," Phineas said snootily.

"No offense, but that dude will maybe buy Ashley and me as a couple, but you two would be a pretty tough sell."

Phineas who was not a stranger to mischief and daring, looked at his young companion. "Well, Mr. Gaspar, we shall see how convincing I can be. As far as I am concerned, our heroine is taking too much time ridding herself of the villain. Watch me and learn," he said, stepping off the stage.

Ashley had started with an obvious coldness. "I assume you're here to see me,"

He nodded. "You are the only reason. I don't think I have too many fans in this place."

Ashley pointed a finger at him. "That so like you. Most people would have said friends, not fans."

"These people weren't friends in the first place," he countered. "Look, can we go somewhere to talk?"

And so it went back and forth. He was insistent they go outside to talk. She was just about ready to leave him standing there when she heard a familiar voice.

"Darling, please, do introduce me to your charming friend," Phineas said in a breathy, overly theatrical manner. He was acting more like Ru Paul than Paul Newman.

Approaching RIchter, he continued talking, giving Ashley no chance to say anything. Staring at the professor, he rambled on, "Imagine, if you will, we are only one rehearsal in and Ashley and I are already planning the myriad ways we can shower attention and affection on each other." He gave her a loving glance. "And let me deal with this before you bring it up, because I know you are dying to: As to our obvious age difference, I can tell you this woman has an old soul. Or as Shakespeare would say, she's *young of limbs, in judgement old.*"

The stunned professor, wearing an open-mouthed look, stared first at Ashley and then at Phineas. He was about to respond when he heard Ashley at the top of her voice, commanding Phineas to stop.

She glared at both men."Kenneth, this is Phineas Flanagan. He had this noble idea of rescuing me from your lecherous grasp and I told him I would handle you myself. He obviously had other ideas. One of which was we were a couple."

Richter shook his head. "Theater people," he huffed. "You have such creative ways of screwing things up." He stared at the actor. "So, I'm supposed to believe this amazing woman would couple up with a Medicare-qualified gay?"

Phineas smiled. "Is that your professorial way of telling me I am an old queer?"

"Hey, take it anyway you like."

Professor Richter then did something that was impulsive, foolhardy and not at all like him. He grabbed Ashley by her left arm and started to move her toward the exit. "We need to talk, outside," he commanded, his voice gravely and harsh.

As he held her arm and began to inch away, the Irish actor moved toward him and grabbed his right arm. It startled Richter who let go of her. Flanagan's grip while not painful was vise-like. The actor's strength shocked and then frightened him. He knew better than to try and free himself. He'd have to wait until Phineas let go.

While he had Richter in his grasp, Phineas caught his eye and began to speak in a voice that carried throughout the small theater. "You probably know about the overworked, hackneyed phrase that the Irish are born brawlers. I assure you I am not, but I was brought up in that world. I had it forced on me from a very early age. My da had two recreations, drinking and beating on my mother and me. When I was old enough and strong enough, I forced him to stop. I tell you this because I grew up having no tolerance whatsoever for unsolicited, gratuitous physical contact. Particularly contact by a man on a woman or a child. Contact such as you just imposed on Ashley."

It might be wise to apologize, the professor thought. He did so and quite effusively to Ashley. To Phineas, he gave his arm a manly shake but only after sensing the man was ready to loosen his grasp. With that, Richter merely nodded and walked away. When he closed the theater door behind him, the cast gave the two left standing in the aisle a round of applause. For what, the cast wasn't sure. They just knew there was some kind of contretemps and their two fellow cast members must have emerged the winners. Phineas acknowledged them by taking an exaggerated bow.

"Don't ever do that again, Mr. Flanagan," Ashley warned him. "I can fight my own battles."

"I do apologize," he said. "You know, I think Franny Gaspar wanted to go in my place. He said I was bad optics being a septuagenerian poof. I paid him no heed."

"Did your father really beat on you and your mother?" she asked as they walked back to the stage.

"Good heavens no," he exclaimed. "Except for inserting your name, that was word-for-word dialogue from a hideous play called *Galway Lullaby*. My father was the dearest of men. Gentle, kind and a man of moderation. My mother on the other hand..."

Chapter 7

One and Done

Gus Latrope walked into Bar OSA at three-thirty on Valentine's Day. As always, he was alone. The unusually large man preferred sitting at the bar closest to the windows facing Shattuck Avenue. He took a moment to settle himself, thankful his perch wasn't the standard barstool that came without any back support. The restaurant was almost empty. Duffy's one other customer was Amazing Grace, a retired teacher, who never explained her nickname. She had a table against the wall and was engrossed in a voluminous biography of some turn-of-the-century woman Duffy had never heard of. He knew better than to ask about the book's subject as Grace did not know how to keep a long story short. One drink would last her three hours and topping that, she was a lousy tipper.

Duffy walked slowly the length of the bar as he knew Gus would study the collection of colorful bottles in front of him before ordering. He scanned them all, left to right; the gins, vodkas, tequilas, ryes, whiskeys, rums and assorted other liquors with exotic names; many of them rarely touched. He had actually timed Gus on one visit. A full inspection ran about three minutes before he'd look up at the barman and in a pleasant, polite manner request a Maker's Mark on the rocks with a splash of water. He never ordered anything else.

"Here you are, Gus." Duffy put a coaster down and the drink on it. "So, how's retirement?" he asked for what he thought was the hundredth time.

Gus owned a carwash in West Berkeley and had just turned the place over to his son, Jeff, who was a younger version of him. Both men had round faces with balding pates atop fleshy bodies that were well-fed. Gus was a year into retirement.

"I'm doing okay, Duffy. My wife convinced me to try my hand at writing," he said. "I've always enjoyed murder mysteries and she thought I ought to, uh you know, give it a try."

"Hey, most guys play golf and throw their backs out. With writing all you have to worry about is carpal tunnel," Duffy said, as if reading a script. "You got a working title for the book?"

"Yeah, I do," he said, excited somebody was showing some interest in his writing. "Funny, I thought I told you. I guess maybe I didn't. Anyway, it's called *The Murderous Waffle-Maker*. See, there's this woman who can no longer tolerate her husband's laziness. She calls him a beer-guzzling, TV binge-watching fat slob which he is. So one morning at breakfast, she decides to kill him. Now the thing is she's a professional colorist. She was going to stab him but the only knives sharp enough to do the job were those plastic ones. She had a purple one and an orange one. Now she had a problem."

Duffy cast a wayward glance at him. "What's the problem?" he asked as if he didn't know.

"What her husband had on clashed with both purple and orange, so the knives were out."

"I see. As a colorist, she maintained rigid standards."

"Yeah, you know how everything has to be just so for people like that," he explained.

"So what happens?" he asked for the first time. Usually, Duffy found a way to escape him before they got too deep into conversation. They were now in uncharted territory.

Gus took a sip of his whiskey. Leaning back, he said, "She ditches the knives and BFT's him with a waffle iron."

Duffy coughed to cover up his laughter. "I assume you mean blunt force trauma."

"Yeah, but that's probably the way the cops would describe it," he said proudly. Checking his phone for the time, he picked up his drink, finished it and started to reach for his wallet. "Got to go. Maybe get a little writing in before dinner."

"You sure you don't want another?"

"Nope, one and done," he said, putting his credit card on the bar.

No sooner had Gus Latrope departed than Ambrose Dowling and Magnus Flaherty arrived. Duffy was delighted to see them, particularly after his brief experience with the retired carwash owner.

"Sometimes, gentlemen, I feel like my life is one giant meme," Duffy complained before they had a chance to order. "Rubbing his chin, he added with a short laugh, "You know, I don't even know the meaning of that word. I think it's got something to do with repetition."

The professor felt qualified to speak on the topic. "Delete it from your vocabulary, Mr. Hart. While it's culturally popular and hip to use it these days, I suggesting skipping the meme and just tell us what is bothering you. But first, a Cuban Manhattan for me and a Tallisker for my companion, the estimable theater director."

"Do you mind if I make your drinks and grouse at the same time?" Turning around to get what he needed, he said over his shoulder, "It's not a big deal, but a lot of my regulars have set routines and they never ever vary. After five o'clock. life gets back to being wonderfully unpredictable around here. But before five, it's *Groundhog Day.* The same people, the same drinks and, worst of all, the same chatter. Take Gus, who just left. He comes in and studies the liquor bottles for three minutes. Yes, I timed him. Then he orders the same drink, a Maker's Mark on the rocks with a splash. Then we talk a little bit, he finishes the drink and pays up telling me he's one and done. Oh, and you know he's writing a murder mystery."

"Aye, I do. The story of the waffle iron-wielding wife," Magnus said. "He cornered me the other day when Arther was bartending. You weren't around. He asked me what the chances were of a story like that becoming a play."

"What did you tell him?" Ambrose asked.

"I told him to stick with trying to be another Agatha Christie," Magnus replied. "Then he said, 'Is that Chris Christie's wife? 'He's a fan of the governor. I left it unanswered and pretended to take a phone call."

"May we move on to another topic, or should I say mystery?" Ambrose asked while staring into his Cuban Manhattan. "Oh, I do love the color of this drink."

"Does this mystery have to do with your cocktail?" Duffy asked.

"No, it does not. It seems two charities we support recently came into large sums of money. Casa Castaneda and the Chase Center for Children each received donations of one hundred thousand dollars. I know this because I received calls from the organizations thanking me profusely for telling the donor about their missions."

"That's a heavy donation," Magnus said with a low whistle. "Who was the donor?"

"They told me it was an anonymous donation," he replied. "Of course, there is no such thing as anonymous. The Poirot in me surfaced and I learned his identity in minutes."

Duffy leaned across the bar. "And who was it exactly, Hercule?"

In most circumstances such as these where Ambrose has information that will shock, disturb, delight or entertain, he would have put some drama into his response. This time, though, he replied directly, "It was Phineas Flanagan."

Magnus was taken by surprise. "That's the last time I buy him a drink," he muttered.

"All I can say is I love the fact that you gentlemen always bring something different to the bar. It makes up for all the Mr One-and-Done's I have to put up with," Duffy said as he watched the aforementioned Phineas Flanagan walk through the front door. "Uh, it looks like you two have some company. I wonder if he wants one of you to be his Valentine? Or maybe both." It turned out to be a prescient question.

Magnus and Ambrose turned around. While they were visiting with Duffy Hart, the place had begun to fill and Phineas had the entire length of the restaurant to traverse before landing at their corner of the bar. All eyes were on him and he loved the attention. Once he'd seen Magnus and Ambrose eyeing him, he waved daintily and in his orotund voice, exclaimed, "And which one of you divine creatures wants to be my Valentine? Either way, I can't lose as you both look bloody scrumptious."

"Neither of us are interested, but don't let that stop you from buying us a drink," Magnus announced, as he watched Phineas strut, not walk, toward them.

He was dressed in his Savile Row best; a bespoke black and white striped, double-breasted suit, a pink shirt with a starched white collar and French cuffs. A blue and white polkadot bowtie and a paisley silk pocket square finished it off.

Phineas noticed all three men staring at him. Feeling they required an explanation, he shrugged his shoulders and commented, "What can I say, gentlemen. Like what you see?"

Magnus moved over one stool to put Phineas between them. "All right, before we start trying to outdo each other with wittier-than-thou repartee, you've got some explaining to do."

He would have to wait, though, as Ambrose had a question already loaded for firing. "Mr. Flanagan, may I inquire as to the reason you are wearing what I can only describe as Prince Charles 'casual wear?"

Sitting down, Phineas straightened the crease in his pants and brushed imaginary lint from his sleeves. "The short answer is it is Valentine's Day, Professor," he replied saucily. After pausing to order a Boodles Martini, shaken not stirred, he continued, "As for the longer version: I woke up this morning, looked in the mirror, liked what I saw and asked me if I would be my Valentine. Blushing, I said yes without hesitation. Think of the pluses of this kind of pairing. Now I know who is coming home with me after dinner. Also, there's no quibbling over the menu or check. Oh, and the conversation is positively enthralling."

Magnus and Ambrose stared at him. Before they could get him back on track to talk about his charitable actions, Phineas took a sip of his Martini, declared it delicious and asked with a trace of a Western drawl, "So, pardners, just where in this here town does one take one's self for a superb Valentine's dinner?"

"Mr. Flanagan, a number of us, including Mr. Flaherty and his wife, are going to Great China which is close by. It is not romantic but you may find yourself waxing poetic over their food. You are welcome to join us," Ambrose said.

Then, turning to Magnus, Ambrose added quickly, "I haven't spoken out of turn, have I?"

Magnus nodded his approval. "No, of course not. I will enjoy having Phineas and his date join us. You don't mind sitting on one chair?" he asked. Then he changed his tone, anxious to learn more of about the unusual donations. "Okay, my friend, Ambrose, and I want to know more about your recent spendthrift ways."

"Ah, you caught me red-handed," he said, throwing his hands up in the air. "I assume I am being charged with two counts of obscene philanthropy. Well, I plead guilty and throw myself on the mercy of the bartender."

Duffy waved him off. "Leave me out of it, please. I just mix and observe."

Phineas gave him a big smile. "Then, please, observe as I confess my sins." He slid his chair back a bit to accommodate his audience of three. "So, gentlemen, I actually have the professor to thank for my sudden decision to donate to two deserving charities. Ambrose went into great detail..."

"Going into great detail is a singular trait of his," Duffy interjected.

"It is, isn't it," Phineas agreed. Gently patting his thinning hair held perfectly in place by an incredibly expensive hair gel, he continued on, "The other day, the professor, when asked, talked with great enthusiasm about the Banter Foundation, its improbable beginning, its unique approach to giving and the concept that you all embrace and which is built around that debatable question of what is enough. It was epiphanic. I became an instant convert."

"Dublin has its share of charities that are in desperate need of funds" Magnus told him. "Why not wait and help your local neighbors?" Magnus asked.

Phineas frowned. "Aye, me lad, I'm afraid Dublin with its many charms is not in my future. Our city on the banks of the Liffey and I have parted ways," he said with a sadness that touched Magnus.

"Two hundred thousand dollars," Magnus exclaimed. "Phineas, that's a princely sum. Do you have that kind of money to throw around?"

Phineas put a hand on Magnus 'broad shoulder. "Do you remembering buying me a pint or two in my acting days?" he asked.

"Aye, but when you were in the chips, you were always a big spender in the pub. I don't regret my generosity. It was marketing, pure and simple and a gesture of friendship."

"In my acting days, money came and went with stunning regularity. When I got into finance, particularly international finance, it came and came and came. Good Lord, Magnus, I've got piles of the stuff. More than I need. So I am giving away a healthy portion of it," he said, taking a final sip of his Martini. "Sorry for poaching your charities but I figured after Ambrose's explanation of how you guys handle things, these organizations and people deserve it. I can be assured I am putting the money into deserving hands."

Putting his glass down, he leaned in toward Magnus. He was clearly uncomfortable but tried to disguise it. By nature, a frivolous person, Phineas doubled down on his flightiness. "Listen, old bean, don't you think it's a smashing idea to have an understudy for me at the ready. What I mean is you never know when I might get a sudden urge to fly off to..." He paused to find a place. "Oh, I don't know. Perhaps, Mallorca, Miami, Maui or, who knows, Milpitas."

Before Magnus could respond to what he thought was an outrageous request, Duffy, noticing Phineas Flanagan's drained Martini, asked if he wanted another.

The tall, elegantly dressed Irishman rose from his chair. He looked across the bar at Duffy and said, "No, thank you. I'm one and done."

With a soft goodby to the three men, he walked toward the exit.

"He could have gone all day without saying that," Duffy mumbled.9

Chapter 8

"He thinks too much.
Such a man is dangerous."

William Shakespeare

Great China's heady, intoxicating aromas were for Phineas Flanagan's aquiline nose a singular thrill. Searching hungrily and happily for more, his sensitive snoot directed his eyes to scan the long table for eight filled with plates of zhen jiang spareribs, spring rolls, kung pao chicken, half tea-smoked duck, sweet and sour pork, ginger scallion calamari and two huge plates of garlic fried rice and seafood chow mein. All was cooked to perfection. He was at one end of the food-laden table. His neighbors were Sylvie Blanchard and her sister, Ashley Porter. Next to Sylvie was Ambrose Dowling and seated next to Ashley was Caitlin Hart also known as The Redhead. Her husband, Duffy, sat beside her and across from Maggie Leyton whose husband, Magnus Flaherty, occupied the other end of the table. Their noses in their various shapes were also having the time of their lives.

Phineas had decided he would host the evening. He'd already informed the others that the check was headed his way and he would hear no argument. Duffy Hart had told him that the restaurant's wine list was formidable. Phineas, claiming ignorance of California wines, told Bar OSA's owner to forget price and order something memorable and plenty of it.

Ambrose turned to look at Sylvie's plate which was piled dangerously high with Great China's best. "Ms Blanchard, you are a mere wisp of a thing. Where do you plan to put all that?" he asked. "There's enough to satisfy an NFL lineman."

Giving her chopsticks a break, she looked up at Ambrose and smiled though a mouthful of food. "This is just the first course, Professor," she managed to somehow say clearly.

"I so hate her for that," complained Ashley, looking up from her plate that had one sparerib, a small portion of duck and some fried rice. "I just smell this food and I gain a pound."

Phineas picked a moment when everyone was happily chatting away. When he noticed Magnus at the other end was not engaged with anyone except his dinner, he rose and went around to where his director was sitting. "Join me outside for a cigarette, Magnus."

Magnus looked up at him. "I don't smoke. Besides this is Berkeley. The closest you can go to smoke is Norway."

"Then just come outside," he said impatiently. "I need to tell you something. Look at the table. No one's going to miss us."

The two men stepped past those standing outside waiting for a table. Finding a spot away from prying ears, Phineas leaned against the restaurant wall and asked, "Are you sure you can't smoke?"

"I am," he said gruffly. "Now what's this about? I hope you're going to explain about wanting an understudy."

"Yes, I am." Folding his arms against the chill "Magnus, I have a confession to make. I trust that like Father O'Brien, to whom we used to confess our venials and mortals, you'll take this to your grave."

Magnus 'problem with his old friend was he never knew when he was serious. Was this more of his playing around. "All right, PD, let me hear what you have to say."

"When I left acting, I did go into finance. I started with a traditional institution and dealt with things in a legally traditional way. Then I went to work for the Conners," he explained, pausing to wait for what he knew would be Magnus 'shocked reaction.

"Conner as in Shamus Conner, the mob boss? The *Dublin Don* as they call him," he said a little too loudly. He was aghast that Phineas would mention their classmate who was voted most likely to be jailed before he was twenty.

"The very same," he said, confirming his employer was one of the city's more notorious gangsters. "And yes, there wasn't anything illegal the scumbag wasn't involved in, and all of it made him, excuse my street language, a shitload of money. Still does even though he's no longer with us."

"Shamus died?"

"Some time ago. Regretfully, in his sleep, peaceful as a well-fed bairn," he laughed. "I was hoping for a more torturous passing. His twin boys, Tommy and Danny, have been running things since and they don't have a brain between them. Which is, in a way, the reason I'm here."

Magnus rubbed his beard. "Shamus was a fiendish piece of shite. Good God, Phineas, it's hard to believe we went to school with him."

"Aye, we did and while he was fiendish as you say, he was a boy to be feared. Although, I did think he was cute," he felt compelled to add with a playful wink. "Then he grew up to be a man to be even more feared. Remember that time when you beat him up in the schoolyard. You were the only one to take him on."

Magnus remembered the tussle that was the playground highlight of the year. The memory made him laugh. "The fight was more of a draw. I just hid my pain and aches better than he did."

"You know, he and his goons never bothered your pub, the Sword and Parrot, or you because of that fight. Shamus had a lot of respect for you."

"I didn't know that. I didn't pay too much attention to his criminal activity, just what I read in the newspapers," he told him. Magnus pulled his phone out of his inside jacket pocket and checked the time. "You know, Phineas, you pick the damndest times to unload. Here you dump all this on me at a come-outside-for-a-minute chat. And you're still not done unloading. That's not fair, me lad."

Phineas looked at his gold Rolex and frowned. "You're right, of course, we should get back. When can we continue this?"

"Tonight," Magnus said all too quickly.

"It's Valentine's Day."

"Do you mind if Maggie is present?"

"Phineas thought about it. "It does crowd the confessional, but no, I don't mind. I'm sure she's the soul of discretion."

"Where do you want to meet?"

"Phineas, I have no idea where you are camping. I only see you at the theater and Bar OSA."

"I didn't tell you?" he exclaimed. "I left the Four Seasons this week and I now have a sumptuous suite at the Claremont in Berkeley or Oakland. A little brochure says each city claims it as its own. I believe it is in your neighborhood."

They started to walk back toward the Great China entrance. Magnus explained he and Maggie were a five minute walk from the hotel. Phineas insisted they meet in his suite. He promised them they'd be home by midnight. Magnus scoffed and told him they'd be back home by nine-thirty.

***

"I hope you don't mind, but I took some duck from your plate," Sylvie said as Phineas again tucked in to his dinner.

"My dear, have at it," he said in reply. "I am more interested in the calamari."

"Excuse me, Mr. Flanagan, could we step outside, please?"

Phineas turned and looked up at the handsome economics professor, Kenneth Richter. Two weeks prior, Flanagan was instrumental in ending a clumsy confrontation between the professor and Ashley Porter.

"I've just returned from an outside chat," he said, putting his chopsticks down. "Now I'm desirous of partaking of the feast you see before me. Besides, if you're calling me outside for something other than a chat, I must advise you that you'd be making a very big mistake."

"No, no. Just a small chat that will include an apology and a thank you,"

Phineas refolded his napkin. "Well, in that case. You are a cute one, aren't you? Here with anybody?" he asked in his typically naughty manner.

Richter pointed to a nearby table where his Valentine date sat devouring rice with rapidly moving chopsticks. Under the table in an expensive dog-carrier was a quiet but bite-happy Silky named Paris. Lani Chang was a meteorologist for a San Francisco television station that also employed Richter for a weekend news show.

For Valentine's Day, she was wearing a form-fitting red dress with a tight high neck and matching red high-heeled shoes. She was of medium height with a figure that looked like she'd stolen it from a UCLA cheerleader. A goodly percentage of diners at Great China were male students from Cal. When they weren't trying keep sight of their food as it was being shipped from their plates to mouths, their eyes were fixed lustily on Miss Chang.

Phineas rose slowly. Looking mostly at Ashley, he said, "Would you please excuse me. I won't be a moment."

Ashley's perplexing expression prompted the professor to acknowledge her. "This has nothing to do with us," he said affectionately, with a smile that was surprisingly ingratiating.

"There is no *us*," she snapped, her confusion turning to anger.

Still wearing that unctuous grin, he waved good by and followed Phineas outside.

Once again, leaning against the wall of Great China, Phineas rubbed his hands together to warm them against the growing chill of the evening. "I seem to be spending more time outside this restaurant than in it."

Kenneth assured him he would be quick. "First, I want to apologize for my boorish behavior two weeks ago during your rehearsal. It was unbecoming."

Phineas acknowledged his apology with a simple nod of the head. "You also mentioned a thank you, although, I can't imagine for what."

"The thank you is the main reason I invited you out here. You see, I'm on the board of Casa Castaneda. I was just informed of your extremely generous donation," he told him. "So I wanted to thank you for that."

"You are most welcome. The pleasure was all mine."

Kenneth reminded himself not to get pedagogical, a common fault of professors. He just wished he wasn't so self-conscious around Phineas. "So I have been thinking..."

"You have been thinking. Really?" Phineas said, teasing him a bit. "In Shakespeare's *Julius Caesar*, Julie himself said, 'He thinks too much. Such a man is dangerous.'"

Richter gave him a bemused look. "It's the professors 'curse. Thinking too much."

"Of course, it's your job. Anyway, sorry for the interruption. Please continue."

"I was going to say it works both ways. You must also get a kick out of making money." Having said that,

RIchter handed him his business card. "As you can see, I am well placed to counsel and suggest a variety of ways to put your money to good use. I guess what I am saying is I am offering you my services." He wished he hadn't included that last sentence.

Expressionless, the actor/businessman nodded. "Professor, I am in the processing of downsizing and that includes money. I'm not in the least bit interested in making more of the stuff."

Richter immediately changed course. It was so fast, it was almost embarrassing as it was so obvious. "My services also include giving it away." Playing it back in his head, he laughed uncomfortably.

"And I assume one of these charities might benefit you?" Phineas asked. "Altruistically, of course."

The professor smiled and, with a silent nod, confirmed it would always be for the best intentions.

Phineas Flanagan stood upright. "I think it's time we get back to our tables. I'm sure Madame Chiang Kai Chic is wondering where you are. It is Valentine's Day, you know?"

With a bemused look, Richter said, "I thought it was Chiang Kai Shek? Oh, wait a minute. I get it. You made a joke, right?"

"Evidently, a bad one. Professor RIchter, your date is a beautiful woman and certainly demands your attention more than I do. We'll talk later."

After swearing he would never tell an economist a joke again, Phineas patted RIchter on the shoulder, adjusted his suit jacket and headed back inside for what he hoped would be the last time.

Chapter 9

"Lovers and madmen have such
seething brains."

William Shakespeare

As he was already ruining the rest of Magnus and
Maggie's Valentine's evening, Phineas decided to ask
Professor Ambrose Dowling to join them in his suite at
the Claremont Club and Spa after their dinner at Great
China. Ambrose told him he would accept the invitation
only if Phineas call it the Claremont Hotel, its name for a
gazillion years before a major chain took the Grande
Dame over and some marketing guru decided to change
it. Phineas, a born and bred traditionalist, agreed
heartily.

Flanagan left the restaurant before the others. He paid
the bill and added a tip so outrageous, the servers and
host were prepared to carry him out of the restaurant on
a large serving tray.

"Ashley, stop looking at Randy Richter's table," her sister told her. "You're going to make him think you're interested and you'll make me think you're jealous." Sylvie turned and glanced at the professor and the meteorologist. "That's Lani Chang. I catch her doing the weather sometimes. She's got like these enormous pointy..."

"Sylvie, I can see she's busty," her sister interjected.

Sylvie stole a quick glance again. "I was trying to describe her fingernails. They are pointy and painted blood red. I loved the shade so much, I bought some."

Ashley took a rib from her sister's plate. "I've never seen you wear fingernail polish."

"I haven't worked up the courage yet."

"I wonder what *he* wanted from Phineas," she mused aloud.

"We'll find out soon enough. Phineas isn't one to keep quiet about anything," Sylvie replied. "Do you think it has something to do with you?"

Clearly unnerved by Richter's presence, Ashley answered sharply, "It'll sound like I'm boasting but everything he does has something to do with me."

That was a little too much for her commonsensical sister. With a short laugh, Sylvie said, "I doubt that very much, my overly beautiful sister."

Leaning across the table, Ashley said slowly and accusingly, "The man is *stalking* me."

Sylvie leaned in, too. Even closer. "Showing up at the same restaurant is not stalking, Ash. It's called coincidence." She sat back and stared lovingly at her sister. "You're not listening to me, are you?"

"Wha...," Ashley uttered. "Sorry, Syl, I'm just really pissed." She pushed back her chair and started to stand up. "I'm going to go over there and ruin that son of a bitch's Valentine's dinner. I'll have him choking on his egg foo young."

Sylvie's eyes watched as her sister rose to full height. "Great China wouldn't be caught dead serving egg foo young," she told her.

"Sit down," Ambrose commanded suddenly, his voice unusually stern. A surprised Ashley did as she was told. "Ms Porter, you are contemplating a capricious act that you will come to regret later. You are better than that."

"And I'm guessing here but I'll bet that weather girl would love nothing better than to get it all on Instagram and Facebook. She looks the type," her sister tossed in for good measure.

***

"Okay, Kenneth, who's the woman at that large table? I noticed you talking to her when you went over there." Lani Chang was pointing one chop stick at him while she delivered her question.

"As you well know, I went over there to talk to the gentleman at the end of the table," he explained to her. "And put that chop stick down. Stop using it as an accusatory tool."

"It does get a point across," she countered. "Kenneth darling, I can see from here that she was saying something to you and she was clearly upset or angry."

"Oh yeah, she was that," he said reflectively. "That's why I keep looking over there. I'm trying to figure out who she is and why she acted the way she did. My best guess is she's a former student and maybe I graded her poorly and she's still pissed off. It happens, but I still sleep at night."

"So what's with the guy you went over to talk to? The one dressed like Mr. Peanut," she said, hooking between her chopsticks what appeared to be a fifteen foot long noodle. Kenneth knew just watching her reel it in would be exciting.

"He's from Ireland. You'll love his name. It's Phineas Flanagan."

She turned to look at the table but Phineas had disappeared. "I call men that age fossils. I know there are other terms like codger, coot, old-timer, et cetera, but fossil hits the mark with him. I will say this, though, the dude's one flamboyant fossil."

"He is that. Anyway I went over there to thank him personally. He gave a rather substantial amount of money to a charity that I am a board member of."

"Don't end a sentence with a preposition," she teased. "You *are* a professor."

Miffed, RIchter stewed, but for just a second. "Turns out he's in the process of giving away much of his money. I think I convinced him to let me help him."

Lani's eyes shone greedily. "And is there any chance some of that money will drift your way?"

"Like sea shells at low tide," he laughed. "Listen, play your cards right and don't let your dog bite me tonight and I might take you to Hawaii. How does four nights at the Halekulani in a Diamond Head ocean-front room sound?"

Lani put her chopsticks down. She reached over and gave Kenneth a kiss full of soy and other assorted Asian flavors. "That sounds marvelous. But why is it I have this odd feeling that you'd rather take that ex-student with you." Nodding her head in Ashley's direction, she exclaimed, "Criminy, my horny professor, if I swung that way, I'd be chasing her, too."

"I love it that you are so romantic," he grumbled.

Chapter 10

"Let me play the fool"

William Shakespeare

Phineas welcomed Magnus Flaherty and Maggie Leyton to his one-bedroom suite at the Claremont Hotel. The evening was cloudless and the view of the bay from the living room was stunning. It was also distracting, because your eyes were continually drawn to it. Phineas did not appreciate the competition so he closed the drapes explaining that he was the star of this evening's entertainment.

Professor Ambrose Dowling arrived minutes later. Surveying the room's luxurious deco. "It seems inappropriate to have the drapes closed on such an illustrious evening," he said, marching toward the windows to open them.

"Phineas prefers them drawn, Ambrose," Maggie Leyton told him.

"Ah, an evening of clandestine conversation. Are you sure I am old enough to participate?"

Maggie and Magnus had settled themselves on the suite's sofa while Ambrose took a chair near them, allowing Phineas to have an attentive audience. While they waited for room service, Magnus looked around, sensing something was missing.

"Phineas, this room has no hanging artwork. There are no paintings, prints, photos. Nothing." he said as his eyes scanned the walls.

"I had them remove everything," Phineas explained, his contorted face evidence of his disapproval. "It's bad enough that I have to live with this pedestrian furniture, but I draw the line at corporate art. It has followed me around for decades and is an annoying pest. Hotels, offices, conference rooms... You name them and I have been in them and none of them had anything hanging that was remotely tasteful, fitting or pleasurable to the eye. I apologize for the bareness, but it is a far more enjoyable environment than the one created by the monstrosities that hung here." He pursed his lips. "Or is it hanged here? I can never get that right."

"Hung will do, Mr. Flanagan," Ambrose said. "May I suggest you ask the hotel to decorate your walls with some of the historic, black and white photos of their early noteworthy guests. They are an entertaining peek into the hotel's colorful past."

Phineas beamed. "I shall do that, Professor. I'm paying a king's ransom for this place. I might was well make one more demand."

Room service was widely praised. Realizing they'd eaten well at Great China, their host had ordered a variety of cheeses and fruits. While the server was there,

Phineas had her make after-dinner drinks from a selection of familiar spirits she'd brought along.

After his guests were settled, Phineas took center stage. The tall, lean, well-dressed man was ready to perform, but first he needed to know if his audience was suitably prepped. "Ambrose, Maggie, has Magnus filled you in on what we talked about earlier this evening?" he asked.

"He has, Mr. Flanagan," Ambrose replied. "I look forward to hearing more."

"I'm all caught up. Magnus tells me everything." Maggie patted her husband's knee affectionately and said, "That is probably the only physical act of love you'll experience this Valentine's night, my dear."

"I will be brief, Maggie. The night is young. You will have your night of romance," I assure you.

"Probably not. It's already past my bedtime," grumbled Magnus.

"Then onward. As Gratiano says, *Let me play the fool,*" Phineas proclaimed. Deciding that standing was too formal, he sat opposite them. Crossing his long legs, Phineas thought about how to tell his tale. He promised himself it was for the best to go light on glibness.

"I was twenty-seven when I left acting to join Bondley-Adams Limited, a financial firm with a somewhat shady reputation. It was headquartered in the International Financial Services Center in the Dublin Docklands. I came to the job with a talent for numbers. The company gave me a crash course on currency. At the time, my local was The Grumpy Grouse, a popular hangout for all us new-to-the-business guys and gals. Often, older money managers and execs would pop in, primarily to hit on the cuter among us. It wasn't a left-brain crowd. You could count the aesthetes on one hand. This was strictly a numbers crowd. They all knew two plus two equals four, but I knew how to make two plus two equal eight. As a result, I was a rising star. One evening, Shamus Conner wandered in with the CEO of Bondley-Adams. I was the reason they were there. Shamus was Mister Charm, sharing with the CEO tales about when we were a couple of boyos and how he used to bully me about."

"I'll bet he didn't bring up our schoolyard fight," Magnus slipped in, hoping Phineas would tell Maggie of his heroics as a young lad.

Phineas did not disappoint. "No, he didn't. Looking at Maggie, he added, Your husband was the only person to best Shamus in a fight and live to tell about it."

Maggie squeezed Magnus 'hand. "And did you fight him to save little Colleen or Bridget's honor?"

"No, nothing like that. He called me a fecking biffo."

"I think I get the gist of that," she laughed.

Phineas issued a loud ahem to continue his story. "So, after our impromptu school reunion, he chased my boss away and then explained to me he was there to hire me. Mind you, I felt more like a conscript than a recruit. He was quite clear about what he expected from me. Put simply, he wanted me to take his dirty four and make it a clean eight. My salary was almost embarrassing. As a bonus, he offered to pay the tuition for my sixteen-year-old niece, Quinn, to study at the Royal Irish Academy of Music. She is a cellist who started out a precocious prodigy and is now a touring soloist."

"That was extremely generous of him," commented Ambrose. "The academy is one of Europe's oldest music conservatories."

"He wasn't being generous, Professor. That was his subtle way of telling me to play by his rules because he knows where my family lives if I don't."

"Sounds like the Shamus Conner I knew," Magnus remarked.

"I followed the rules for years with an award-winning steadfastness," Phineas said almost proudly. "Shamus had told Bondley-Adams to provide me with an office, but I was rarely there as my job took me to countries far and wide. I traveled grandly; five-star hotels and first-class air. I made a lot of money for Mr. Conner and his thugs."

"So you were laundering his dirty money," Maggie said disapprovingly, though thinking his narrative would make a grand movie.

Phineas wore a penitent look. "A variation of it, Maggie. The money I washed grew several sizes larger.

"Gotcha," she uttered.

"Shamus and I were the same age, but by twenty-seven he was already an established mob leader. He turned out to be a decent employer. He kept me away from all their illegal activities of which there were many. I never knew any of his associates or goons personally. You pick the term you prefer. Personally, I think one reason he kept me out of the loop was because of my sexual preference. Homophobia ran rampant through this bad-ass, testosterone-fueled crowd."

Magnus was getting impatient. "So Phineas, what changed and why are you, for the lack of a better way to explain it, worried about your mortal future?"

"Magnus, I appreciate your wanting me to move this along. I promise to edit wisely but let me tell my tale, please."

"It's your party, Phineas. Please continue."

"There came a time early on when I decided I ought to take my fair share of these ill-gotten gains. So, instead of making eight out of the four with eight for them, I made seven for them and one for me. Then when his demented twin sons took over, it was six for them and two for me. You have no idea how much I managed to store away in such a short time. I chose a bank in the sunny climes of the Caribbean. The money's there under my company name of FTC Holdings."

Maggie had a thing about initials. She had to know what they stood for. She asked Phineas.

"Fuck the Conners," he replied with a wry smile. "Sorry, I should have said feck. It goes down much better."

Magnus couldn't help himself. He raised his hand and asked, "So now Shamus is dead and his twin boys are running things. What changed?"

Phones frowned. He rose from his chair and began to pace the living room while he talked. "When Shamus was alive, he was what we Irish call a bleedin 'bowsie, a very disreputable character. But his crimes were local and the money went international. When Tommy and Danny took over, the crimes went international as well. These two goons jumped in bed with the Russians, Ukrainians and gangs from all the countries that end in STAN. Oh, and toss in few malevolent Arabs and Italians, too," he explained.

Ambrose Dowling decided to weigh in: "Mr, Flanagan, in business that's called expansionism. It would seem only natural. Personally, the nature of their business is repellent to me large or small. And you were a part of it no matter what its size and scope, so I I fail to see how this growth affects you. It certainly can't have anything to do with conscience."

Phineas sat back down. "Ouch, Professor. All right, I admit what Shamus and I did was inexcusable. I hope it might be forgivable," he said in a low voice. "The twin's expansionism, as you called it, became a turning point for me. The people they are now aligned with are truly nasty. Heinous doesn't begin to describe them. And the twins themselves are as thuggish as you get. I wanted out. You see, the twins, unlike Shamus, wanted me close. I soon found myself dealing with unsmiling men shaped like boxcars with names like Ivan and Igor."

Magnus leaned forward. "So what happened? Did they find out about you embezzling their dad and them over the years?"

"Good heavens, no," he replied, gesturing grandly as if he were on stage. "They're not bright enough and way too unimaginative to find out about my personal retirement account."

"But they *are* after you," Magnus said. "Or, at least, you seem to think they are. Something has you worried."

Phineas sat back down. "Two months ago, I told them I was going to take a holiday, explaining I needed a break. It seems they interpreted that to mean I quit. That's what a trusted source told me. And that's really unsettling because theirs is not a business that gives you a gold watch and pats your fanny on the way out. They would end our relationship by ending me. As soon as they find me, that is."

Maggie seemed puzzled. "You told them you were just taking a break, Phineas. How can that be misinterpreted?"

He shrugged his shoulders. "I think because I told them I would only be gone for a week and that was eight weeks ago," he answered, giving her guileless look.

Magnus leaned forward. "So what else have you learned from this trusted source who, I hope, has your best interest at heart."

Phineas thought a moment. Was he too quick to put his faith in Shamus Conner's wife? He remembered telling her jokingly that she was his Deep Throat. Anything that was worth his knowing, Mary Eileen Conner provided it. She was a tough Dubliner who brooked no nonsense from her gangster husband. She was, in many respects, as potentially dangerous as the Conner boys but inexplicably she had taken a liking to Phineas. She enjoyed his joie de vivre and what she called his *savoir-fairy*. When she learned that Tommy and Danny were up in arms over his absence, she let Phineas know. She told him the twins were convinced he was on the run because he had probably stolen money from them. Their reason for thinking that? "Don't all poofs try to steal you blind," her son had told her.

As to Magnus's question of her loyalty, Phineas said he was sure his source could be trusted. "I learned today that Tommy and Danny were talking about dealing with me personally and there would be no problem finding me. That meant only one thing. They would seek out my niece, Quinn, and ask her."

"Does she know?"

"She didn't until I called her this morning and told her to tell them if they call on her," he replied.

"Whatever for?" Maggie asked incredulously.

"Because those boyos are brutal sadists who believe in doing anything to get the answers they want. *I don't know* is never acceptable in their grimy awful world. It's better Quinn knows and tells them."

Magnus shook his head. "You are an amazing sort, Phineas."

"She's a cellist, my dear fellow. They'd think nothing of breaking her hands."

The plush suite that wasn't quite up to Phineas Flanagan standards fell silent. All four sat silently for a moment, each of them pondering the predicament of the man slated to play Antonio in *Merchant of Venice*.

Maggie broke their silence. "Phineas, is it their intention to kill you?"

"That would seem to be the case, my dear," Phineas replied. "And yes, I am scared out of my extraordinary wits." Okay, he thought, a little glibness might help lighten the mood.

Ambrose rubbed his chin. "Mr. Flanagan, we, that is the three of us, and the others in the Banter Foundation, have been involved in any number of shenanigans and unusual adventures but none so threatening and daring as this," he said.

"He's right, Phineas, but I'm sure there's something we can do to help you," Magnus remarked.

Maggie held up her hand and waved it with enthusiasm. "Oh, there is definitely something we can do," she said with unrestrained confidence.

With vexed expressions, Phineas, Ambrose and Magnus all stared at the pert Hollywood screenwriter.

"And what is that?" asked her husband.

"We kill him before they do."

Chapter 11

"Okay, play dead. Count to fifty."

A child's game rule

Phineas walked to the window and opened the drapes. The view once again became part of their Valentine's Day gathering. He remained there, staring at the glittery spectacle.

Without turning to face his guests. he said over his shoulders, "Ladies and gentlemen, we have now arrived at the scene of this drawing-room comedy where the director speaks."

Kicking his stage accent up a notch, he continued, "The director says, 'Cue Phineas Flanagan for his reaction to Maggie's preposterous idea. Phineas, my dear, I want shock and surprise but I want you to keep it subdued as your character is cool in every circumstances. Are we ready to shoot? All right, walk toward Maggie, Phineas. Don't forget heel to toe. And we are rolling.'"

Phineas 'movements were that of a young man; fluid and graceful. Arriving at the sofa, he sat on the edge next to Maggie. Poised and erect, he looked like a toothsome swain ready to profess his undying love to the woman who had stolen his heart.

"Maggie, you said and I quote, 'We will kill him before they do. 'I know I am *him*. I also know who *they* are. But who are *we*?"

Maggie ran her hand through her short hair. "Us," she chirped, pointing to Ambrose and her husband who appeared to be falling asleep. She nudged him and he awoke with a grunt.

Ambrose held up a hand. "Does your imaginary director allow other characters to insert themselves into the scene, Mr. Flanagan?"

"Of course, he does," he laughed heartily. "That was just my silly way of dealing with Maggie's rather startling suggestion. What is it you want to say, Ambrose?"

"I want to add that it won't be just the three of us killing you off. I am guessing here but I think Maggie intends on employing the full force of the theater group and the members of the Banter Foundation."

Now that he was awake, Magnus added with a friendly wink, "Aye, Phineas, you remember the old adage. it takes a village to kill off an Irishman,"

Ignoring him, Phineas returned to his conversation with Maggie. "This may sound like a silly question but your answer, if it's in the affirmative, would be a great comfort to me. Is this a pretend killing?" he asked, almost seriously.

"Yes, it is. And may I add that it will be the very best pretend killing we can muster, " she said with the same cockiness she exhibited when she pitched a screenplay in Hollywood.

Flanagan popped up from the sofa so as to better address all three. "While you two might assume I think Maggie's idea is farfetched, I assure you I embrace it fully."

"I should think it would be fun to have my wife plan your demise, theatrically speaking, that is," Magnus said.

Ignoring him a second time, Phineas turned to Maggie. "My dear, I knew when I left Ireland, I would be on the run forever and dear Dublin would exist for me only in my dreams and memories. The Conner boys, you see, would never let me happily retire. My knowledge of their operations puts me in this perilous position."

"What about the money?" Ambrose asked.

"Ah, the money," he repeated. Phineas gave that serious thought. "Professor, I feel confident enough to say they know nothing of my assets. I would have heard even if they had an inkling. Let us pray, it stays that way."

Maggie put him back on track. "So you left Ireland and planned to..."

"Recycle Phineas Dermot Flanagan and take on another identity. A friend in the Docklands knew of an excellent forger who lives in San Francisco. I have already hired him to create all the documents I am going to become a seventy-two year old bon vivant named Reginald Pennington.

"REGINALD PENNINGTON!" shouted Magnus in a thunderous voice. "Will you please explain the logic behind that daft choice?"

Phineas shrugged his shoulders. "With my Queen's English accent, I appear more English than Irish. As for the name itself, I think it suits me. Besides, I have always liked the name Reggie. Think about it, Magnus. I even dress like a Reggie Pennington."

Maggie was busy taking notes on her iPhone. She looked up at their host and said, "Do me a favor. Call your friendly forger and ask him to add a death certificate for Phineas Flanagan to your list of valuable documents."

Ambrose held up a hand. "A death certificate lists cause or causes of death. How do you plan on handling that?"

"Excellent question, Professor." Maggie closed her eyes and thought hard. "What was on my father's certificate? Let me think."

"I remember," Magnus said, turning to stare at her beside him. "He died of extreme happiness after raising a talented, free-spirited and beautiful daughter. It says so right on that formal document."

Maggie blushed, took his hand and brought it to her face. "That's the nicest Valentine's Day present ever."

Phineas Flanagan, witnessing this display of giddy romance, brought both his hands to his cheeks and cooed, "No wonder I had such a crush on you when we were acting together."

Ambrose brought everyone back to earth. "We still need a cause."

Maggie's eyes signaled she'd remembered. "I got it! Cardiopulmonary arrest." She shrugged her shoulders. "Beats me as to what that is. I don't pay much attention to medical stuff. For our purposes, though, it sounds good."

"My great grandfather, Phineas the second, died from delirium tremens caused by acute alcoholism. Father said he was great fun while he was with us."

Ambrose folded his arms. "Speaking of colorful causes of death: My grandfather, who was a bit of a wanderer died from Bronze John while traveling in Panama in 1906.

"Oh? Let me guess. He died of an overdose of sunscreen," Phineas remarked.

"While that does seem to be an intriguing way to go, he died of yellow fever," Ambrose said. "However, I must remember that sunscreen line."

"Those are two fascinating suggestions, gentlemen, but I think we will stick with cardiopulmonary arrest," Maggie told them. "Phineas, do you want to make a note of that?"

"Don't worry. I will remember and I will tend to it immediately, Maggie,"he said, returning to the chair he had occupied earlier. Sitting down, he leaned forward to be closer to the two people on the sofa. He wore a huge giddy smile as he felt a great weight had been lifted off his shoulder. He had been so busy constructing Reginald Pennington, he never once gave a thought as to how to make Phineas disappear. He had said blithely to Maggie that he was going to recycle Phineas, but he had no idea what that meant. He had entertained the idea of having him die but it sounded complicated.

"Maggie, Magnus and you, too, Ambrose, I can't tell you how appreciative I am to have friends like the three of you," he said with a cheerful earnestness. "It's odd, you know, that I never came to terms with what to do about Phineas once I became Reggie. Thank you for helping me get out of this nasty mess. To think, I just needed to be murdered."

"Whoa, Phineas," Magnus exclaimed. "No one is being murdered here. Maggie, Ambrose and I are not murderers. However, we're going to do a great job in killing you. There is a difference."

Maggie looked at the two men. "Listen to you two, carrying on like little schoolboys" she said scoldingly. Phineas, all you need to know is that our tinkering with your mortality will be a credible and suitably creative production."

Magnus jumped right back in. "Maggie's right. I hope you understand that

it's going to take a concerted group effort and and that means a lot of people are going to have to know why." He pointed at his Irish schoolboy friend. "And *you* are going to have to share with them the story of how you got yourself into this tidy mess. And you can't leave anything out."

Phineas popped right up and his eyes brightened. "How about assembling everyone involved in this grand charade and I'll put on a one-man show. I am a fantastic monologist and because it is such a spell-binding tale, one that is so near and dear to me, it is only I who can do it justice."

"Mr. Flanagan has an excellent idea. I can take charge of bringing everyone together. Just give me a time and date," Ambrose said.

"Maggie, I am curious, though, about one thing. I realize your ambition is to convince the Conner twins of my death. So obviously, I must be missing. Do you want me to go into hiding? I'm guessing Tommy and Danny will visit the theater where you'll produce the death certificate and tell them in as mournful a tone as you can produce how I came to be deceased. Then you'll call me out of hiding after giving the Conners directions back to Ireland and Bob's your uncle."

Maggie rose from the sofa and stretched. "I've been sitting too much today," she complained, as minor aches began to dance through her body. "Phineas, you are not going into hiding. We need you there because we'll need a corpse. This may sound like a contradiction in terms but we need a corpse that is very lifelike. I suppose I really mean dead-like," she giggled. "Remember, the Conner boyos, as you call them, will probably want certifiable proof you're dead."

It was as if Phineas 'imaginary director just asked him to produce an expression that blended fear, doubt and worry. His face was awash with all three. "So for the first time in my life, I am to play a corpse." He drew a breathe. "Maybe not. When we were kids, we used to play a shoot'em up game and when you were you killed, you'd play dead and count to fifty. I only counted to thirty-five," he boasted.

Maggie approached him. "We are theater people, Phineas. Our creative resources are limitless. We are going to use all the tricks of the trade from both stage and movies," she told him. "The Conners will go back to Ireland convinced you were dead. Then we will all welcome Reggie Pennington to our little world."

Phineas, seeing her eyeing the exit, prepared to wish them all adieu. "Well, my friends, it's a plan that is still raw and undeveloped but Maggie has convinced me there's a way of avoiding the deadly wrath of those two cretins, and for that I am grateful."

They had all gathered in a little cluster near the double-door entry to his suite. Their goodbyes were said in a variety of fashions. Only then did Maggie fail to stifle a mischievous urge. She put an hand on Phineas 'arm and stared up at him affectionately.

"Oh,I forgot a minor but important detail," she said with a disarming sweetness.

"What's that, my dear?"

"Would you rather be buried or cremated?"

Chapter 12

"Are they still called undertakers?"

Sylvie Blanchard

Maggie Flaherty took complete charge of killing off Phineas Dermot Flanagan. A screenwriter by trade, she approached this group project in much the same manner as she would a film. First, she wanted to to see it all in her mind from start to finish. Or, as Phineas joked, from death to resurrection. She made copious notes and her to-do list was the length of her arm. Maggie knew they needed at least a week to prepare. A few more days would be a blessing. And it was a blessing they received.

Early Tuesday evening, February 19th, Phineas had phoned Maggie and Magnus. In an animated and agitated manner, he told them he'd heard from both his niece, Quinn, and Mary Eileen, Shamus Conner's widow. He described Quinn's call as riveting and frightening. When the Conner twins visited his niece, demanding threateningly to know where he was, following Phineas' explicit instructions, she let her well-known Irish temper flare and proceeded in telling them her son-of-a-bitch, no-feckin'-good uncle had skipped off to Berkeley, California to try and revive his acting career. When asked to explain her red-faced rage, she said her uncle had just informed her that he had rewritten his will, leaving her a lousy two thousand euros. She said he had decided that when he passed, he was going to leave the bulk of his estate to charity. The clever ruse worked as they left her unhurt. Even though compassion was not part of their makeup, the two thugs did attempt to console her.

Mary Eileen's phone call came on the heels of Quinn's. She was more than eager to help her former husband's financial advisor. She had good reason. When Shamus died, her sons had cheated her out of the money promised her in her husband's will. Instead, they gave her a pittance of an allowance which denied her the style of life her husband had provided. Unknown to the boys, Phineas promised their mother enough money to get out of Dublin and out of the twin's toxic and violent world. As miserly as they were to their mother, though, like all dutiful sons, they always looked in on her. On this, their most recent visit, they informed her of their plans to deal personally with Phineas. They told her of their puzzlement over the length of his absence and, sticking with their pig-ignorant view that all gays are inherently untrustworthy, they were certain he had absconded with some of their hard-earned. No sooner had they left than Mary Eileen let Phineas know her sons would be arriving in San Francisco on the last day of February and were planning to visit Berkeley the next day. Their plan was to deal with Phineas and then leave Berkeley because everything they had heard about the university city convinced them they would be surrounded by the political, social and religious dingbats of the world. Mary Eileen wondered where she went wrong in raising them.

Maggie had told Phineas to get his story ready as they would assemble everyone the following day at the theater. After an early rehearsal, they would map out his mortal demise which included Phineas first explaining how to he came to have two vicious and violent Irish thugs who look alike chase after him. In a lighter mood, she asked him jokingly if he would like to give a name to their imaginative operation.

"*The Phineas Resurrection* has a fitting ring to it," he had answered drolly. "Although, it sounds frighteningly like a Jeffery Archer novel and, speaking as an ex-altar boy with lingering beliefs, I don't feel comfortable appropriating the word resurrection. Let's keep it simple. How about *Flanagan's Wake?*"

After ending her call with Phineas, Maggie and Magnus took the next twenty minutes and reached out to Ambrose, the Harts and Sylvie Blanchard whose jobs were to alert everyone about the next night's assembly. That done, Magnus suggested they go to the Berkeley City Club for a drink at Morgan's bar with its reputation for being a library-quiet establishment.

Maggie plucked a small olive out of her Martini. "I'm really excited by all of this," she said in a low voice, holding the olive up for close inspection before putting it into her mouth.

"You know, Maggie dear, it's a positive joy to watch you confront a Martini. You do the same thing every time. The first to go into that beautiful mouth of yours, even before you take a sip, is the garnish which always gets a rigorous going-over before you eat it. Don't ever change that custom as I am charmed by it."

She produced a coy smile and promised not to. "Magnus, just think we have the opportunity to save a man's life." With a playful wink, she added, "Even if it means killing him."

"Aye, Maggie, but what concerns me is the number of people needed to make it all happen." he said.

"Secrets can be kept by groups," she stated with a calm assurance that she was right in in her belief. "I mean, look at the CIA. They must have thousands of people in their employ. And they are all about secrets."

Magnus's harumph was almost too loud for Morgan's bar tranquil ambiance. "Maggie, the CIA leaks like a sieve. It has from its beginning and will continue to do so. And these are people who have security clearances. I'l bet when they get caught, they have their eyebrows ripped off, the word *leaker* tattooed on their private parts and..."

Maggie stopped him in time as he'd run out of imagined torturous actions taken by the CIA. She put a hand on his drinking arm. "Okay, my Large Irishman, I get your point. Mine is I choose to believe our friends and the theater company will give us their wholehearted trust and they'll keep mum about what we're up to."

Magnus Flaherty stroked the hand that held his arm. He loved the feel of her skin. "You choose to believe, then so do I. This is your plan, so tell me what you want me to do."

She reached into her over-sized catch-all bag and brought out a notebook. "Tell me first about an Irish wake."

"Sure. The history of the wake is interesting. It all began when women in the neighborhood came to the deceased's house to wash the body and then wrap it in white linen. They then festooned it with black and white ribbons" he explained. "Now here's what's really unusual. No crying was allowed until the body was washed and clothed for fear of evil spirits carting the soul away. Pretty soon the somberness of a wake waned and the celebrating of the deceased's life waxed. There were all sorts of pranks that were played and special songs that were sung. Among the men, feats of strength were performed by lifting the corpse like you would a weight."

Maggie made no notes. "There'll be none of that at our wake," she said sternly.

That didn't stop Magnus from continuing. "You'll appreciate this. Often, the family hired women keeners who were paid to wail, howl and cry."

"No keeners, please," she mumbled. "Magnus, don't make me sorry I asked you about a wake."

"Suffice it to say, it has evolved."

She took a small sip of her Martini. "Here's what I foresee happening. We hold the wake next Friday before the curtain rises on your first dress rehearsal. We let everyone know that Phineas had made a deathbed wish that he be celebrated on stage and we thought it only fitting to schedule it then as he was going to play Antonio."

"I will have everyone at the theater prepared for this," he promised.

"We're going to need an undertaker." She heard herself say undertaker and giggled, thinking it old-fashioned. "Do you think they are still called that?" she wondered.

"My da used to call them cold cooks. I have also heard them referred to as death-hunters, but you don't want to go using those expressions. I think nowadays they call themselves funeral directors," Magnus replied.

"Okay, but in this case, *I'm* the funeral director," she asserted.

"Aye aye, Ma'am," he said with a casual salute.

"Anyway, Ambrose is tackling that job," she said, reaching across the table and taking his hand. "Magnus, darling, I don't think what I'm about to tell you is going to sit well with you."

Her husband gave her a wary look. "And why would that be?"

"It involves Phyllis Hathaway," she said.

Her husband's reaction was immediate. "What?" he shouted.

They both signaled apologies to the three elderly couples nearest their table.

"This is like drinking in an old people's home," she whispered.

"Maggie, darling, we are the same age as those people, give or take a year or two," he whispered back.

"Well, we don't act it or look it. Old, that is," she huffed, leaning back and folding her arms.

Magnus thought it best to just raise his glass and silently toast agreement.

"So what I want to tell you is Phyllis 'brother owns a funeral home and creamatorium, somewhere east of here," she told him.

Magnus grinned. "It's a crematorium, not a creamatorium. A creamatorium is where you go to buy unlimited supplies of whipped cream."

"Oh, that would be right up your alley, Mr. Cool Whip," she teased, knowing his fondness for the sweet treat. "Anyway, she's helped us before and the Hathaways are big donors to the theater. I'm certain Ambrose can talk her around. To make this work, we are going to need a specially-constructed casket and a hearse."

"She hates me, Maggie," he reminded her. "Remember, I'm the one who planned the real marriage of her son in the last act of *As You Like It*. And to a woman Phyllis didn't even approve of. Thus, I denied her the wedding of her dreams for her son. The woman still barks at me like some crazed chihuahua."

"She is more the prissy poodle type, darling," she laughed. "In her defense, though, she did step in and help us last year. Look, she's a rich, society woman who likes occasionally to step out of her insulated world. This is yet another chance for her to do that. Let's let Ambrose work his magic with her."

"Aye, you're right. The wily professor will get you what you need. That I am sure of. Somehow, someway, he'll charm that hairsprayed monster." Magnus finished his Martini and placed it on the table. He signaled the lone server for the bill.

"Maggie, a final word. I don't mean to be a squeaky wheel, but I have to say the number of people this enterprise requires concerns me greatly."

His wife's smile was a comfort. She put a hand on his arm and, leaning forward, told him she agreed with him.

"The problem, my Large Irishman, is everybody has to be in on it to make it work. I tried looking at it with the idea of just letting essential people know what we're up to but it won't work. Once those thuggish twins arrive at the theater, we can't afford any foulups or missteps. Everyone must play their part."

"You know, my pretty pixie, Shakespeare had something for almost all conversations," he said with a curvy smile that his wife didn't appreciate.

She looked at him sternly. "Magnus, don't you dare."

Ignoring her, be began: *All the world's a stage and all the men and women merely players; they have their exits and entrances; and one man in his time plays many parts...*"

Maggie looked around the room. "Sh, please, Magnus. Whenever you quote the Bard, your voice rises and people in the next city can hear you."

"Ah, Maggie, you could have at least waited until I got to the part about the infant mewling and puking in the nurse's arms. I love that line."

"Excuse me, but isn't that from *As You Like It?*" The question was asked by one of the elderly gentlemen seated at a table close to them.

Magnus looked over at the bearded man whom he guessed was in his late seventies. He was dressed in workingman's jeans, a plaid flannel shirt with red suspenders and well-walked-in sandals over thick, wooly socks. Like a napping pet, a worn, wide-brimmed Tilley rested on the floor. He looked like he would be more at home in a bar in the Gold Country than the Berkeley City Club. Magnus smiled at the gent and said, "Yes, it is."

"Any chance you know the rest of it. I'd buy you a drink to hear it, particularly with that charming brogue of yours," he said in a geezer-like voice.

"And I'd love to recite it for you, particularly as I am now in the sixth age," Magnus replied.

The man shifted in his seat. He glared at a robust Magnus. "Nonsense, I don't see your shank shrinking and you still have your big manly voice," he laughed.

Magnus leaned forward. In a confidential tone, he said, "I would love to, sir, but my wife would kill me."

Maggie with a raised voice, added, "Oh, go right ahead, darling. I'm already killing somebody this week."

Chapter 13

"We that are true lovers run into strange capers"

William Shakespeare

Sylvie listened carefully as the professor chatted enthusiastically about Maggie's inspired project dubbed *Flanagan's Wake*. She had just one question. It was an innocent inquiry that she had saved for the end of their conversation.

"Ambrose, what's a wake?"

Normally, the chatty professor would have, with delight, answered her in entertaining detail. However, on this Thursday evening, he was pressed for time.

"Ms Blanchard, whilst I rarely advise this, in fact, I condemn it for all things related to personal health, I recommend you consult Google," he said. "I'm sure it overflows with information about this funereal ritual."

"Will do," she said cheerily, sensing he was in a rush. "I'll see you tomorrow."

"You will, Ms Blanchard. And may I say I'm surprised we got through this phone call without your sister interrupting us for some fashion advice," Ambrose laughed.

"Yeah, me too," she responded dryly as it as no laughing matter for her.

Her sister's timing was off by two seconds. As soon as Sylvie put down her phone, Ashley implored, "I really need your help, Syl."

She was standing in the doorway to her bedroom where clothes and shoes were strewn about on her bed. A cat would have found it inviting. Ashley was wearing a light blue jacket over a white tank top and ash-grey, fitted pants. On her left foot was a dressy black boot while on the other was a low-heeled soft-yellow shoe. "The shoe or boot? I can't decide."

Sylvie, used to her sister asking about outfit, said, "I didn't know you were going out."

"A group from work is meeting in downtown Oakland for drinks. I'd normally pass but I don't feel like staying in tonight. So what's it to be? Shoe or boot?"

"Definitely, the shoe. The boot makes you look like a mild-mannered dominatrix."

Ashley's hazel eyes widened. "That settles it. I'm wearing boots." She did a model's turn and returned to her messy bedroom.

"I guess I'll just sit here all night and gorge myself on veggie-sticks," Sylvie shouted at her disappearing sister. "Not that I am trying to make you feel sorry for me."

Plopping down on their sofa, she curled up on one end of it. She began to think about what she'd do with the rest of her Thursday evening. She could visit

Ambrose. He was always good for conversation and great-tasting cheese and chardonnay, but he had already admitted to being busy. Okay, she told herself, this is the perfect time to read *Merchant of Venice*. She wasn't in *The Merchant of Venice,* but she felt as the theater manager, she should always be versed in the company's current production. She reached for her Kindle where she had downloaded all of the Bard's plays and sonnets.

"Okay, sorry to interrupt your veggie-stick binge but I have one more question," Ashley said, flying back into the room and standing over her sister at the edge of the sofa.

Sylvie glanced at her feet. Ashley was wearing the yellow shoes. "Cool, Ash. I really do like those on you."

"Forget the shoes. This is an earring question. Hoops or my diamond studs?"

Sylvie scanned northward from her sister's feet to her face. Everything in between seemed to be in stylish order. She tilted her head right and left and then issued a judgment. "Definitely the hoops."

"You are a doll." Ashley reached down and kissed the top of her sister's head. "I am on my way in just a sec. I shouldn't be late."

No sooner had the front door closed, than Sylvie's phone rang. She reached behind her to retrieve it from the side table. The screen displayed a number, no name. She didn't recognize the area code. Usually she would let it ring, thinking it a robo-call, but with all that was going on at the theater, she thought it best to answer.

"Hi, Sylvie, it's Samson Webb."

Realizing who she was talking to and forgetting he was on a phone, she swung her legs off the sofa and sat very ladylike. She even ran her fingers through her hair to try and look better. Surely, he was calling for Ashley.

"Samson, my sister's not here," she announced. "Can I take a message?"

"No message needed unless you want to say hi to her for me. You are the reason I called."

"Really?" she exclaimed, her voice going up almost an octave, Or so she thought.

"Yes, really," he echoed in a warm and friendly voice. "Actually, I am calling to ask an enormous favor?"

"Sure, anything," she said nervously.

"Maggie has asked me to help her with *Flanagan's Wake,*" he began to explain. "I need to be in Hillsborough this evening. I have a seven o'clock appointment with a famous illusionist. He's agreed to help us if he can. I was wondering if you could drive me down there. The problem is we'd have to get going right away."

"I, uh..." Caught off guard by first his call and then his offer, she wondered how to respond.

"Look, I know this is last minute. I understand if you can't do it."

"How would you get there then?"

"Uber or Lyft, I suppose," he replied, sounding disappointed with his other options.

"I can drive you," she volunteered, surprising herself. "And I won't ask for a tip."

"Are you sure?"

"About driving you or not asking for a tip?"

"Both, I suppose. How about I kick in for gas money?"

"Are you staying at the Claremont Hotel?"

"I am."

"I'll pick you up..." She looked at the time on her phone. She would have just enough time to go to the bathroom and grab a sweater. No time for makeup or a change of clothes. "I'll be there in fifteen minutes," she told him, sliding off the sofa and rushing to her bedroom.

Bay Area roads and highways will sometimes reward drivers with what can only be called a spurt of smooth sailing. Sylvie Blanchard and her passenger, Samson Webb, were enjoying one of those rare moments. Her well-maintained, always clean, old Honda Civic purred its way to Hillsborough. They would have no problem reaching their destination on time.

"Samson, if you're going to be here for several days, why don't you rent a car?"

"I don't drive," he said, turning his attention to the driver rather than the passing scenery.

"You don't like to drive?" she asked, sneaking a quick glance at her passenger.

"Promise not to laugh?"

"I won't laugh. Unless it's funny ."

"I *can't* drive," he told her. "I don't know how to drive. But I'm a hell of a good passenger."

"Getting a driver's license is like a rite of passage," she said. "I thought everybody knew how to drive."

Samson shifted in his seat. "I was born into a Hollywood family. My father is a cinematographer and my mother is a makeup artist. You name the country or state and I'll tell you where I was schooled. We always seemed to be on location so, as a result, I was tutored on set. Bringing the family along was always part of their contract. What I'm getting at is driver's ed just wasn't part of the curriculum."

"That's a roundabout way of explaining it," she commented.

"You're right. Too much information. I'm always guilty of that. What I was trying to get at is wherever we were filming, I would head out and tour that city or region. I got around pretty good on public transportation and fell in love with it. A bonus was I got lots of ideas riding a bus, subway or train."

Sylvie threw him a quick smile and returned to watching her driving. Samson noticed her attention to the road. "I wish some Lyft or Uber drivers paid as much attention to their driving as you do."

"And the speed limit," she added. "So tell me about this famous illusionist."

"His name is Ronaldo Reyes. He lives in Las Vegas where he has a multi-year contract with a major casino. His partner's parents live in Hillsborough and they are visiting for a couple of weeks."

"So why are you meeting with him?"

"Let me give you a little background first. I got to know Ronaldo because I hired him when I was directing the first *Scepter Code*. I wanted him to show us how to have people escape what seemed to be impossible imprisonments or bondages," he explained. "This time, though, I don't have a job offer. Plus, I am going to try the seemingly impossible."

"What's that?" she said with a small laugh.

"I'm going to ask him to tell me how a certain illusion works. And after that, I am going to try something that might be even more challenging."

"What could that possibly be?"

"I'm going to ask you if we can have dinner afterwards," he replied. He held up a hand in warning. "But don't answer now as I haven't asked yet."

Sylvie knew she was blushing. She swore she could feel the reddening all the way down to the soles of her feet. By nature, when intimidated, she was inclined to employ sarcasm. "Do you usually ask your Lyft or Uber drivers to dinner?"

"No, I haven't done that," he said. "I did, though, put a driver named Omar in one of my films."

Still blushing, she said, "That's cool. Okay, I'll wait until I am asked formally."

"You're not going to give me an itty-bitty hint as to how you might answer," he asked blithely.

"Uh oh," she sighed. "I don't know that I can trust myself alone with a man who says itty-bitty."

"That's nothing. When I'm really worked up, I've been heard to say gee whiz and holy-moly."

"Have you ever been tempted to step out there and get s little edgier. Maybe say darn?" she asked, hitting the steering wheel for emotional emphasis."

Samson folded his arms and struck a thoughtful pose. "Yes, I have. But you want to know the real truth. I grew up in a family environment where nobody swore.

We all have tribes and mine was my family and their colleagues. They weren't a cussing crowd so I wasn't. Never any lectures about the right or wrong of it. It simply wasn't a part of our world."

"Are your parents famous?"

"No, they're not famous but they are well-known and well-regarded in the industry," he answered. "Between them they have three Oscars, seven nominations and a couple of Emmys. That gets them lots of work. When we were younger, my sister liked to dress the Oscars. She named them Magda, Zsa Zsa and Ava."

"When it comes to famous threesomes, I'm afraid I only know Huey, Dewey and Louie and Larry, Moe and Curly," she laughed.

"The Gabor sisters were three Hungarian beauties who were the predecessors of the Kardashians," he explained. Noticing the freeway sign, he checked the map app on his phone. "Looks like we better start getting directions. Hillsborough is coming up."

Sylvie parked in front of a Mediterranean mansion with a large, manicured lawn. She remained on the street instead of using the circular driveway.

"Do they allow Honda Civics in this neighborhood?"

"I'm sure they do," he said, removing his seat belt. "Do you want to come in with me or wait here?"

Sylvie considered the invitation but thought otherwise." As much as I would like to see the interior of that palatial estate *and* meet a famous magician, you ought to go alone. I think Ronaldo would be more inclined to show one person the magic behind his magic rather than two people. Am I being silly?"

"No, that's a valid point. Listen, while I'm gone, think about that other challenging question I mentioned." He stepped out of the car and leaned in. His smile was as warm as his voice. "I promise I won't be long."

He wasn't. Sylvie barely had time to consider what was behind Samson Webb's surprising dinner invitation. Was he flirting with her while they drove down or just engaging in a conversation that turned silly? Did he simply need a ride to Hillsborough and thought a dinner invitation was a nice payback? And, as she often asked herself in similar situations, was he just trying to get close to Ashley through her. She did have enough thinking time to resolve that one. The answer was an emphatic no because he had repeatedly expressed no interest in Ashley romantically.

Sylvie watched as he walked back to the car. Once recognized in Hollywood as a black-leather-clad, Goth-style, smart-ass brat, an image created for him by image-conscious agents, Samson, after the success of his first film, rebelled. He returned to being his mild-mannered, well-behaved and well-dressed self. Tall enough and slim enough, he wore clothes well. That evening, he was in a Harris Tweed sport coat, opened white dress shirt and pressed khakis. Sylvie thought he might have taken fashion advice from Ambrose. There was a difference, though. Where Ambrose was professorial and wrinkled, Samson was fashionably cool and well-pressed.

"How did you do?" she asked, waiting for him to fasten his seat belt before pulling away.

"Ronaldo was tightlipped about his illusions and tricks, but that's okay because he volunteered to take charge of that part of the wake."

"And that part of the wake being?" she asked, looking quickly at her passenger and realizing she liked his eyes.

"From what Maggie has told me, Phineas Flanagan will, for a bit of time, be in an open coffin," he explained. "Once the casket is closed, he has to disappear which means he has to exit the casket while it's still on the stage and we're all mingling about. Maggie says there'll be no opportunity for him to just step out of it between the stage and the crematorium. He has to somehow disappear. She has her reasons."

"And Rolando can make that happen?" she asked while deciding his eyes were cerulean blue. A most appealing color, she thought.

"Yes, he can. I asked him how difficult it would be and he said, 'Easy-peasy.'"

"I hope so, Samson," she said, turning to again glance at her passenger. "You don't mind that I call you Samson?"

"Not at all," he exclaimed. "Another step forward in getting to know each other."

"Then you won't mind my asking a rather straight-forward question?" she asked nervously.

"Fire away."

"This dinner invitation. Is it your generous way of saying thanks for the ride to Hillsborough, or..." She paused and then added, "something else?"

The movie director leaned forward in his seat so Sylvie could see him and the road. "Definitely something else. I'm asking you out on a date, Sylvie."

Her hands tightened on the steering wheel. That maddening blush returned and she muttered, "Oh, shit." Then just as quickly, she amended it.

"Oh, shoot."

Chapter 14

Sisterly love gets put to the test.

Just after midnight, Sylvie arrived at her Berkeley apartment. Aware of the squeaky front door and that her sister may be asleep, she paid careful attention to opening it as quietly as possible. Her considerate effort didn't matter. Ashley was on the living room floor in sweats on a yoga mat doing what is called Navasana or the Boat Pose. Sylvie didn't understand the boat analogy because Ashley looked like she was pretending to be the letter V.

While remaining in that difficult position, Ashley welcomed her home with an admonishing tone to her voice. "Where have you been, Syl. I was beginning to worry."

Sylvie tossed her keys on the small table by the door and walked into the living room and fell onto the sofa. "This is *my* latest yoga pose. It's called One-Tired-Mama."

"Very funny. So what have you been up to?"

"Right after you left, Samson called..."

That's as far as she got. Both ends of Ashley's V collapsed. Sitting up, she asked breathlessly, "You took a message?"

"He wasn't calling you."

She didn't understand. Baffled, her older sister said, "That surprises me. There's no other reason for him to call."

Sylvie popped up from her One-Tired-Mama pose. Miffed, she snapped, "I'll give you a hint. You live with the other reason he called."

"You?" she said, almost laughing.

"Yeah, little old me. By the way, he did ask me to say hi."

Clearly astonished and not apologetic, Ashley asked. "I don't mean this to sound insulting but why would he call you?"

Sylvie could have told her that he needed a ride to Hillsborough. Instead, she decided to unnerve her. "He asked me out on a date," she said, blushing a little from her truthful admittance. "I drove him to Hillsborough where he met with a magician who is going to help us and then we went to dinner at Bar OSA."

Ashley readied for another yoga pose. "Sylvie, think about it. He needed a ride to Hillsborough and back and decided to thank you with a dinner at Bar OSA. That's not what I call a date."

Her sister sat back on the sofa and crossed her legs, a smug grin suggesting she'd hit the nail on the head.

"Gotcha," Sylvie remarked. "It was just his way of showing his appreciation for what I did for him."

"Afraid so, sis," she said, "I hope you had a good time."

"Oh, I did," she said haltingly and pensively.

"What's on your mind?" she asked as she threw her arms in the air and bent her knees. She was now in the Chair Pose.

"I was just thinking. I wonder what big favor do I have to do for him tomorrow to justify his taking me to dinner after the meeting." With that, Sylvie slipped off the sofa and waved a goodnight to her sister.

Chapter 15

A proper fitting for a wooden onesie.

Amelia Palmer felt Friday morning would be slow as she unlocked the front door to Vintamelia, a vintage clothing store she co-owned with her partner of many years, Berra Hannigan. The shop was on Ashby Avenue in the heart of Berkeley's Elmwood district. In addition to the store, the pair owned a large costume rental company in Emeryville called Amelia-Berra Rents which catered to theater companies of all stripes and movie studios worldwide. They took a gentle ribbing from their clients who noticed that the town's only film studio, Pixar, specialized in animation and had no need of their special services.

Amelia was proud of her ability to gauge how busy they would be on any certain day. "Berra, why not take the day off. I'll handle things," she told her partner who was busy opening the store's computer.

They were a contrasting pair. She was tall and thin. A pretty woman, she wore her hair in a style popular in the

Forties and Fifties; shoulder length and wavy. Amelia often wore dresses, preferably from the different eras represented by the store's inventory. Berra was short and boxy with curly, black hair that resembled a poodle's furry coat. Her eyes were green and her mouth was angled, giving her a cute lopsided grin. She, too, enjoyed, wearing vintage clothes. That Friday, they were both in tea length swing dresses from the 1950's.

Before Berra could respond to Amelia's suggestion, their door opened and in marched Maggie Leyton, Magnus Flaherty and Phineas Flanagan. With a look of surprise, Amelia rushed forward and gave Maggie and Magnus affectionate hugs. Berra was right behind her to give the same open-arms welcoming.

"Amelia, Berra, this is Phineas Flanagan," Maggie said. He's playing Antonio..."

"You're doing the *Merchant*," Berra said excitedly.

"Aye, and that's why we're here," Magnus told the two women who were shaking hands with Phineas.

"Mr. Flanagan, dressed as you are in that decidedly English outfit, I'll positively swoon if it's accompanied by a matching accent," Amelia gushed.

"And I, dear lady, must ask if you two have just come from a Martini-and- cigarette soiree with Lucy and Ricky Ricardo," he quipped in his best Queen's English.

They both looked down at their petticoat-less dresses and laughed. Amelia turned to Maggie. "I'm going to guess. You're here because you've decided to put the play in a modern time setting. At least our version of modern," she giggled.

"We have," Maggie said, "1948."

Berra rubbed her hands together. "Great year. You've come to the right place. We can easily dress the entire cast."

Amelia jumped in, "Maggie, we'll get the clothes — we don't call them costumes—from our Emeryville location. I think it's best the cast goes there to be fitted."

"Any chance we can hold a dress rehearsal in a week's time?" Magnus asked nervously.

"If you can get everybody to Emeryville for fittings no later than Tuesday midday, we'll have them ready for you," Amelia promised. She smiled as Magnus gave her a thumbs up.

Maggie moved toward Phineas who was browsing through a rack of men's clothes, occasionally holding one up and making a comment only he could hear.

"Amelia, we brought our Antonio along because we would like to buy his costuming... Oops, sorry. His stage apparel. While we just need one outfit for each of the cast members, Phineas here will require two coats and they should be polar opposite of each other,"

Amelia and Berra gave each other thoughtful glances. Berra spoke for them. "The cut of men's suits from those days is remarkably similar. However, we can handle it through color. Perhaps, a black pinstripe double-breasted and a..."

Amelia interjected with enthusiasm, "A flashy sport coat. That will do it, Berra. Something Cary Grantish or Gregory Peckish. I'm assuming he'll stay in one pair of pants."

Berra was curious as to why they were purchasing his outfits as opposed to renting them. She asked Magnus who was standing next to here.

"This way, if they are damaged, we don't have to worry," he said casually.

"Damaged?" Amelia repeated. "Don't tell me you've rewritten the play and Shylock gets his pound of flesh."

"Actually, I put them up to it," Phineas said in a raised voice while he walked the aisles checking the Vintamelia inventory. "I told Maggie that if I look as good as I think I am going to look a la 1948, I will make them part of my wardrobe."

Berra looked at Maggie. "I love listening to that accent. You have my permission to be a chatterbox."

Maggie put a hand on her shoulder. "Don't encourage him.I'm glad he's in a quiet mood."

Contrary to her prediction, Amelia noticed a number of customers coming into the store. Anxious to tend to Maggie and her needs, she invited the three into the back room while Berra grabbed some coats for Phineas to try on. Amelia excused herself to tend to the new arrivals.

While they waited, Maggie, in an almost motherly voice, asked the Irish actor a question she knew would unnerve him. She loved unsettling him. "Phineas, which coat would you like to die in."

Having already gotten to him with questions of cremation and determining the cause of death, he had developed an immunity to her ribbing. "Maggie, my dear, if you mean what do I wish to be wrapped in while lying inert in the coffin, I really don't know. Surprise me. However, remember my death-coat goes to the crematorium never to be seen again. So I would suggest we make it the least colorful of the two."

"That sounds very practical," Maggie commented.

"It does, but on the other hand, I am known for being a bit showy. Perhaps, it's only fitting I go out in something splashy."

"Will you two listen to yourselves," Magnus, rising from a chair he'd found in a dressing room. "We have a lot to do before we stick Mr. Dead Duck Flanagan in a pine box."

"Dead Duck Flanagan!" Phineas exclaimed. "Honestly, Magnus, your wife and I were just enjoying some conversational sparring. We'll stop if you don't ever use that clumsy term again."

Amelia and Berra returned with an armload of men's suits 'coats, all circa 1948. They piled it on a large table and invited the three to pick and choose. Phineas rushed over and began looking for just the right suit to die in. While he did, the two store owners rushed out to handle new customers.

Once they were out of the room, Maggie inched closer to Magnus. In a low voice, she said, "You know those two better than I. How do you feel about me letting Amelia and Berra know what we're up to."

Never letting an opportunity go by to touch, hug or hold his wife, Magnus put an arm around Maggie and pulled her close. "Ah, you are, without knowing it, a genius."

She cuddled closer and replied, "How so, my large Irishman?"

"It is often said a secret is safe between two people if one is dead. Now you offer us another maxim; a secret is safe as long as everyone knows it."

She wrenched herself affectionately from his grasp, pausing to give his arm a soft punch. "Okay, I get your point. Anyway, I like them both and I know how much they love the theater. They're definitely on our side."

Amelia and Berra listened intently as Maggie, often interrupted by Phineas, explained the extravagant wake they hoped will convince two hitmen that Phineas 'term as a human expired before they could their grubby hands on him. She ended by inviting them to the rehearsal that Friday evening where everyone involved would hear her plan. The pair said unhesitatingly they would be there.

Berra had one question for Maggie. "I imagine Phineas will have to escape the coffin while it's on stage and be ready to put on the other coat. How will he wiggle himself out of the jacket he's wearing in such a confined space?"

Maggie didn't have an answer. She speculated he would first leave the coffin and then be free to switch coats. Perhaps, Berra had hit on something. He needed to be coatless upon exiting so that he could escape the area below the coffin as quickly as possible. "I don't know," she admitted. "Do you have an idea?"

Berra's lopsided grin hinted that she was going to make a wild stab at remedying their problem. "Okay, this may sound silly, but you know how basketball players have these tearaway warmup outfits. Maybe we reconstruct the coat so all he has to do is rip it off." She thought about what she said. "Well, maybe not *rip* it off, but get out of it quickly."

"Aye, that might work," Magnus said. "But honestly, I shudder at the thought of having to maneuver around inside a wooden onesie. That's not my idea of fun."

Phineas looked up from the pile of coats. He held two that he liked. "Magnus, darling boy, I haven't heard that since my grandfather, Phineas II, died of a life wasted delightfully so on excessive drink, smoke, unattractive women and oysters morning noon and night. "

Berra thought it all amusing. "It's a better term than the one I grew up with. My mother referred to a coffin as a womb of doom. I shiver every time I say it," she said. "Anyway, Phineas, it looks like you found your two coats. Which one do you want to lie in state in?"

Phineas patted her shoulder. "Oh, Berra, I do like the way you put that. I think I will go out in this dark blue, double-breasted and come back in that crazily-patterned sport coat that does remind me of Cary Grant in *His Girl Friday*. Here's hoping I can wear it with as much panache."

"Okay, into the changing room with you, Mr. Flanagan," the husky voice Berra commanded him. "Let's get this coat sized for you. As for the Jimmy Cagney gangster suit, leave it. Amelia and I will make it so you can shed it in seconds."

***

Cafe Strada was packed. Students were between classes and looking to caffeine-up before their next round of intellectual stimulation and challenges. Like the students, Professor Richter, too, was between classes. He had picked the cafe when Phineas Flanagan had called him the previous day asking to see him. Luckily, he found a corner table outside. He waited patently and wondered why the meeting. He didn't have to wonder long as Phineas appeared at the table. His head spun about taking in the busy scene.

"Oh my, Professor Richter, I believe you have discovered the fountain of youth. Look at all this untamed beauty," he exclaimed. "Do we have time for coffee? I've just come from a fitting and I am in need of refreshment."

Richter inched away from the table. "My treat. What are you having?"

"A straight ahead black coffee," he said, looking around at the other tables. Seeing the array of exotic concoctions, he realized he was a lone wolf.

Richter returned, anxious to learn why the Irishman wanted to meet with him. While he watched Phineas wait for the coffee to cool, he asked, "Is there something I can do for you?"

Flanagan laid a hand on the table. "Please, call me Phineas." Taking a furtive sip of the coffee, he explained his presence. "Professor Richter, I have a friend, an Englishman named Reginald Pennington. He is a fascinating creature who is looking to turn his life around, and I believe you might be able to help him."

"Tell me how I can do that," he said, sipping his cappuccino.

"Reg was one of the best money launderers in Europe. We won't throw numbers about as I don't want to scare these attractive innocents close by. Anyway, he ran afoul of a French lawyer who was corrupt to the core. This cur laid a financial trap for him. He was subsequently arrested and ended up doing time in a French prison. Reggie is now out, repentant and living here in the United States. He's on a crusade to educate anyone and everyone about the, if you will, art of the money launderer. HIs stories are hugely entertaining stuff."

The professor wondered what he could do for him. "How can I help?"

Phineas leaned back in his chair. "Reggie is coming this way to also seek employment. He's interested in meeting financiers, bankers and the like. I thought if you interviewed him on your podcast..."

"How do you know I have a podcast?" he asked.

"I know a lot about you, Professor Richter. I don't hand just anyone fifty thousand dollars willy-nilly. I have done my homework," he said with a smug smile.

The economist's heart skipped a happy beat. Now he could turn the dream of taking Lani Chang to Hawaii for a few days of Mai Tais on the beach into reality. "So you're going to fund my research?" he asked.

"It appears so," he replied. Phineas took another sip of his just black coffee. "This is quite good. Anyway, I know besides your podcast which reaches a respectable audience, you have five minutes every Thursday evening at five-ten on the local PBS station. If you were able to interview Reggie for the podcast and edit a couple of minutes to also promote him on your radio feature, it would go a long way in giving him a legitimacy that would help him open doors. Of course, anything else you can do would help immensely."

"When do you see this all happening. When do I meet Reggie What's-his-name?"

"His name is Pennington and he's in New York. He will be out here a week Saturday," he answered. "Here's the thing, my academic friend, like a lot of us who occasionally are presumptuous when we shouldn't be,

I'm afraid we're in a bit of a rush. Reggie has lined up some informal interviews over that weekend and I promised him some advanced publicity."

The professor checked his watch. He recorded his podcast on Thursday and he could have a couple of minutes ready by the afternoon. He'd have to move things around but it shouldn't be a problem. He told Phineas it sounded doable and then explained he had to get back to class.

Phineas popped up and reached across to shake his hand. "Excellent. You will not be disappointed. The stories he has are first-rate. All I need is a phone number for him to reach you."

Richter removed a business card and wrote another number on it. "I'll look forward to hearing from him and I look forward to hearing from you regarding my funding."

"And you shall, dear boy, you shall." Phineas held up a hand. "Oh, I should tell you we sound remarkably alike, Reggie and I. Both of us are guilty of having that posh accent known as the Queen's English or BBC English. The difference is I learned mine, Reggie was born with his."

The tall, slender Irishman watched Professor Richter rush off to class. He enjoyed being surrounded by such youth and energy. I may stay for another coffee he told himself and enjoy these surroundings of vitality, youth and beauty.

Chapter 16

"I'm in a spot of bother."

Phineas Flanagan

Phineas Flanagan didn't speak right away. He stood quietly at the edge of center stage and surveyed his audience of friends and acquaintances. He realized every one of the attendees was there because they would play some part in the production of an elaborate hoax designed to save his life. With a closed-mouth smile, he surveyed the room as if he wanted to remember where everyone was. His timing was excellent. He seemed to sense when they would become restless from the quiet.

With a humility that surprised his longtime friend Magnus, the tall, slender actor told the assembled, "I am one of you. And for that I am exceedingly grateful."

With those two sentences, he'd won their hearts and he was elated. This strange man who was years older than most of the cast and decidedly extravagant in his behavior and manner had just told them he felt he was one of the gang.

When the cheers abated, he folded his arms and looked skyward. In all his years, he'd not experienced this kind of comity and belonging. In his acting days, he mostly remembered a highly toxic environment fueled by acid-tongued cattiness and outrageous fits of ego and jealousy. Of course, he knew that he was one of the cattier and boastful players among them.

When he went to work for a mob boss, his duties kept him mostly away from the more threatening and thuggish of the workers who all were convinced, like him, they toiled in a hostile environment that didn't encourage friendly rapport. So here he was in a small theater filled with people whose names he knew mostly and whose particulars he was aware of. He was truly humbled and thankful they were there to support him.

Lowering his head, he told the audience why he was there. "I'm in a spot of bother."

He paused, overcome once again by a feeling of community that he'd not felt in years, if ever. "And Maggie Leyton, a sainted woman if there ever was one, has come to my aid. It was her idea that I should first tell you my personal story which is, I must admit, a gripping yarn. But let me post a warning. Even though I'm known as a man of Irish magniloquence, I'm sure Maggie wants me to edit carefully my story and explain it in an opaque way that keeps it from sounding like a confession. A legal confession, that is. I dare say, I don't want to be perp-walked off this stage before the fun begins. By the way, I have already confessed my sins to Father McGinty over a couple of G and T's in the House of Shields, a wonderful bar in downtown San Francisco. Buying the G and T's were my penance, by the way."

Phineas took advantage of the laughter, to pause. There was a stool behind him. He decided to relax for the brief moment or two he was on stage. Settled half on and half off the stool, he continued.

"What you need to know is for years, many years, I handled the finances for an Irish crime syndicate. In those years of obscene and illegal profits, I managed to syphon off a euro here and there without my employers ever knowing. Pretty soon I was awash in the stuff. These improprieties are not something I am proud of, but there they are." A physical shrug was his only explanation of how he felt about these criminal actions.

"So you launder money?" someone in the second row asked.

"Yes, Charlene, I do and I can have it back to you in 24 hours pressed and cleaned like it was newly printed. I am kidding, of course. Laundering money is a good term for the movie and book versions of what I do, but my financial dealings were much more complex. During these years, I spent most of my time in what many of you would think are glamorous environments. I danced back and forth from exotic places like London, Dubai, Zurich, Monaco and Paris. My work also took me to some countries that weren't so glamorous but were home to investment-savvy oligarchs. When the mob boss under whom I toiled died, things began to change for the worse. He was replaced by his twin sons who give white collar crime a bad name. My work environment suddenly became more dangerous. Men with whom I could kept a social distance were now part of my everyday. These thugs are homophobic and detest people with minds. So,

I decided to pack up and leave. Mine is a business where you don't give a two-week notice. I have been gone now for a time that has drawn their attention and ire. Thanks to trusted allies, I know the twins are headed this way in a week's time and they are intent on finding me for two reasons. The first is to find out if I have cheated them out of their ill-gotten goods and if I have, to force me to tell them where it is. Then they will retire me permanently."

"You mean they would kill you?" asked young Charlene who had a minor role in the play.

"Yes, Charlene, and they are very good at that sort of thing." Phineas lifted himself off the stool. Moving it aside, he approached the microphone stand which he had ignored and centered it for the next speaker. He continued talking while he fussed with it.

"I had an exit plan, you know. I'd assume a new identity, pare down my assets through charity and with enough to live luxuriously, hide away in some distant paradise. That is not to be. And the reason it is not to be is you," he said, pointing to those who sat in the front part of the theater. I so enjoy your company, your enthusiasm, your personalities. I like being around this tiny theater. I'm sure you see how that that complicates matters."

"We'll be sorry to see you go, Mr. Flanagan," Ambrose said from the first row. "But then we'll look forward to whomever replaces you."

There were sounds of agreement from the others.

"Thank you." He smiled at woman in the first row. "Now I'd like you to meet the woman who will take charge of seeing that this transmogrification of me goes without a hitch. Maggie Leyton."

Maggie squeezed her husband's hand and rose from her first row chair. Phineas walked to stage left and took her hand as she stepped onto the stage. "We're crazy, Maggie. You do know that. But I'm just fine with it," he whispered as she walked past him.

Maggie hopped aboard the barstool and took the microphone from the stand. She turned it on and tapped it to see if it was hot. "I don't have Phineas 'sonorous tones. I need this little guy," she said. "I want to ask you all a question. Can I trust you not to tell anyone outside this theater about what we're planning to do?"

She paused and waited for responses. It seemed trust was something she could rely on.

"Ms Leyton," Ambrose began. "Or do you prefer Mrs. Magnus?"

"Do you want me to keep him quiet, Maggie," shouted her husband who was sitting next to him.

"No, let the professor speak."

"What about those of us who might be tempted to tell the tale of this extraordinary hoax after the fact?"

Maggie looked over at Sylvie who was sitting next to Samson Webb. "Sylvie, how many people do we have here?"

"Thirty-six," she sang out. "Not counting Phineas, of course."

'Wait a minute," he cried out. "I don't die until Tuesday. Thus, I am still part of the living contingent."

Maggie acknowledged his presence. Pursing her lips, she continued on. "I have some technicians and others who will be joining us through the week, so let's round that number out to forty. That means there will be forty different versions of what happened bouncing around in the stratosphere at some time or another. But, as you said, Ambrose, it will all be after the fact. The news cycle is so fast these days that most stories are beaten to death in one afternoon. I'm not worried. But, let's not get ahead of ourselves. We have a lot of work to do and little time to do it and this is when I am really counting on you all keeping quiet as church mice."

In a composed voice, Maggie explained what would be happening in a week's time. She told them they needed to know because so much would be going on through the week that it would be difficult to work in secret.

"My plan is to hold an Irish wake on this stage. The deceased will be none other than our beloved Phineas Flanagan who, we will have learned, died the previous Tuesday from cardiac arrest in his hotel suite. When Magnus and I discover him, we find among his possessions a letter expressing that he be so honored. The reason for his having a such a letter is he knew he was suffering from heart disease and an attack was always possible. The wake will precede the dress rehearsal next Friday. Our timing will be to the minute and worked out as we get closer. Now through the coming week, you'll get instructions on where you ought to be and what you should be doing during that time. Some of you will have more to do than others, but all of you are necessary if we are to pull this off successfully."

Maggie held up her notebook. "I am approaching this as if I were making a movie. So, consider me the director. For the next seven days, we will be constructing the set. The Banter Foundation people are here because they have valuable access to people we need. In military intelligence, they have a phrase called need-to-know. We are in a unique situation where you all need to know what we're doing. But how we're doing it will be confined to a small group."

Charlene couldn't help herself. The young actress with the child-like voice asked, "Will Phineas be in any sort of danger? Heck, for that matter, will any of us?"

"No one is going to be in any danger," she said with brimming confidence. "Having said that, there will be a few minutes of tension and that is when the twins from Dublin arrive to view the body of Phineas Flanagan. We are going to work tirelessly to see that they are so convinced he is dead, they will leave us feeling cheated out of a killing. And they will always have to wonder if Phineas stole any money from them. To that end, we will play this through to cremation."

Charlene gasped. Shaking her head, she muttered something about having so many questions. Maggie gave her a comforting smile which she extended to the whole room.

"Yes, there will be questions on questions," she assured the assembled. Then, slapping her leg, wrapped it up. "Okay, kids, time to go to work. We have a lot to to. And remember that old World War II saying, Loose lips sink Phineas."

Sylvie tried her best to pay attention to Maggie and for the most part, she did. She was glad she was alert enough to answer her when asked about crowd size. Her distraction was sitting beside her. The gentleman was doing nothing purposeful to cause her to lose her concentration. His physical closeness was solely to blame. Sylvie's seat-mate was Samson Webb who had insisted they sit together for the Phineas and Maggie's presentations.

They were in the second row; Sylvie in the aisle seat and the movie director next to her. Occasionally, she would glance at the woman on his right. A trim, vivacious and extremely well-dressed woman with deep blue eyes in her early thirties.

Sylvie thought back to Thursday evening and how seeing his this woman for the first time had shaken her. After Samson had met with Rolando, the magician, in Hillsborough, she and Samson went to dinner at Bar OSA. He explained that Duffy Hart would assure them the kind of privacy they might not get somewhere else given his celebrity. They lingered. They talked. They laughed. They infrequently found subtle ways of touching each other and make it seem like the perfect thing to do. When Duffy pleaded with them to go so he could close, Samson suggested they have an after-dinner drink at the Claremont. When they had pulled up to the hotel entrance, without explaining himself, Samson had jumped out of the car and quick-stepped his way toward a beautiful woman. Sylvie had felt her heart sink into her stomach. She was now convinced Samson had indeed just needed a ride and dinner was a payback. She was tempted to drive away but the valet had already opened her door to hand her a ticket. She stood there in the cool February air, shivering not because of the chill, but shaken by the familiar hug that the woman was giving the man who had so charmed her at dinner.

"She's going to check in," he informed her, returning to where Sylvie was standing. "She's exhausted so she won't be joining us. I'll catch up with her later."

"Who is *she*?" his dinner companion asked.

Samson gave her a quizzical look. "You don't know?"

"No, I don't"

"That's my sister," he explained. He rubbed his hands to warm them. "I can't believe we talked for as long as we did and I didn't mention Pen."

Sylvie felt all her body parts returning to where they were meant to be. "I'm sure I skipped something as well, 'she laughed haltingly.

Penelope Withers, his married sister, had also chosen the movies as her profession. She was one of Hollywood's most successful makeup artists. Samson had recruited her to work on Phineas Flanagan, first as a corpse and then as another man entirely.

As they strolled into the hotel lobby, Samson asked Sylvie, "You, uh, didn't think, Pen was someone else, like a girlfriend."

Trying to stay calm and casual, she responded, "Of course not," she said with a dismissive laugh. "I never gave it a thought."

Chapter 17

"Going Up?"

When Ambrose Dowling called Phyllis Hathaway early Friday evening, he had not expected her full-throated approval. Thus, he was completely unprepared for the ride of his life. Saturday morning, he found himself buckled into the plush leather passenger seat of a brand new, top-of-the-line, eighty-thousand-dollar Range Rover. The British racing-green SUV with its tan interior was barreling down Highway 580 toward Livermore, California. The pilot was Phyllis, who in her years of driving California freeways, never bothered looking at a speedometer.

An ashen-faced Ambrose suggested they had no need to rush. Turning to face him, she responded cheerily, "Are you that sort who drives sixty-five mph and not a smidgen more?"

"I am," he said almost proudly and most assuredly nervously. "I also appreciate it when the driver keeps their eyes on the road. `

"Oh, Ambrose, you are such a fuddy-duddy," Phyllis laughed, taking her hands off the steering wheel. "This car practically drives itself. It has all sorts of darling road sensors. We are quite safe."

They were on their way to Livermore where Phyllis' brother owned a funeral home. While Phyllis left east-bound traffic in the dust, he thought back to Friday evening when he called her. He had wasted no time in describing his reason for the call. Not mincing words, he told her the Banter Foundation and their beloved theater required the complete services of an imaginative, rule-bending funeral home director and she was his only hope of finding one that answered that description. Duffy Hart had done some investigating and found there was someone in Livermore with a colorful and iconoclastic approach to dealing with the end of life. When he saw the director's name, Malcolm Midgely, he remembered that being Phyllis 'maiden name. To Ambrose's surprise, when he called her to make his case, Phyllis came on board with no reservation.

"There is one stipulation, Professor Dowling" she said in her clipped voice. "I want to be at that ceremony. The wake, as you call it."

"That's not a problem," Ambrose had informed her. "Although, you can't tell Mr. Hathaway. This is all terribly hush-hush."

And that was that. At ten o'clock the next morning, Phyllis and he were just ten minutes away from her brother's business. That time was taken with Phyllis adhering to the speed limit on two lane roads that wound southward from the freeway through long stretches of vineyards, wineries, tasting rooms and small estates. It was a scenic route but of no interest to Ambrose who was not appreciative of a true country setting. For him, if he desired nature, the Berkeley Rose Garden answered all his needs.

Suddenly, there it was. To his left, a hundred yards ahead, there appeared two massive doric columns with an ornate iron gate between them. It may have been, for all intent and purposes, the entrance to a luxury resort or an ultra-private golf community.

A large metal sign in italic font appeared over the entrance. It read *GOING UP?* Below it was a smaller sign that read *A Midgely Funeral Home, Crematorium and Memorial Park*.

Ambrose looked in astonishment at his driver. "Mrs. Hathaway, am I correct in assuming your brother's funeral home's name is *Going Up?*"

Phyllis cackled. "Malcolm's a bit odd. He's a theology freak. I'll tell you all about it, unless he's in a proselytizing mood and gets to you first. Then you'll get it with an enthusiasm and passion I don't share."

Phyllis headed for a large, three-story Mediterranean-style building whose newness matched her Range Rover. Ambrose turned this way and that, trying to take it all in. There was an eerie calmness about the place. It was as if the birds were ordered to flutter more and chirp less. Ambrose first attested this unusual quietude to not yet seeing a person. However, he had a feeling that when he did, there would be no such thing as raised voices.

Phyllis and Ambrose walked through the double-door entrance, the click of her high heels echoing through the open foyer. To their right was a small, paper-free, white escritoire and behind it sat a young woman modesty dressed in a beige suit. Recognizing Phyllis, she rose quietly from her desk and walked toward a closed paneled door to tell her boss his sister had arrived.

In seconds, Malcolm Midgely bounded out of his office. He was a jovial blimp of a man. Tall, rotund with a chubby face and just enough hair to darken and spray into place, he reminded Ambrose of a professional sports 'team owner or an editorial cartoonist's version of a Republican politician from Florida. He certainly didn't look like a funeral director.

"Hello, dear sister, as always you look magnificently manufactured," he said in a booming voice, getting as close to her as he could, considering his girth, for a two air-kiss greeting.

"You never change, Mal-Mal," she said with a tight smile, "you can still turn a greeting into an insult."

Malcolm registered surprise. "Well, believe it or not, sis, it was just my way of telling you that you are particularly well turned-out, especially for a Saturday morning. Nowhere in Livermore will you find anyone dressed so well."

She noticed her brother stealing glances at Ambrose. "Malcolm, this is Professor Ambrose Dowling. He is the reason we're here."

Malcolm stuck out his hand. "Ah, the professor who has mischief on his mind."

"I'm afraid it's a little more than mischief, Mr, Midgely," he said, shaking his hand.

"And I know what you're thinking," the large man said, jabbing Ambrose in the chest. "You are wondering why I don't have a more cadaveric look. How come I'm not a tall beanpole with brooding dark eyes, sunken cheeks, stringy hair and a voice that frightens even bats?"

"You misjudge me," Ambrose replied. "I had no preconception. But it's unimportant."

"Phyllis told me in very broad terms what your plans are to save a man's life and what extraordinary steps your are taking to make it work."

"We plan to hold an Irish Wake next Friday..."

"They can get out of hand, you know," he said. "Drunken elegies. corpses removed from coffins and propped into corners and various other shenanigans."

"This will be run more like a state funeral. Everything timed to the second," he replied.

Malcolm took Ambrose by the arm. "Let us three take a walk to the Empyrean Gardens. Champagne and salty treats await." Turning serious, Malcolm's perpetual smile left his face. "Before we set out, let me ask one important question. Am I correct in assuming all sorts of laws, regulations and social norms will be broken to pull this off?"

"You are correct in your thinking, Mr. Midgely."

His red-faced jollity was back in a flash. "Oh goodie, I wouldn't want it any other way."

The three sat in comfortable high-back wicker chairs. An attractive, young woman, again modestly attired, served them glasses of Dom Perignon champagne. There was a plate of cheeses, cold meats and a variety of crackers set between them. Malcolm quickly finished his first glass. As his assistant poured him a second glass, he attacked the appetizers as if had hadn't eaten in days.

In between bites and sips, he asked Ambrose, "And what kind of services do you seek from *Going Up?*"

"All of it, Mr. Midgely. However, we need the casket right away as certain adjustments are going to have to be made to it."

"Are these adjustments anything we can do for you?"

"Thank you, no," he replied. "We have employed a famous magician or illusionist named Rolando who will at the start of the week be tinkering with it."

"Ah, I see," Malcolm said, popping another cheesed cracker in his mouth. "I've heard of him. He's good at making things disappear."

"I must add that from the wake forward, we'll require your special presence to remove the casket and bring it out here for cremation. Everything done as if there were a real body in it."

"Then we would be talking about our Top Floor Service, the only difference being the funeral service would at the theater and not in our special chapel. It is costly, Professor."

"Money is no problem, Mr. Midgely."

"Trust me, Mal-Mal, the Banter Foundation has money and lots of it," Phyllis added.

"And you want us to cremate no one, but go through the process?"

"We do," Ambrose said.

"It's cheeky to say but that's going to make for one hell of a small urn," he joked with a rumbling giggle.

"Once the cremation is complete, we hope you will proceed with whatever you do. We'd prefer a normal-sized decorative urn," Ambrose told him.

"Oh, that certainly can be done. We can also dig up some ashes for you, if you want them."

"Knowing Maggie Leyton's penchant for dotting every I and crossing every T, I think that would be in order. Ms Leyton, by the way, is in charge of this grand scheme."

Malcolm took his champagne flute, threw back his head and finished what drops remained. "I figure *Going*

Up will have broken five laws and any number of regulations by the time we hand over the urn and wish you God-speed." Malcolm observation was said in a tone of voice that suggested it didn't really matter.

All three rose simultaneously. Malcolm signaled Phyllis and Ambrose to follow him. "Let us go look at caskets," he said cheerily. "And while we march along, I'll explain the difference between a casket and a coffin."

"I have read that it's primarily shape and cost," replied Ambrose.

"Right on the mark, Professor. But, I understand, you have special needs, so I think we'll first look at caskets. My thinking is a coffin might not do the trick."

Malcolm walked them back to the main building. His employees likened his stride to that of an overweight penguin's waddle. Once inside, he directed them to a large showroom where a range of caskets were on display in three rows.

Throwing his arms out, he exclaimed with pride, "Behold, the finest of final resting places. They come in mahogany veneer wood, teak, solid mahogany, cherry veneer wood, solid pine, pink steel and stainless steel. The interiors are mostly ivory velvet."

"I believe I can make this easy for us all," Ambrose said, reaching into his sport coat and retrieving a piece of paper. "This is what Rolando requires."

"Ah, the magician," Malcolm replied. "Let's see what his needs are." As he read, he made small mutterings. Crumbling the paper, he told them he had just what Rolando desired. "He's selected pine. And he's requested a few adjustments that we can easily do here. They are offbeat enough that I will take care of that myself. Let me show you what he's asked for and then we'll begin the paperwork."

Malcolm Midgley sat behind a huge desk which Ambrose thought looked eerily like a casket. It was free of clutter. Phyllis and the professor sat opposite.

"The best way to handle this is to pretend we have a real deceased and then proceed as we would normally do," he said, pulling from a top drawer an attractive file folder full of forms to be filled out. "So when did Mr. Phineas Flanagan pass away?"

"Tuesday, February 26th. You can pick a time," Ambrose replied.

Malcolm smiled. "I don't think i have ever post-dated a death. Oh well, there's a first for everything. Normally, I would have my assistant, Naomi, handle all the paperwork but I think I am the Lone Ranger in this instance."

Phyllis was surprised at how quickly they were able to wrap up that portion of their visit. Malcolm stored the papers away and rose from behind his massive desk.

Coming around to Ambrose, he extended his hand. While shaking, he assured the professor that the specially adapted casket would be delivered to the Ashby-upon-Avon theater first thing Monday morning.

"As I understand it, we will be at the wake or service on Friday, March first. There, Mr. Flanagan, will lie in repose in an open casket. At the prescribed time, we will close the casket, carry it to the hearse for the drive out here to our crematorium where it and its contents will be cremated."

"That is what Ms Leyton requests," Ambrose said.

"And I can be assured that no live Phineas Flanagan is residing inside," he said with the slightest of giggles. "By the way, here is a brochure that describes what I call the theology behind *Going Up*. You may find it provocative."

"I will read it on the way back to Berkeley."

"We'd chat more about it but I don't dare proselytize in front of my sister," he said, winking at Phyllis who quickly thanked him.

"I assume there are a number of floors in Going Up as there are the nine concentric circles of hell in Dante's Inferno," Ambrose mused.

"There are eleven levels of eternal pleasure," Malcolm answered. "Ask Mr Flanagan what floor he'd like to stop on."

Chapter 18

Sometimes a little
Abracadabra is needed.

Maggie Leyton was impressive as commander-in-chief of *Flanagan's Wake*. She had taken over Sylvie's small office at the theater and from there, by email, text and phone, directed the army of people she needed to pull off successfully the grand goodbye planned for Phineas Flanagan on Friday, the first of March. She was just wrapping up a long phone call with her longtime friend, Doctor Phil Seton, when Phineas appeared in the doorway. She waved him in.

"Yes, Phil, I can't think of anything else to add. I'd just put an emphasis on thirty minutes max." she said, smiling at her new guest. "Okay, we'll see you tomorrow. I'll put you up at the Claremont. Old stomping grounds for you at one time, if I remember correctly. Please plan on staying through Saturday, so we can celebrate."

Putting her phone on the desk, she glanced briefly at her email. "Good morning, Phineas," she said over her shoulder. "You do realize this is your last full day as Phineas Dermot Flanagan?"

"You forgot to add the Fourth," he said with his trademark wry smile. He sat with his legs crossed in one of the two small chairs in front of Maggie's desk. "My day began with a phone call to my niece, Quinn. I have recruited her to help us."

"And how can she do that?"

"Maggie, dearest, as you say, timing's everything." he began to explain. "I still don't know how you plan to have me play dead, but obviously, it can only be for a certain amount of time. As I see it, everything's got to work around the Conners 'schedule. When they come. How long they stay."

"So how does Quinn fit into all of this?"

"I booked her on the same flight the Connors are on. Even put her in First Class. I think you'll approve. When the Conners discover her presence, she's going to tell them she learned I died and she wanted to pay her respects. That, of course, will require telling those two idiots where and what time I am being respected." He clapped, proud of his independent action.

"You know, Phineas, you're making this all doubly difficult because, at your request, we're not just killing you off but turning you into another being, all at the same time," Maggie noted with a show of slight irritation,

Phineas leaned forward. "The idea of slipping out of that casket and reemerging as Reggie on stage ready to rehearse with the others seems...." He looked to the ceiling. "Oh hell, I don't know. It just seems appropriate and sensible," he said in his defense.

"Let's just say, your speedy transmogrification complicates things," Maggie said. "But, we're this far along so we'll see it through."

"Sorry for being difficult."

Maggie didn't respond. Instead, she thought through more carefully about what Phineas had said. Picking up a drawing of the stage, she said, "Actually, having you blend into the on-stage crew is a plus. I mean, where else can you go? You certainly can't stay under the casket."

"By the way, who is Phil?"

"He is a doctor and an old friend who knows more about medicine than the entire Mayo Clinic," she said. "His plan is... Oh, I don't know the medical terms, but he's going to put you into a sort of suspended animation thanks to his extensive knowledge of voodoo and the use of their hallucinogens."

As an actor, Phineas reacted to the word *voodoo* with displayed horror. His face contorted, he muttered, "You mean voodoo as in weird spinning dancers with wild eyes, pounding drums, poison plants and... I saved the best for last, zombies."

Maggie, enjoying his apprehension, replied, "That about describes it. But that's more the Hollywood version. Although, zombies do exist, he tells me."

"Yeah, they do in mostly catatonic, schizophrenic states."

***

While Maggie and Phineas planned for his faux death the following day, Magnus, Sylvie and Samson were watching a crew from the *Going Up? Funeral Home* move a gleaming mahogany veneer wood casket toward the stage. Directing them was Ronaldo who would see to it that Phineas had an escape route.

Ronaldo, who made no effort to give them a last name was no more than five feet, four inches tall, but he carried himself as if he were the tallest person in the room. He was a handsome man, dark-haired with fine features and eyes that were a brilliant blue. What was most noticeable about him was his glaring stare. He looked at everything with an intensity that was both charming and magical.

"Is there a part of the stage where I can work on the casket and not interrupt your rehearsals?" he asked Magnus who towered over him.

"Aye, we can have them put it in the back, stage left," Magnus replied, pointing to a welcome spot for the casket.

"Hm, this would be so much easier if you just let me do a little abracadabra," he said with both a smile and a seriousness. "But as I understand it, you want the casket to remain intact but you require an escape route for the man inside."

"Is that a problem?" Sylvie asked.

"Nothing is a problem, Sylvie," he said, walking over to the casket that was now placed on the floor of the stage. "I do have some work to do on the casket to make it easy to escape from and I'd like to do that with some privacy."

Sylvie ran her hands along the the top of the casket. "It's so lustrous. So what's mahogany veneer wood as opposed to just mahogany?"

"Mahogany veneer is a medium grain wood often used for refacing. The color usually runs from pinkish-brown to reddish-brown. This casket, as you can see, is more to the reddish-brown side. I like its satiny texture," he explained to them all.

Samson stood next to Sylvie. He was close enough to want to take her hand but he didn't dare make such a move in front of Magnus and Ronaldo. Once the weekend had started, the two were inseparable. They dined, walked, watched television and talked. They talked incessantly. They still hadn't kissed. The reason being each had a disarming shyness that set their romance on slow-growth. Samson, fighting off the temptation to grab her, went over to the casket.

"So you need to work in private, Ronaldo?" he commented. "How do we make that happen?"

"As I see it, there's no magic involved here, Samson, just a lot of technical trickery. Thanks to years of doing shows in Vegas, I have adapted nicely to toiling in the nighttime hours. Leave me here for two nights and I will have a casket designed so that Phineas Flanagan can escape at will. Now I need something from you," he said, looking at Magnus.

"And what's that?" Magnus asked, wondering if he had the courage to ask Ronaldo if he would do a fund-raising show for them at the theater sometime.

"I'll need a platform which the casket will rest upon. I'll have exact measurements and a specifications by late this afternoon. Can your backstage crew handle the construction of it?"

"They can and they will," Magnus said with confidence.

Maggie Leyton always had what she called a stealth walk. Inevitably, wherever she went, she seemed to surprise people. This time the three of them were unaware of her presence until she said aloud, "Ronaldo, there is one other thing you should know about our little escapade."

Unblinking, Ronaldo bowed in her direction. "I have been told you are the commander-in-chief. I am here to serve."

"The corpse will be..." She paused, displaying frustration. "I'm so bad with medical terms."

"Let me help you," he said. "You want me to know the corpse, Mr. Phineas Flanagan, may not have the ability to escape on his own due to whatever drugs used to keep him, for all intents and purposes, in a death-like state."

She smiled humbly. "Something like that."

Ronaldo walked away from them. He wandered the stage, giving new meaning to looking around. His arms folded, he stepped off the stage and walked to the middle of the theater. And there he stood for a long moment.

"May I call you Maggie," he said aloud.

"Please."

"Maggie, how do you see this wake playing out?"

She jumped down from the stage, a tricky maneuver for a woman in her early seventies. The frown on Magnus 'face expressed how he felt about it. Maggie approached the famed illusionist.

Pointing to the stage, she began to explain. "I see the casket in the center front downstage, positioned with the front facing that way," she said pointing to the rear of the stage. "There's a reason for that."

"And that reason?"

"Phineas, once freed from the casket, can emerge from the platform with cast members on both sides helping disguise his move while we distract the Connors. They will have him backstage in a flash." Her eyes were sparkling. Excited, she asked, "What do you think?"

"Risky at best," Ronaldo replied. "What if he's still drugged up. I, of course, can construct an exit that would cushion and protect him. But there he is, inside the platform. It would require two big men to pull him out and get him offstage while you're charming those two gangsters."

Maggie mouth went to one side to the other as she thought of Ronaldo's response. "Do you have a better idea."

Ronaldo's shoulders straightened and he assumed a pose designed to impress an audience. "Yes, I do and it's my stock and trade. It's what I'm really good at. It will take a bit more planning, but it can work." He said this so matter-of-factly, it was as if he were a mechanic suggesting something as mundane as an oil change.

Magnus, Sylvie, Samson and Maggie all wanted to ask him. Sylvie got there first,

"What is your thought, Ronaldo?"

"It's simple, really. I'll make him disappear."

Chapter 19

"There is no following
her in this fierce vein."

William Shakespeare

There was no following her. Mary Eileen Connor had slipped into Gaelic and now in a state of torment, was trying to explain herself to Phineas. It was almost seven in the evening in Dublin and he knew she'd probably taken a healthy swig or two of her beloved Irish whiskey. Mary Eileen was known for her fierce temper and Phineas could tell from the emotion heard in her Gaelic flow that she had recently experienced a bout of dyspepsia and was now the worst for it. He could only let her finish.

"And you didn't understand a fecking word I said, did you, Phineas Flanagan?" she said, breathing heavily after she had pretty much ripped through the entire Gaelic vocabulary.

"No, Mary Eileen, I missed the entire, but I'm sure, eloquent soliloquy. However, I know Shamus spoke highly of your Irish temper and your frequent use of Gaelic."

"Oh, Phineas, I do miss the man. All of him except his *winkie,* that is," she confessed, her voice full of love for her late husband. "Sadly, he was just not talented in that department, bless his dearly departed soul."

"Mary Eileen, I didn't need to know that," he told her. Anxious to know why she called and why the Gaelic outburst, he asked.

"My boys dropped by earlier today," she began to explain. "They noticed my new candy-apple red Mustang convertible in the driveway and wondered how I came by it given the money they know I don't have."

"Let me guess, your famed Irish temper got the best of you," Phineas remarked nervously.

"Oh, it did, Phineas, it did," she sighed. "I don't know why those boys treat me so cheaply and cruelly. There's something psychological at play here and I am not smart enough to understand. Anyway, even though they are my sons, I have had my fill of the two of them and I let them know it."

"Oh dear, I hope you went after them in Gaelic. At least, those two dimwits wouldn't know what you're talking about."

"Oh I wish that I had," she replied. "I'm sorry, Phineas, but I let them know that if it weren't for you, I would barely be above the poverty line given the way they screwed over me regarding the inheritance. Without thinking, I blurted out that they think they're good at what they do but to me they're a couple of gombeens. Then I let them know how you right, under their stupid noses, siphoned off millions."

"And how did they react to that?" he asked, trying not to sound uneasy.

"First, they just stood there, dumbfounded. When I finished yelling at them, Danny looked at Tommy and signaled they should go. They didn't say a word. They just up and left. Danny did stop and kick the tire of my car in anger. I think he'd like to do more than that to you," she said. "I'm so, so sorry."

"Apology accepted. Now go for a nice drive in your new car with the top down," he suggested, forgetting the time change and the Irish weather. "I will be ready for them on Friday. Let me ask you, Mary Eileen, would it bother you if you don't end up seeing your boys for awhile. What I am trying to say is would you miss them if they ended up spending some time in The Joy or someplace miles from Dublin.?"

She knew The Joy well. Since 1853, Montjoy Prison in Dublin had been home to those who ran afoul of the law. "Phineas, even as their mother, it would please me. I actually think Shamus, a loving father, wouldn't mind seeing those two pea brains put away either."

"I will do what I can," he said with a hesitant confidence.

***

Maggie decided to let Phineas Flanagan die in peace that Tuesday. She told him she would visit him later in the day. She did insist he not stray from his suite at the

Claremont Hotel. It was around eleven and she wondered how to attack the rest of her day. Magnus had gone off to the theater and she was quite alone with her thoughts. One particular thought took center stage. Ronaldo, after quipping that he would make Phineas simply disappear, expressed a real desire to serve them by doing just that. He told them it would not be as simple as he suggested. Rather, it would require some effort on his part to make it happen. So Maggie, as the boss, had a decision to make. Accept Ronaldo's offer or have Doctor Phil Seton drug him. It was a choice between illusion and the original plan of having Phineas leave the casket, drop into the interior of the platform and have cast members pull him out. At wit's end, she decided to call Ambrose Dowling. She thought him wise and prudent and could help her make a decision.

"Ah, Ms Leyton," Ambrose said cheerily. "I appreciate my phone letting me know who is calling so I can adjust my greeting."

"I'm so glad I caught you," she said. "Ambrose, I need your help."

Maggie explained in detail about her difficulty reaching a decision as to what strategy would be more responsible and smart in presenting Phineas Flanagan in an open casket so that two Irish thugs would be convinced he's dead.

"I suppose it comes down to illusion or drugs or maybe both," she said wistfully. "What are Professor Ambrose Dowling's thoughts?"

"It's Tuesday. I don't do my best thinking on Tuesdays." he explained. "However, you seem to be in a quandary so it behooves me to step up and try to provide wise counsel regardless."

"Maybe I should call you tomorrow when you're in a more serious mood."

"Please, I was just stalling," he replied quickly, even though he did have this thing about Tuesdays. "I remember a story George Burns once told. He had a chronic cough. He went to a doctor who prescribed a drug to be taken four times a day for two weeks and because of the drug's side effects, he would also be taking a second pill. Deciding on a second opinion, he went to another doctor and told him of his chronic cough. That doctor stared at him for a second and then shouted, 'Stop coughing! 'Guess which course he chose."

"Okay, a questionable analogy but I see your point."

"Are you willing to take on faith the illusionist or accept the science of modern medicine?"

"What would you do?"

"I probably would bounce back and forth between the two choices for several days and then pick one, but back it up with the other."

"I don't know how we'd do that," said a frustrated Maggie. "You either put your whole trust in Ronaldo which means we would have no idea what he's going to do. Or, we stick with the original plan and hope we get the right dosage that will put Phineas under for a specific time. It's an agonizing choice.'"

"Yes, it is," he agreed. "Ms Leyton, I suggest you seek more opinions. Talk to your husband, Sylvie, Samson and anyone else who is close to this. Or, perhaps, you can put it in Phineas 'lap. He's the one who will be playing dead."

"That, Professor, is an excellent idea," she said with enthusiasm. "I'm meeting with Phineas at the Claremont at four. I will gather everyone and have them meet me there. I hope you can join us?"

"I can and I will. I certainly don't want to miss the opportunity of chatting with a corpse."

Maggie thanked him for his thoughts. Deciding he was right in seeking the opinions of the others, she began calling the others. She also included Ronaldo and Doctor Phil Seton who was arriving at the Claremont just in time for their meeting.

***

No sooner had Ambrose put his phone away than his doorbell rang. It was Sylvie. He wondered whether he had enough cheese and chardonnay. After all, it was close enough to noon and he knew whenever she stopped by she came withher usual appetite.

Rushing into his living room, she found her favorite place on his sofa. "You don't happen to have..."

"That is why, young lady, you see me headed toward the kitchen," he said. "Settle yourself and I'll be right back."

The cheese and wine in front of them, Ambrose sat nearby and asked, "What brings you here on a Tuesday, Ms Blanchard?"

"I knew you'd be home. I know you have this thing about Tuesdays," she answered.

"It seems everyone knows about my aversion to Tuesdays," he said, laughing. "So, aside from the treats in front of you, what brings you by?"

Sylvie had debated confiding in Ambrose but she needed to talk to someone and her stepsister, Ashley, was not a good option. So, after slathering a cracker with brie and taking a sip of Chardonnay, she asked with a contrived casualness, "What do you think about Samson Webb?" The question asked, she consumed the entire cheese-laden cracker.

"A better question is what do I think of you two as a couple?"

Sylvie finished her cracker. Wiping her mouth which didn't wash off her blush, she answered in a low voice, "Yeah, that's really what I wanted to ask you."

Ambrose sat forward in his easy chair. "I think you two are ideally suited. When I have been in your company, I have enjoyed seeing your bashful and hesitant flirtations. You two seem to be taking your time and there's nothing wrong with that. And, I might add, this week requires extra vigilance with an Irish wake pending."

Sylvie leaned forward. "I agree. Okay, what I am having a hard time with is his celebrity, his fame. He seems to let it roll off his back. When he's around me, he acts like a regular or ordinary guy." She paused to think about what she just said. "I don't mean regular or ordinary in a bad way."

"I'm sure you don't."

It's just that I'm uncomfortable with the celebrity side of him," she admitted, grabbing another cheesed-up cracker.

"Then, Ms Blanchard, I suggest you do the same as Samson who seems to handle it well," he replied, popping up from his chair. "Let it roll off your back, too. Now, young lady, I hate to cut our visit short but I have things I must accomplish before Maggie's four o'clock meeting at the Claremont. I believe she intends to invite you as well. Look for her call."

"Great," she said excitedly. "I will be back here at three-thirty to pick you up and I won't take no for an answer. We can talk more about Samson and me in the car."

***

Phineas Flanagan was extremely resourceful and very good at thinking on his feet. In minutes, after his call from Mary Eileen, he had crafted a plan. Fate was on his side as he managed to successfully put it into action before expiring at exactly one-thirty that Tuesday afternoon. Luck was with him as he was able to contact his niece with new instructions, two former associates of the Connor mob who were looking to oust the twins whom they referred to as spanners or idiots and, finally, a longtime contact he had with the *Garda*, Ireland's national police force. That done, he enjoyed an excellent room-service lunch and then a long reinvigorating hot shower. He decided to wear the suit he wore when he introduced himself to Berkeley, the Banter Foundation and the theater. He loved tying bow-ties and paid particular attention to the one he chose for that afternoon. Obviously, he would remain Phineas until Friday when he becomes Reggie Pennington. But there was a symbolism to this day and it weighed heavily on him. Satisfied with his appearance, deeming it dashing and sophisticated with a flamboyant air, he opened the suite's double doors at 3:55pm. Grabbing his brolly, he walked over to the long sofa and with ease, stretched his long frame out on it. After placing his umbrella on the floor beside him, he crossed his arms on his chest, closed his eyes and waited for Maggie and her cohort to arrive.

"A poor player that struts and
frets his hour upon the stage."

William Shakespeare

They crowded together, standing silently over the soft beige sofa that contained the dapper, unmoving body of Phineas Dermot Flanagan. They had arrived en masse at exactly four o'clock. Magnus and Maggie were joined by Ambrose Dowling, Sylvie Blanchard, Samson Webb, Ronaldo and Doctor Phil Seton.

Magnus, his eyes trained on the inert man lying on the couch, intoned, *"He should have died hereafter. There would have been a time for such a word."*

Ambrose picked it up from there. *"Tomorrow and tomorrow and tomorrow creeps in this petty pace from day to day to the last syllable of recorded time."*

Nudging the professor, Samson indicated he wished to participate. *"And all our yesterdays have lighted fools way to dusty death. Out, out brief candle!"* He put his all into the last four words.

While he was catching his breath, Magnus relieved him. *"Life's but a walking shadow..."*

Before he could continue, Phineas rose up, giving voice to the next line: *"A poor player that struts and frets his hour upon the stage. Yada, yada, yada."* That said, he returned to his corpse-like position. With his eyes closed again, he ordered them to stop: "The rest does not apply. The silly idiot's tale, the rage and the signifying nothing has nothing to do with me." With that, he fell quiet, but only for a second.: "And don't step on my brolly."

"All right, everybody, as touching as that was, we need to move on," Maggie said, picking out a chair to sit on. "And, Phineas, it's time to rise and shine. We need the sofa."

They all scattered to find seats. Samson and Sylvie waited for Phineas to rise and then took a share of his sofa, trying to sit as close as they could to one another. Maggie waited for them to get settled and then introduced Doctor Seton who had taken the small chair by the escritoire. He rose and took a slight bow. The doctor was a tall, well-built man with a kind and intelligent face.

"I have always enjoyed madcap adventures, and this is certainly one of them. Thank you, Maggie for summoning me. By the way, it's a pleasure to meet you all. From what you've told me, my duty is to put your friend here into a drug-induced, suspended animation for a time.

"Hopefully, for a small amount of time, 'Phineas mumbled.

"Of course."

"Maggie said you will turn me into a zombie," Phineas added, sitting at one end of the sofa with his long legs crossed, one hand holding the brolly as if he needed it to sit upright.

"I did not," Maggie snapped. "I told you, Phineas, that Phil has extensive knowledge in voodoo."

"And I do, Phineas," the doctor added. "I can assure you that my procedure will be safe and you'll come out of it as healthy as you were before the drugs. The only side effect is you'll have a strong desire to bay at the moon occasionally and feel a need to visit cemeteries at midnight. Otherwise, you'll be good as gold."

Phineas 'blue eyes widened. "Surely, you jest?"

"Surely, I do." he echoed.

Magnus raised his hand. "Phil, will he really appear dead?"

"For all intent and purposes, yes. To the average person, he will certainly look dead to the world."

"What do you mean by the average bloke?" Phineas asked.

"It's interesting, but diagnosing death is an age-old problem," Doctor Phil replied. "Some say death is cessation of all vital organs, some credit various other medical conditions. Be assured, though, between Pen's magic use of makeup and my drugs, you will appear to be quite dead for a designated time."

Phineas popped up. Putting his umbrella down, he marched to the hotel's phone. "It's dangerously close to five o'clock. Anyone care to join me for a cocktail and some appetizers?" Ambrose laughed as he spotted Sylvie putting her hand up. Her appetite is remarkable, he thought. Perhaps, I should alert Samson. The professor joined Phineas at the desk and offered to write down the orders. While they waited, the eight of them engaged in convivial but purposeless conversation. It was only after the drinks were served and a toast was made that they returned to the topic of how to get Phineas Flanagan out of a casket.

Maggie got them back on that topic by asking Ronaldo and the doctor directly, "Can you two work together?"

Ronaldo smiled at the question. "I would be honored to work with Doctor Seton. I can certainly give you an easy way for Mr. Flanagan to escape the casket, and no one will be able to detect any change in its construction."

It was Dr. Seton's turn. "And I, too, can work with Ronaldo. I am a huge fan."

Ambrose Dowling decided he would bring up what was surely the elephant in the room. "I am personally delighted there's a mutual accord between the doctor and the illusionist. However, we do have two opposing approaches to how this will all play out. We have heard the from the doctor and we know what he plans for this ruse of ours to work. Now I think we should hear from Ronaldo."

"The gentleman will not have to escape the coffin or casket," the magician told them in a soft but convincing voice. "He will vanish. I shall make him disappear."

Magnus rubbed his beard. "Aye, that's all well and good, Ronaldo, but I'm sure you are aware of how difficult it is to put our solid support behind something we know nothing about. With Doctor Seton, we have science and transparency."

"I agree, Magnus," the magician replied. "What I would do to make Mr..."

"Please call me Phineas," Flanagan interjected, staring intently at Ronaldo.

"Thank you. What is required is very similar to one of my signature illusions, so I hope you understand I that I can't share with you how it's done," he explained. "I must work alone. If you choose to put it in my hands, you'll just have to put your trust in me," he said with a confident smile.

Maggie took a sip her gin and tonic. "Okay, I'm game to put this to a vote."

Phineas had returned to the sofa. Instead of holding his umbrella, he now held a Boodles Martini with several olives. "Maggie, dearest, I am the one who has to get into that wooden sleeping bag. I should have the dominant say in how I want to be handled. Don't you agree?"

There was a general nodding of heads. Only Magnus remained still. Maggie, instead of nodding approval, said, "Phineas, you have a point. How can we best handle your temporary confinement?"

Phineas ran a finger slowly around the rim of his Martini glass. He stared thoughtfully into it. "In my former business, I learned early on to trust only my instincts. Trust nothing else. I am doing that now." Turning his head, he looked over at the illusionist. "Ronaldo displays such a calm coolness and confidence. His convincing manner impresses me. No offense, Doctor Seton, but I prefer to vanish than to be drugged."

Seton smiled graciously. "No offense taken, Phineas. I have seen Ronaldo perform and his illusions are nothing but out of this world." He turned to Maggie, "You mind if I stick around and witness this grand hoax. Who knows, I might be of some use."

"Phil, you are more than welcome to stay. And I am certain there will be a role for you to play," Maggie assured him. "So, Phineas, you would like Ronaldo to take charge of getting you safely out of the casket?"

Instead of answering her directly, Phineas got up from the sofa and walked toward Ronaldo. Extending his glass to him for a toast, he said, "If this goes grandly, perhaps, we can do it again in Las Vegas during your act."

Ronaldo toasted him. "I already have an able assistant. And let me give you a tip. Only a foreigner would say Las Vegas. The rest of us call it Vegas."

"I *am* a foreigner," he sniffed. "So, Mister Magician, anything I can do between now and Friday."

"Don't really die," he replied. "That would take all the fun out of it."

Maggie, sensing things were wrapping up, rose from her chair. "Phil, to help set the scene, perhaps, you can pose as Phineas 'personal doctor."

"I would be happy to do that," he said cheerily. "By the way, is there a death certificate?"

"There is," Maggie told him. "Phineas has every official document known to any bureaucracy. He has all he needs to go from Flanagan to Pennington. We're set."

"Is the meeting over?" Sylvie asked, looking at the movement in the suite and eyeing hungrily the snacks laid out on the coffee table in front of her. Samson popped up and extended a hand to help her up.

"If you don't mind keeping company with someone who's been dead for just three plus hours, please stay, you two," Phineas said to the couple, "I hate to drink alone and I can't possibly finish those goodies myself."

Chapter 21

Warning! Never answer your cellphone while dead.

Twenty-four hours had not yet passed since Phineas Flanagan died of a heart attack and he was already bored stiff. No pun intended. Maggie had ordered him to remain in his hotel suite incommunicado and he was obeying, albeit, reluctantly. They were comfortable enough lodgings, but he yearned for a little more movement than shuffling from the sofa to the bathroom to the bedroom. Wednesday came to town in a wintry mood. It was a cold, showery morning, but strolling in such inclement weather seemed preferable than watching television. He'd never been a fan and daytime programming intensified his dissatisfaction. He was convinced that without commercials for drugs or therapeutics to cure or manage erectile dysfunction, incontinence, high blood pressure, depression and myriad other maladies, television would cease to be. He found day-time show hosts insufferable and the programs juvenile. He begged Maggie to drop off books. She promised to stop by that afternoon.

Phineas did not consider himself a contemplative person. Self-reflection was something he rarely indulged in. However, this Wednesday, planted on his sofa, dressed to the nines, he gave considerable thought as to who he was and who he was about to become. Overall, he gave himself good grades. Now in his seventies and, except for being dead for another three days, in excellent health, he decided that he could as Reggie Pennington be a bit more outrageous. Not outrageous exactly. What was that adjective Ambrose used when they were describing themselves as fossils, he asked himself. "Flamboyant," he shouted gleefully to an empty room when it came to him. Yes, he would, as a certified fossil, be more flamboyant, but in a charming manner. Enjoying the time he was giving to self-appraisal, he also gave some attention to his sex life which he realized was nonexistent and had been for some time. He realized he was content with that. He'd tired of meaningless sexual encounters with anonymous men, always younger, immature and brasher. They now seemed more trouble than they were worth. However, he told himself he would not run from a serious relationship if it came to be. Admitting that always reminded him of his longtime, unrequited love. And that reminded him he needed to contact Magnus for help in finding her. Yes. Her.

Phineas stretched his long legs out and crossed them at the ankle. Relaxed and happy with his self-assessment, he closed his eyes and let his mind wander. What happened next was by accident.) Chalk it up to learned behavior. Still, it was very wrong. His cellphone rang and he automatically answered it. He'd already said hello before instantly disconnecting the phone. "Shite, shite, shite," he uttered angrily. Phineas looked at recent calls to see if he recognized the number. "You're dead, you pillock. Dead people don't answer phones," he said, scolding himself. Okay, he thought, perhaps it was just a robo-call or wrong number. He reminded himself not to make that same mistake again.

***

Professor Kenneth RIchter was confused. He wondered why Phineas had hung up on him? Deciding to give himself a half-day off, he had turned his midday class over to his teaching assistant. The professor had no specific agenda for the rest of the day except to call Phineas about his promise of funding his project. He also had a question about his interview with Reggie Pennington on Thursday.

If Richter had taken time for some brutally honest self-reflection like Phineas had, he might have discovered that much like an overweight doctor who smoked, a psychiatrist with more neuroses than his clients or an engineer who can't screw in a lightbulb. Richter, while a brilliant economist, was small-minded when it came to his personal finances. A failing that limited even his greed.

The professor found himself at the bar at Bar OSA. He hadn't planned to visit the restaurant. He had been to the Walk Shop around the corner to buy new shoes and decided Spanish tapas would make a good lunch.

"Hey, Professor, this is a rare treat," Duffy Hart said, standing across the bar from him. "I thought we were off-limits to you? You know, this is Professor Ainsworthy's hangout. The professor, of course, being your wife."

"Ex-wife," he muttered, looking at the drink menu. "I'll have a vodka Martini, shaken not stirred."

"Certainly, James," Duffy joked, turning to make the cocktail.

"It's Kenneth," RIchter said, correcting him. The professor sensed the restaurant owner didn't like him.

Duffy turned back and stared. "I meant James, as in James Bond."

The professor thought a moment. "Oh, yeah, of course. Only natural we'd drink the same cocktail," he said, adding an awkward laugh.

When Duffy returned with his drink, Richter leaned forward and asked, "Doesn't Phineas Flanagan come in here a lot?"

"Did," he answered, pulling his ragged bar towel out of his back pocket. He began to clean the already spotless counter.

"What do you mean *did?*"

"Of course, you wouldn't know. He died of a heart attack yesterday," he explained. "A real tragedy. He was in his hotel room and collapsed in the early afternoon. Turns out Phineas had a faulty ticker and none of us knew about it."

The professor sat up straight. With a quizzical look, he stammered, "But I... I mean I just talked with him today."

Duffy sensed trouble. "What do you mean, you talked to him?"

"I called his cell and he answered. And he didn't sound like a ghost."

"What did he say?"

"He said hello," he answered. "Then nothing. He must have hung up on me."

"It was probably someone else," Duffy suggested. "I'm sure the place is just crawling with people. One of them probably picked up the phone and then realized they shouldn't." He hoped that explanation would lessen Richter's interest.

RIchter shook his head. "No, can't be. Flanagan has a unique voice. I'm sure it was him."

"All I know, is what I heard," Duffy said with a shrug. "Are you ordering food, professor?"

"I am," he said, picking up the menu. "So he lived in a hotel, huh?"

"Phineas went first class all the way. He had a lavish suite at the Claremont."

The professor ate little and quickly. He left after paying his bill but leaving no tip as he felt that wasn't necessary because he was being served by the owner. Later, Duffy told The Redhead and Lauren Ainsworthy, Richter's ex-wife, of his actions. Both got a big laugh, promising to tip Duffy exceedingly well after their lunch.

Richter had had no plans for his half-day holiday. After leaving Bar OSA, he decided to go home. He had finally gotten around to decorating his waterfront condominium and he looked forward to spending more time there. He had no aesthetic eye and a tendency to be frugal in matters of furniture, furnishings and design. Thus, the decor was fitting for a young bachelor just starting out in the business, not an established, older professor at a major university. His pride and joy was an intricate sound system and a sixty-five inch flat screen smart TV that he was struggling to understand their many complexities. Lani Chang, a TV meteorologist and girlfriend had given him some minimal instruction as to how to tame the media beasts, but he'd never gotten around to it. So it was, he would that afternoon try and master it.

The trouble was he couldn't get the abrupt phone call to Phineas out of his mind. He was convinced it was Flanagan who answered his cell. How could he be dead, he wondered. After one feeble attempt to learn how to add closed captions, he decided to clear his mind by visiting the Claremont, nestled in the Berkeley/Oakland hills.

The professor ignored public parking, choosing the hotel's costly valet parking.

It was worth it as he loved the attention he received. There were about a dozen people under the three lane porte cochere. When the parking assistant asked for his name, he gave extra voice to the answer. A quick scan of the rest of the crowd, revealed he was zero for twelve when it came anyone recognizing him.

With s slightly damaged ego, Richter entered the impressive, white building. The lobby began as a long narrow stretch before opening into a larger, grander space. To his right was a long counter accommodating five front desk personnel. Mid-afternoon, usually quiet, meant only one or two people at check-in. As he passed, this head swiveled in that direction when he heard, "Professor Richter?"

It was a husky, almost male voice that beckoned him to the front desk. There were two woman behind the long counter. Richter, judging from what he heard, decided it was the woman who was stout and square with an equally square face and grey hair assembled in a stern bun. She wore a scowl, looking like everyone's vision of a nightmarish mother-in-law.

He approached her and, with a hesitant smile, announced himself. "I'm Professor Richter. You called me?"

She didn't speak and her head never came up from the computer screen that held her attention. Instead, she just pointed to the clerk to her right, an attractive, young woman dressed in a modest, front-desk uniform. With large dark eyes, she radiated a sincere cheeriness rather than the prescribed peppiness the average guest was used to and certainly more welcoming than her coworker.

RIchter moved three steps to his left and changed his expression. He now wore his best media smile. "I'm Professor Richter," he said again, noticing her name-tag read Paulina.

She put both hands to her face, expressing surprise. "This is like so cool. I am a huge fan of your Sunday news 'show. You ought to be on with all those network types and not just local," she gushed.

"Well, thank you." Looking at her more closely, he added, "Paulina."

"I graduated from Cal last year," she said proudly.

"Go, Bears."

"Yeah," she giggled. "Go, Bears."

They stood there, silent for an awkward moment. Richter loved looking at her. She was a pretty woman, tall with a lithe figure. Her dark brown hair was worn in a ponytail. She looked, he thought, Slavic.

"Am I keeping you from... Oh, I don't know, maybe a meeting" she asked nervously.

"No, not at all. No meeting. So, Paulina, is this a day job or did you just come on duty?" he asked, his smile beginning to wear on him.

"Oh, I'm off in an hour," she chirped. "I can't believe this. You know, I am a news freak and I particularly like reading and hearing about financial news. I find it fascinating. And you are so knowledgeable."

"If you have no plans for after work, perhaps we can meet for a drink. We can delve into world affairs together," he laughed, standing straighter, convinced she might be taller than him.

She didn't hesitate. "That would be great. How about I meet you in the Limewood bar? That's the bar and restaurant right as you enter the hotel," she said, pointing in that direction.

"I look forward to it," he said, checking his watch. "Say, I know this is probably against hotel rules but I want to surprise an old friend of mine who is staying here, but I can't remember his room number."

Her answer was a dismissive wave. "Easy peasy. I can find him for you. What's his name?"

"Phineas Flanagan," he replied.

She brightened even more and exclaimed, "Mr. Flanagan? Oh, he's so nice and what a character. I understand he's an actor."

"He is that and a lot of other things," he said, wondering why she would not have heard of his passing.

Paulina gave the professor the number to his suite and told him she was excited about meeting him for drinks. She was anxious to know what he thought about the United States leaving the Paris Accord.

"Maybe we'll also talk about just Paris," he flirted.

"Why not," she giggled in her small, gravelly voice.

The professor walked away thinking when things go right, they really go right.

Emerging from the elevator, he checked the hallway signs to check room directions. He was to turn left. As he did, he heard voices. Several doors down, Sylvie and Samson Webb were knocking on what he guessed was Flanagan's suite. He now knew what he had to do. When he heard the door open, he rushed forward silently, arriving at the suite's entrance just as Sylvie and Samson were about to enter. Crudely, he pushed his way in much to the shock and surprises of the other three.

Looking up at his host who stood inches over him, Professor Richter greeted him. "You look awfully well, Phineas, considering you suffered a heart attack and died yesterday."

"We didn't invite him, Phineas," she said, her voice full of scorn for the man she was talking about "I have absolutely no idea where he came from."

Composed and always polite, Phineas turned to allow his guests entry. "Please, make yourselves comfortable. And you, Professor, I promise to tell all."

Chapter 22

"Thanks for the nifty insults, Will."

Sylvie Blanchard

After Phineas had bade them enter, he escorted Professor Richter, Samson Webb and Sylvie Blanchard into his living room. He told them where he wanted them to sit. He showed his invited guests to the sofa. Next, he selected for his intruder the room's most uncomfortable chair, the small seat that accompanied the escritoire, a small French writing desk. He then took a wingback accent chair close to Richter who immediately had begun to fidget, trying to find a comfortable position.

"So, Professor, to what or to whom do I owe the pleasure of your unexpected and, I might add, unwanted visit?" Phineas asked with the gracious sarcasm of a seasoned diplomat.

Richter was so taken off guard by this strange welcome, he took a moment to remind himself that he was in charge and he was not to let the Irish actor get the best of him.

"As I said, I *will* tell all," Phineas repeated, seeing the puzzled looks on Sylvie and Samson's faces. "However, I am curious as to why you are here."

"I was at lunch this afternoon and I was talking to Duffy Hart. He told me you died of a heart attack yesterday which I thought strange as I had just called you and you answered," he told his guest. "So I decided to find out for myself if you were really dead, which you obviously are not."

Phineas confirmed his observation. "Obviously, I am not. But I will be for two men who are on their way here from Ireland who intend to see that I really do die."

Samson leaned forward on the sofa. "Phineas, do you really want to tell him your plans?"

"Samson has a point," Sylvie added, glowering at the professor, a man she throughly despised.

"It's fine, I assure you," Phineas told the pair who were sitting on the edge of the sofa, straight as pencils, staring angrily at Sylvie's old teacher.

"Professor Richter, I meant what I said about being threatened by two very violent men. I worked for their father and then for them for a short period. I am of no use to them anymore and in their line of work, and I might add, my line, that's a typical severance package."

"Organized crime, huh?" he asked.

"I suppose you can call it that, even though it is ridiculously disorganized at times," Phineas answered. Making a steeple with his hands, he put them to his lips and began to think. He knew he could throw Richter off the track. He had several ideas. Now he just had to pick one. And just like that, he did.

"Professor Richter, can I trust you to keep what I am about to tell you under wraps?"

RIchter didn't answer right away. He, too, was thinking about how to play this. Like Phineas, it came to him in a flash. "I don't know what I'm supposed to keep under wraps. Maybe it's something illegal or morally wrong. I'd need to know more."

Phineas was magnanimous in his reply. "Of course, I understand," he replied.

"I don't, and I think he's full of bullshit," Sylvie blurted out.

Richter turned toward her. "Well, I can see I did right in not choosing you as my TA."

While she stewed, Phineas was about to explain what they planned when there was a knock on the door. "Excuse me," he said as he headed to answer it.

It was Maggie and Magnus, arms full of food and books. They marched in, first spotting Samson and Sylvie and giving them a welcoming nod. Then they both saw Kenneth RIchter.

"What's *he* doing here?" she asked, putting her bag of food on the closest table, all the while glaring at the professor.

"Why not ask me directly, huh?" Richter said with a smirk. "You know, asking Phineas and not me is not what I call polite. I think an apology is in order."

Magnus still held the books. Looking for a place to put them, he walked toward the escritoire, placing them inches from Kenneth Richter. Towering over him, he leaned down and said in a low, threatening voice, "Phineas is going to tell us why you're here. My wife is not apologizing to you. Now I just looked around and I don't see that there's any place for Maggie to sit. So I strongly suggest you offer her your seat. And don't think about moving to the sofa because I am headed there. I suppose you'll just have to stand." That said, he lightly patted Richter's cheek and went over to the sofa where Samson and Sylvie happily snuggled closer to make room for the large Irishman.

Phineas clapped his hands. "A bit of solid drama is always worth acknowledging. Now, ladies and gentlemen, may I have the floor?"

Seeing he had their approval, he first explained how Richter came to be in the suite. He apologized to Maggie and promised it would not happen again. Phineas then addressed RIchter who was given his chair back by Maggie who felt his standing gave him an appearance of dominance over the group.

"Professor, these four clever people concocted a scheme that we think will remove the threat that, frankly, has me a trifle scared," he said.

Maggie rolled her eyes wondering where Phineas was headed.

Phineas crossed and then recrossed his legs. "I won't bore you with minutiae but thanks to trusted contacts in Ireland, I know how and when the Connor twins, those are the thugs, are coming to Berkeley. My niece will at some point inform them of my death. She will also tell them she's headed here for a funeral service, otherwise known in Ireland as a wake."

Now Samson and Sylvie began to fidget. Why would Phineas reveal all to this jerk?

Phineas ignored their puzzled stares. "So in order for this to happen, Professor, I have to die and I needed a place to show these two bruisers that I really am deceased."

Now Magnus harrumphed, signaling that his childhood friend had gone too far.

And still Phineas continued. "Well, to our amazement, we managed to find a funeral home that didn't mind breaking a few rules. So here's what we have planned for Friday."

Four of his five guests were on tenterhooks. They were all sitting forward and their expressions signaled Phineas that they were not happy.

Their silent protest didn't work. Phineas marched on. "So, Professor, at four o'clock, Friday, I will lie in rest at *Going Up Funeral Home, Park and Crematorium* in Livermore. It will be attended by just a few people." he said, pointing to his other guests.

Richter put a hand up. "So how come someone like Duffy Hart knows about it?"

"He's catering the event," Phineas replied. "Plus, we included four or five more people whom we trust so that there's a respectable number of mourners." There was a sly smile on his face.

"And these mobsters will know to come out there?" Richter asked.

"My niece, Quinn, also from Dublin, will take care of that." Suddenly, Phineas straightened up and his eyes brightened as if he just had a great idea. "Why don't you come, Professor. I would really appreciate it."

Magnus, Maggie, Samson and Sylvie sank into their seats and looked visibly relieved.

Kenneth Richter looked hesitant. Noticing, Phineas thought he would add an incentive. "We talked about fifty thousand for your urbanization project. I can, perhaps, speed up getting that money to you."

"Sure, I'd be happy to drive out there," he said. "Should be quite an entertaining time."

Phineas uncrossed his legs, popped up and walk over to the professor. Extending his hand, he said, "Good. I'm glad to hear that."

Richter let go of his hand. Still seated, he looked up at the slim man who stood over him. "Uh, one slight correction. It's now one hundred thousand. Fifty just won't let me achieve what I want to with this project. And given these strange circumstances, I think one hundred thousand also insures my discretion."

Sylvie Blanchard left the sofa as if she had been shot from a circus cannon. In seconds she was standing by Phineas and looking down at Richter. She was beet-red, her fists were clenched and she was rocking slightly.

"You swag-bellied, motley-minded, panty-sniffing old coot, how dare you..." She paused to take a breath. "How dare you come in here and try to profit once again from my sister's work." She turned and looked up at Phineas who was amused by her unexpected outburst. "Phineas, this clot-pole, coed-seducing..."

Phineas put a hand on her shoulder. "Easy now, Sylvie. Calm yourself. You'll have plenty of time to tell me all."

With a raised voice, Magnus, said, "Bravo, Sylvie, the Bard would have been proud."

Over her shoulders, she said, "Thanks, Magnus, Will does have some nifty insults, all of which apply to this semblance of a man."

"None of them deserved, by the way," Richter said coolly. "You are really a nasty piece of work, young lady."

"Oh, stop trying to sound like Donald Trump," she spat as Samson pried her loose from Phineas and returned her to the sofa.

"I think it's time you left, professor," Phineas told him. "I will call you with the address and time of the service. Can I count on your presence?"

Richter stood up. He still had to look up at Phineas. "I've received a few nice checks in my time for attending events. I can sure handle one for one hundred thou. Call me with the details."

He started to walk away. His heart was pounding and he was far more upset than he let on. Sylvie had rattled him but he'd be damned if he was going to show it. As he passed the sofa, he looked over at Samson. "You better find a muzzle for that girlfriend of yours."

Magnus was beside RIchter in an instant. Putting a hand on his shoulder and pressing enough to cause Richter to wince from the pain, he advised him to leave without another word.

When the door closed, Sylvie glanced over at Phineas who actually seemed to enjoy the drama of the afternoon. It certainly was a step up from daytime TV.

"Please tell me you're not going to pay him that money," she pleaded.

He shook his head. "Of course not, I think I will instruct Mr, Midgely at *Going Up* that when Professor Richter arrives, he is to give him a note with two hundred dollars in it and several suggestions for dinner in the what I understand to be the beautiful Livermore Valley." He clapped at the cleverness of his mischievous suggestion. "And once again, we find ourselves near enough to five o'clock for a cocktail. I'm taking orders."

Chapter 23

Now you see it. Now you don't.

Thursday, the Bay Area woke to yet another grey, wintry day. While this kind of dull, colorless weather can lessen the charms of some locations, others refuse to let it affect their special allure. The city of Berkeley was one of them. Or so it seemed to two men who, as visitors, were enchanted by its uniqueness. They were Rolando, the Las Vegas magician and Doctor Phil Seton, a Los Angeles emergency room doctor. Each was there to participate in the Maggie-inspired-and-directed scheme to save Phineas Flanagan's skin and other anatomical parts.

The planned Irish wake was just twenty-four hours away. Everything seemed frighteningly on schedule. The two men were at the theater for most of the day. Doctor Seton had borrowed Sylvie's office and was busy filling out a number of forms that described in detail how Phineas met his Maker.

Rolando, after giving a thumbs up to the curtained platform, gave instructions to a crew as to how he wanted the casket to be situated on it. Once it was in place and to his liking, he began to roam the theater, examining the entire area with an intensity that fascinated those who were around him. They knew better than to distract or interrupt him.

Both he and the doctor had finished their chores at the same time. A gregarious man, Seton invited Rolando for a drink. They decided on Bar OSA. It was only four o'clock and they felt they had a good chance at finding a place at the bar. An eccentricity both shared was a preference for a bar over a table.

They were in luck. Bar OSA was lightly populated. They chose two stools at the end far end of the restaurant and settled in. The doctor ordered a Bombay Sapphire Martini and Rolando a Manhattan. When Duffy suggested a Cuban Manhattan made with a fine rum, a house specialty, Rolando changed his order. When the drinks arrived, they picked them up and toasted.

"Here's to science," Rolando said cheerily.

"And here's to magic," Doctor Phil Seton offered, lifting his Manhattan for the first taste. "Although many scientists might argue that doctors aren't scientists. They sometimes take a dim view of us."

Rolando laughed, "Nonsense. Although, if you think about it, there's so much contrariness, confusion and ignorance about the physical makeup of humans. I'm sure you've treated a patient or two in a manner that flew in the face of science."

"You're right. I have. Some of us more than others. You can count me among the some," he laughed. "Not to change eh subject you are so well known. I mean an internationals figure. I'm surprised you can move about so anonymously."

The magician sat straight on the stool. His expressive hands were flat on the counter. "I think there are two main reasons. When I am performing, staging is everything. I am made to look imposing, larger than I really am. We strive for larger than life. As you can see, I am a diminutive man off stage. Also, most people assume that a famous person would not occupy the same space they do. Added to that, my street clothes, while I think they are fashionable, are designed so that I don't stick out."

"One thing I notice are your eyes. When you stare at a person, you seem to be looking into them, not at them."

"I can call you Phil?" he asked.

"Please, I have a hard time with Doctor Phil." he said.

"Oh, because of the ubiquitous, media-mad Doctor Phil? I get it. Anyway, the eyes are a big part of my trade," he said.

"Would you rather be called a magician or an illusionist?" the doctor asked. Shifting positions, he turned sideways to more comfortably talk to Rolando. "Actually, I have a second question: What goes into an illusion? I would imagine distraction plays a major part."

"Yes, it does," Rolando answered, picking up his drink. "How about another toast. This one to distraction."

Seton turned to pick up his Martini and it was gone. There was no one near them and the counter was empty. "My drink? Where did it go?" He signaled Duffy who was steps away.

"Can I help you?" the bar owner asked.

"Did you take my drink?"

"No, afraid I didn't."

Mystified, he looked at looked at Rolando. He was clearly puzzled. "So what happened to my drink?"

Rolando smiled. "Nothing happened to your drink," he said.

The addled doctor turned to looked at the bar counter and there in front of him, he saw his barely drunk Martini. "You... You made it disappear," he gasped in amazement. "I gather you won't let me know how you did that."

Rolando, still holding his Manhattan, said, "No, that I won't do. Now, let's change the toast. Here's to illusion and the major part you played in it."

***

Phineas was attempting in an obvious clumsy manner to explain his relationship with Kenneth Richter and yesterday's encounter with the professor, when he suddenly asked Magnus, "Do you remember Aisling Walsh?"

"Aisling Walsh," his friend repeated, pronouncing it correctly as Ash-ling. He was reclined on Phineas Flanagan's sofa, tired from a day spent at the theater. Phineas had served him two fingers of Tallisker and told him there were several fingers left. Magnus wondered why Phineas had brought up her name. "I do remember her. Aisling was a classmate of ours for a couple of years. A prodigy, if I remember, who went off to higher levels at an early age. What about her? And how does she relate to Kenneth RIchter?"

Phineas stood at the window looking at the bay view but paid it no attention. He turned to Magnus. "This may come as a shock to you, Magnus Flaherty, but I loved her, Probably still do. At lease she still occupies a place in my heart," he said with a touching sincerity.

"Aye now, you're having me on," Magnus said, propping himself up and looking at his friend with a goofy smile. "You told me Shamus Conner was your schoolboy crush."

"This happened years later," he answered, moving over to the accent chair nearest Magnus. "I was is London on business, she was in town for a conference molecular such and such. We were staying at the same hotel." Breathlessly, he uttered, "Oh, Magnus, it was a reunion for the ages. When her conference ended, she stayed on a few days and we got to know each other in a most intimate fashion. We took the city by storm. There was no happier couple in all of London. I don't think I ever felt as fulfilled as I did that week.

A stupefied Magnus looked at his old school mate. "Uh, how did your... I mean, didn't you tell..."

"How did the fact that I'm gay fit into this? Is that what you're trying to say?"

"Aye."

Phineas put his head in his hands. His eyes were closed. After a thoughtful pause, he looked up at his friend and began to explain. Or, at least, tried to. "I don't know how to answer that, Magnus. It shook me to the core. That I will tell you. I know this. I had fallen in love with her. I do have to say, it was, probably for the benefit for all concerned, an unrequited love. I never expressed my true feelings to her and I knew at the time, while we were deliriously happy, she would be going home without giving me a promise of staying in touch."

Magnus took a sip of his Tallisker. "You said there were more fingers to be had?" he asked, holding out his glass.

Phineas took the glass and walked over to the French writing desk that he'd converted into a small bar. "Magnus, from an early age, I always knew I was gay and would live within the limitations that come with that kind of recognition. Having said that, I never let my sexuality define me as a person. I always thoughI I'm me regardless of whether I was gay, straight, bi or someone who got off on eating animal biscuits while naked. Who I was sexually was something I didn't give a lot of thought to."

He poured another two fingers of the peaty scotch and handed the glass back to Magnus. Exasperated, he murmured, "Or am I just kidding myself. You know, I don't usually think about these kinds of things." Phineas stretched a bit and added in a more relaxed tone, "All I do know for certain is love is transcendent and delightfully contagious."

"Phineas, I, uh," he said, faltering. "I am trying to pretend that we are in my pub in Dublin. You're at the bar and I'm behind it. As a witty publican, what would I say in response to your sudden and surprising outburst?"

"Probably something like, 'Cut the blarney and have another pint,'" Phineas chortled.

"Had you any other serious relationships? Male or female."

"No, I have spent most of my life in hotel rooms in many different locales. Mind you, I am not complaining. However, this Bedouin existence doesn't work when it comes to building partnerships. My love life was sort of one and done."

"So back to the first part of our conversation. What does Aisling Walsh have to do with Kenneth Richter?"

Phineas put his drink down. "It's Doctor Aisling Walsh-Coburn now. She is a highly regarded molecular biologist who is also a professor at UC Berkeley. Magnus, she's right here, in our own backyard as Americans like to say." he announced. "I have kept up with her and know that she is now doing vital research. Research, by the way, that will continue if funding continues."

"So you've known she was in Berkeley?"

Phineas nodded. "Of course, I've followed her career with avid interest."

"So she's the reason you came here," Magnus said, rubbing his beard and trying not to sound like a detective interrogating a suspect.

"No," Phineas said, shaking his head. "*You* were the reason I came to Berkeley. I came to San Francisco because that's where the gentleman resides who provided me with certain papers necessary for my transformation. It was then that I read an article about you running a theater here.

"And you don't have any interest in meeting with Aisling?" Magnus asked.

"It would be terribly awkward. For her, we were a moment in time. However, my being here will make what I want to do for her so much easier. You see, she is to be the last recipient of my largess. I have saved the biggest charitable contribution for last and it is going to her. It's a rather substantial amount," Phineas said, pausing to take a sip of his drink. "I learned quickly that donating money can be complicated in certain circumstances and a huge university system is one of those circumstances."

"Aye, the Banter Foundation often runs into the same problem."

"Perhaps, we can work together as my first resource has dried up."

"What do you mean?"

"It's one of the reasons I befriended Kenneth Richter," he explained. "Little did I know I'd be dealing with a philandering, street-level fraudster. I learned what he did to Sylvie's sister. I thought he could help me work my way through the maze called UC."

Magnus 'eyes brightened. "I have a better idea. After your wake, I'll introduce you to Richter's ex-wife. She's also a professor at Cal. She is, like Aisling, a highly regarded member of the faculty. She is Arete to his Hecate," he said, an analogy Phineas would understand.

"Ah, Magnus my lad, you remembered your Greek gods and goddesses," he laughed. "If only Father Brendan were here."

"Don't even think that. If he were, the boozer would have polished off the Tallisker, leaving us with a finger to fight over."

***

They sat at a corner table across from each other, looking like star-crossed lovers to the other diners at Fenton's Creamery, a popular, century-old ice cream parlor on Oakland's Piedmont Avenue. Between them, in the middle of the small table, was an elaborate concoction of three large scoops of vanilla, chocolate and strawberry ice cream, topped with pineapple, strawberry, hot fudge, almond and whipped cream. They each held a spoon at the ready.

Sylvie looked across at Samson and smiled. "What flavor are you going for first? You know, it will say a lot about you," she said with a mischievous air.

Holding his spoon high, he looked at his choice. "There's only one first choice and that's chocolate."

"Yea," she exclaimed. "Nice to know we have that in common."

"But what does it tell you about me?

She shrugged. "I haven't the slightest idea. I don't even know why I said it," she giggled, running her spoon-fee hand through her short hair. "I think it may have been something I read or saw in a movie and I thought it was cool. So, come on, let's attack this sweet treat."

Samson wiped some chocolate from his face. "Sylvie, can we talk about..."

"Excuse me, but are you Samson Webb?" The inquirer was a nerdy-looking man in his twenties. Dressed in old jeans and an even older *Star Wars* tee-shirt, he had managed to sneak up on them as Samson and Sylvie were so wrapped up in their own company.

Samson looked up at the young man and then glanced past him to a table in the middle of the room where six other similarly dressed men and women were sitting, all of them looking in their direction.

"Guilty as charged. Yes, I'm Samson Webb," he said cordially.

"This is so cool. I'm Rich," he said, offering his hand. He pointed to the table behind him. "We're all from Pixar. We thought it was you."

"You guys do terrific work," Samson said, noticing Rich glancing over at Sylvie. "And that's my friend, Sylvie Blanchard,"

Rich shook his head and beamed. "Wow, so with that name, you must be like a

famous French actress."

She smiled and replied, "I'm a not-so-famous Berkeley theater manager."

"That's cool, too," he said diplomatically. "Man, Mr. Webb, I could talk about movies with you for hours."

"I'm sure you could, but then this delicious banana split would melt," Samson pointed out, hoping he'd get the hint.

An obvious ice cream aficionado, Rich responded,"Yeah, for sure. Anyway, nice meeting you. Come by Pixar anytime. Ask for Rich Cummings and I'll give you the grand tour."

A soon as Rich departed, Sylvie apologized. "I completcly forgot. This place is a hangout for Pixar people. I should have warned you."

"Nonsense, that was no problem," he replied. "Now dig in before this really melts."

"But you were going to ask me something."

"I can do that and eat at the same time." Asking her turned out to be difficult as he stammered, "I, uh, wondered... Let's see... I wondered If you were... Well, I mean, I think you are. At least, that's what I feel."

"Is that supposed to be a question?" she laughed.

"I'm usually not this tongue-tied," he said, putting his spoon down.

"So, what you want to ask me is do I like you with the same intensity that you do me?

Samson blushed. "That pretty much sums it up."

"And now you'd like an answer?" she asked coyly, taking the last bite of the chocolate ice cream. She tried to hide the pounding of her heart.

"I would really appreciate it," he mumbled. "I am hoping it's yes."

"I can better answer once we're alone," she said breathily.

Samson leaned back, wearing a big grin. "And from what movie did you get that line?"

Chapter 24

"And a Bloody Mary for
my cello, please."

Quinn Mallory

Tommy and Danny Connor, who adamantly refuse to respond to Thomas and Daniel, had recently binge-watched reruns of *Miami Vice*. Their latest viewing had a profound sartorial effect on them with both desiring to look like Don Johnson. As a result, for their flight to San Francisco, they boarded business class looking like two, expensively dressed drug dealers. Tommy was wearing a white Zegna linen suit with a light blue shirt, the top three buttons opened to show off his hairless chest. He finished the outfit with soft tan loafers and no socks. Danny, preferring a more casual approach wore a costly black tee-shirt, lightweight designer jeans and a Marc Jacobs faded pink sport coat. He, too, finished it off with tan loafers and no socks. The twins were less than an inch over six feet and solidly built. They were not identical but close enough. Their heads were large and square with each sporting a broken nose. Their complexions were Irish linen white. With their blue eyes, light brown hair cut stylishly and perpetual scowls, the twins made an unusual fashion statement. Never had two men looked so out of place as they climbed aboard the plane that would take them non-stop from Dublin, Ireland to San Francisco, California.

With one small carry-on bag each, the made their way to their seats in business class. Three seats from their destination, on the same side of the aisle, Tommy spotted Quinn Mallory, all buckled in and enjoying the airline's welcoming glass of champagne.

"And what are you doing on this flight?" he asked, his manner stern and his tone threatening. Danny stood next to him and just to be sure she heard the question, he asked it, too. He had a habit of repeating what his brother just said.

Phineas Flanagan's niece was an attractive woman in her mid thirties. She was a perfect fit for a cello; tall enough and slender enough to look like she belonged behind the large stringed instrument. Her hands were long and slim, but strong from years of playing. Her best feature was, perhaps, her eyes. She was one who couldn't disguise her feelings as her eyes were a giveaway. Toughened by years on the concert circuit and countless hours of practice, she appeared formidable and seemingly fearless.

She didn't answer them right away. Instead, she studied them from top to bottom. With barely a smile, she said, "You two better hope that U.S. Customs doesn't go in for profiling or you'll never leave the airport. Why on earth are you dressed like a like a pair of Miami hoods?"

Her comment angered Danny, but Tommy merely let it pass. Brushing imaginary lint from his suit coat, he asked again with a little more menace in his voice, "So, why are you on this flight?"

Quinn put her magazine down and looked behind her. "You know, you're keeping people from getting to their seats. Wait until we're at 35,000 feet and we can move around. I will come visit you two lugs and tell you." With that, she picked up the airlines 'publication and buried her head in it.

The takeoff was uneventful and soon Ireland was now east of them. The captain had given his little spiel in a garbled, static manner. What Quinn got from it was the weather was good and it was going to be a smooth flight. Shortly thereafter the flight attendant was in the aisle asking for drink orders.

"I'll have a Blood Mary and one for my cello, please," Quinn requested.

Smiling, the attendant asked, "Is he or she over twenty-one?"

"The cello is a she. And, yes, she's over twenty-one by one hundred and fifty years or thereabouts," she answered with an engaging smile.

"Ah, that's why you have her in business class. I really should upgrade her to first class."

"Not without me," Quinn laughed.

"Wait a minute. You're Quinn Mallory, 'he exclaimed. "I saw you in London a year ago. Let's see. It was Britten's *Suite for Cello.* You played magnificently."

"Thank you," Quinn responded shyly, patting her cello's hard-white case affectionately. "You did well, too, Anne Bonney,"

"Wow," the attendant said. "Named for a Celtic warrior." He thought a moment. "Listen, I'm the purser on this flight. I'm putting both of you in first. It's practically empty. Get your things together and I'll have Bloody Marys waiting for both of you."

Quinn stopped by the seats occupied by the twins. "Okay, you wanted to know why I am on this flight. I'm going to San Francisco to attend my uncle's wake tomorrow," she said with a tremor in her voice.

An Incredulous Danny asked, "Whoa now, are you telling us he's dead?"

Quinn frowned at one half of Dublin's most feared criminals. "Yes, that's a basic requirement for having a wake."

Tommy was expressionless. "So what happened to him?"

"Heart attack," she replied without showing any emotion. "He's always had heart problems. Phinny - that's what I call him — collapsed Tuesday afternoon and evidently there was nothing they could do to revive him."

Danny muttered, "Shite"

Quinn said sardonically, "Aye, and it's a damned shame his failing health got to him before you two clowns did." With that, holding her cello and purse, she moved into first class.

Ken, the purser, was a silver-haired, trim man in his late fifties who could have been mistaken for the plane's captain as he walked the aisles of business and first. He immediately found a secure place for Quinn's cello and then briefed her on the luxury amenities of first class of which there were many.

"I couldn't help noticing you talking to those two men who, dressed the way they are, must think we're headed to somewhere in the Caribbean," he laughed quietly.

Quinn looked up at the purser. "You are looking at Dublin's dumbest mobsters. They're headed to the Bay Area to kill my uncle Phineas, but he spoiled all their fun by dying last Tuesday of his own accord. Anne Bonney and I are on our way to his wake," she said, smiling up at Ken as if she had told him the men were priests in disguise, hoping for a short vacation.

As he began to walk away, he shook his head and uttered, "Oh man, I have to write a book someday."

Quinn, whose concert contracts always included first-class air, was accustomed to the plush comfort and pleasure the front of the plane offered, and within minutes she'd made herself at home. Her plan was a late Thursday night dinner, an after-dinner drink with her Kindle, then to bed until it was time to refresh herself for deplaning at nine Friday morning. She was undisturbed for the remainder of the flight thanks to the purser who made it clear to Tommy Connor, after he tried in vain to visit her early in the flight, that he and his brother were not welcome in first class.He also told him they must keep their feet off the bulkhead while they were seated.

Customs was perfunctory and fast. Quinn could hardly not notice that once they had all deplaned, the Connor twins remained behind her. Once outside, near the cab stand, Quinn stopped and turned to face them. "God, please tell me we're not staying in the same hotel," she prayed out load. "So where are you two headed?"

"We're at the Mark Hopkins on Nob Hill," Danny said, consulting his iPhone.

"Oh good," she sighed. "There is a big body of water called the Bay separating us."

Tommy decided to play nice. "Look, Quinn, I know we got off to a bad start..."

"A bad start? Oh, you mean when you came to my house and literally threatened to break my fingers unless I gave you information on my uncle?"

"He stole from us. Turns out to be lots of money."

"You don't know that."

"We do now. An outside auditor told us that millions of dollars have gone missing over the years. And guess who handled our finances all that time. We want our money back. Now that seems more difficult with Phineas dying. If he is dead that is," he added.

She snorted. A cute, feminine snort. "Right, I came all this way to play at his wake and now you're trying to tell me the corpse is going to be a no-show," she scoffed.

Tommy shot back, "It's happened before. But we caught the creep."

"Yeah, we caught the creep," Danny repeated.

Quinn looked at the both in amazement. This is all going so well, she thought. "Okay," she said, throwing her hands up. "What do you want from me?"

"Maybe he left a will," Danny mumbled.

"And you think Phinny left you two anything?"

"But he did leave a will," Tommy said.

"He did. I told you that already. I get two thousand euros," she said cooly. "If he has more, I don't know what his plans are for the funds. Maybe he went all Robin Hood on us and gave it away to something like a sanctuary for parakeets a lisps. I don't know."

"If I remember, you were really upset when you learned that you only got two grand," Tommy pointed out.

She shrugged. "I thought maybe I deserved more. It was a moment in time. But I do all right, thank you. I don't need his money." She got Anne Bonney ready to go as she eyed the waiting cabs. "I'm going now. Nice to see you both. Maybe you should have a nice time in San Francisco and take a fight back tomorrow so you can continue to wreak havoc on Dublin. What a shame you had to come all this way for nothing."

But Tommy had other ideas. "No, we're not going anywhere, Quinn Mallory. So when and where is this wake?"

Quinn held Anne Bonney close. She smiled warmly at the Connor twins, thinking this is all going so well. I can't wait to tell my dear deceased uncle.

Chapter 25

Scenes from an unusual
Friday morning

Maggie awoke refreshed, but anxious. Magnus, who slept like the bear he resembled, was still asleep. She nudged him. "It's Friday, my large Irishman. Come join me in the real world. We have lots to do."

Magnus awakened one eye at a time, making all sorts of incomprehensible snorts and coughs. Finally, he spoke. "Now, Maggie, it is still dark. And I might remind you this will be a long arduous day, so it stands to reason we should begin at daybreak."

She learned over and shook him gently. She smiled at how comfortable he seemed to be and how happy she was having him as a bedmate. She marveled that, while he slept soundly, he did not snore. A light sleeper, Maggie was grateful. She looked down at him with his full beard, ruddy complexion and, remarkable for a man his age, a head full of hair that was still a reddish brown. "There are times I feel like I went to bed with Davey Crockett and woke up with Daniel Boone."

"Ah, two fine outdoorsman. Thank heavens, you didn't say Lewis and Clark. They always struck me as being sort of iffy in an outdoorsy way," he told her. "But Maggie, I'm a true city lad. Camping and the great outdoors are unknown to me."

She nudged him. "Okay, that was fun. Now to business. Did you know Rolando is taking the casket this morning. He called me yesterday to inform me."

"I do. He's recruited Malcolm Midgely to drive one of his hearses here from Livermore to transport it wherever Rolando wants it," he explained, joining Maggie in sitting upright. "He told me he intends to have it formally delivered back to the theater today just before four with Phineas in it. As you know, Rolando doesn't expand on his plans."

With a furrowed brow, Maggie asked with concern, "Did we make the right choice, Magnus. Should we just go back to plan A and have Phil dope him up. We can always find a way to cover up a clumsy exit. If not you and George Crowder will have to protect Phineas from those two gorillas."

"I don't think it will come to that," he laughed. "Now, Maggie, If you want to change course, best to do it now. But I think we stick with Ronaldo. I've spent a lot of time around him. He has an almost scary level of concentration. Of course, he's not going to tell any of us anything he doesn't want us to know as he's an illusionist, and we have to live with that." He reached over and took his wife's hand. "Trust him."

Still doubtful, she nodded to her husband. "Okay. I'll trust him but I'll be nervous."

"We are all nervous."

Maggie had one more thought before getting out of bed and attacking this special day. "Magnus, why does Phineas want to become someone else? I mean, once those thuggish miscreants go back to Dublin, convinced he's dead, why can't he just keep his own identity and get on with life. Why does he have to become Reggie Pennington? Who, by the by, sounds like he's right out of a Trollope novel."

"For that matter, so is Phineas," he reminded her. "Anyway, you want an answer. There are two reasons. The first is as Phineas he would have to live the rest of his life knowing he's wanted by some very bad people. Trust me, criminals have excellent memories and unlike a law enforcement agency, they're generally successful at finding their man. Aye, Maggie, it would be a dark cloud indeed that he'd be living under."

"I guess that reason alone justifies his actions," she uttered. "So what's the second?"

"I think he wants to be rid of Phineas Dermot Flanagan," he replied, pausing a moment to find a way to explain his thinking. "I believe he doesn't like Phineas Flanagan. He doesn't like what he's done. The money he managed came from murder, extortion, drugs, prostitution, sex-trafficking, et cetera. I think he's guilt-ridden and wants a do-over, a fresh, stain-free start. He can't do that as Phineas because he thinks the old Flanagan will haunt him."

Maggie thought a moment. "Phineas can still haunt Reggie Pennington. He can't escape that."

Magnus turned to face her, admiring the way she looked. Even after a solid eight hours of sleep, she appeared put together. "You know, my pretty, if he ever goes back to church and in the confessional admits to the long list of Flanagan's foibles, he'll spend the first two years as Pennington saying the *Rosary, Our Father* and *Hail Marys.*"

"Or he can make a large donation," she mumbled cynically.

Magnus turned to get out of bed. "Aye, sometimes it's all about money, isn't it? But Maggie my dear, there are some nights that the *Our Father* has helped me." He defied his age and sprang up. "Come on, Boss, we've work to do."

***

After hearing a light tapping, Phineas approached the suite's double door. With his eye pressed against the peephole, he saw his niece. He reacted instantly, shouting, "Quinn!"

Shouting back, she said, "Begorrah, the corpse talks."

He swung open the doors and literally tried dragging her in. She held her ground. "Hold on, I have Anne Bonney with me."

He was thrilled and excited by the sight of his niece, his only family. "Yes, yes, of course. Bring her in and park her here..." He looked around and found an appropriate corner. "Over there."

Phineas managed a longer look at the traveler. "I see a purse and a cello. You're not staying long?"

"I shipped my bags to the hotel," she said, walking to the window to look at the view. "Oh my, this is truly spectacular. I'm just down the hall so I must have this joyous sight as well."

"Indeed you will. Quinn. By the way, I can't tell you how appreciative I am for all you've done to help put this, uh... What would you call it?" he asked.

"I think madness is a good fit."

"I agree, but we are so far along and there are so many good people involved, there's no turning back." Phineas checked his watch. "Ten-twenty. How about breakfast and champagne to welcome you to America, or more specifically, to Oakland and Berkeley?"

Her eyes lit up. Quinn explained while she was well-rested from the flight, she was peckish. She plopped down on the sofa and gazed up at her doting uncle. "I'll make it easy, Phinny. I'll have a waffle, strawberries and whipped cream and a side of crispy bacon. I gather the hotel doesn't know a dead person occupies this suite?"

Phineas shook his head. "Oh, that's just between, uh, a few people," he said unconvincingly.

She spotted the hesitation."So how many, dear uncle?"

"I think the final tally would be around fifty," he said in a low voice, hoping she didn't hear him.

Quinn shot upright and hollered, "Fifty! Oh good lord, Phinny. Fifty people all know you are leaving Flanagan in the dust and reemerging as a posh, to-the-manor-born Brit."

Feeling he needed to defend his new identity, he said, "Reggie is not that at all." He paused and gave more thought to what he wanted to say. "Okay, he's posh. But chrissakes, Quinn, I already am. He's just going to be a more souped up version of me. I plan to give him a little more horsepower."

"You don't even drive and you're throwing around car metaphors like a race driver. There's a hypocrisy there, I think," she laughed. "Seriously, how do you expect fifty people to keep this charade to themselves?"

Phineas waited to answer, first phoning in their breakfast order. He walked over to his doubtful niece and sat beside her. "My precious cellist... Try saying that three times fast." Quinn gave him a stern look. "Ah yes, you want an answer. Only a few trusted friends know about Reggie Pennington. The rest think we are staging a fake wake to prevent harm coming to me from two thugs who wish to kill me. They are the cast and crew at the theater and this maddeningly crazy, eccentric group of wealthy characters who enjoy giving money away in the most unorthodox of ways. There are about twelve of those. All good people I count on as friends."

"Then, I look forward to meeting them."

Phineas checked his watch again. "Listen, my dear, we'll eat breakfast, chat and then I am tossing you out. At noon, I am expecting Rolando who is the key to getting me in and out of the casket."

"I'm almost afraid to ask this, but who or what is a Rolando?"

"He's an illusionist from Las Vegas. He's going to make me disappear."

She rolled her large blue eyes and sighed. "Oh please, dear God, make all this go well."

"And what are you going to play at your uncle's funeral?"

"There's an appropriate song from the musical *Stop the World—I Want to Get OFF*. It's called *What Kind of Fool Am I*."

Phineas chortled. "It's apparent you inherited the famed Flanagan wit." He put his finger to his mouth and thought a moment. "I was thinking of something more along the lines of *Carrickfergus*. It's all about love, life, drunkenness and death. Emotionally, it has a very high chill factor."

She gave him an affectionate kiss on the cheek. "For you, dear Phinny, soon-to-be Reggie, I'll play it for you. Don't cry noisily in the casket."

"You know the song?" he asked.

Quinn's eyes widened. "Know it? In my final year at RIAM...Oh, I will continue to thank you for financing my final year," she noted.

"Look at my investment, you're a cellist superstar," he said.

"Anyway, four of us, two violinists and two cellists got together. We called ourselves the *Stringers*. We played weddings, funerals and wakes to make some extra spending money. Anne and I have played *Carrickfergus* more than Tony Bennett has sung *I Left My Heart in San Francisco*."

***

Ashley Porter and Sylvie had worked out a weekday morning routine fit for two people sharing a small apartment. While Sylvie dressed and prepped breakfast,

Ashley used the one bathroom they shared. Then while she dressed, Sylvie scooted into the bathroom taking one-third the time it took Ashley to put her face on. They breakfasted together and both could be out the door to report to their jobs at the same time. This Friday morning, the mood was different as they knew they were just hours from participating in the grand hoax they called *Flanagan's Wake.*

"I've never seen organized-crime guys," Sylvie said, adding more cinnamon to her Belgium waffle. "Do you think we'll see the evil in them or will they just look like every other guy."

Ashely looked up from her iPhone where she was reading the New York Times. "I think the latter, Syl. But I don't know. Maybe there's something different about them. How they move, How they talk to you. I guess we'll find out. One thing I know is they won't be happy with your boyfriend filming them," she pointed out, adding a special touch to the word boyfriend.

Her sister let it pass, though she did enjoy hearing him described that way. "Samson will be filming the wake. I'm sure he'll be discreet when it comes to those two guys."

Ashely tossed her napkin down and took a final sip of coffee. "Syl, about Samson"

Sylvie got up from the table to clean the dishes. She held a hand up like a school crossing guard and warned her sister, "Don't go, there, Ash." It was an adamant demand.

As if an older sister is going to do anything her younger sibling demands. Ashley plowed ahead anyway. "I just don't want to see you hurt. Samson is a man who has enjoyed enormous success and fame and at an early age. It's nigh on impossible for him not to be infected by all that notoriety. It changes men. Probably women, too. But we're talking about a man. I just don't want to see you used and then discarded."

Sylvie was angry but she understood Ashley and her glass half-empty attitude when it came to the opposite sex. She knew her sister had far more experience with relationships and, because most of them were, in Ashley's own words, disappointing, she knew she would be suspicious of Samson's motives.

"Ash, Samson and I have spent most of this week working on the wake. Yes, there's been some romantic moments. But we're both cautious. I love your concern, but I'm okay. He's a good man. And here's the good news. You'll be proud of me. If he somehow tosses me aside, I won't feel bad because I have a backup man in mind," she said, hoping her lower lip didn't quiver, a sure sign she was kidding.

With keen interest, Ashley asked who it was.

"Kenneth Richter," she said, trying hard not to laugh.

Ashley did, though. And heartily.

***

Rolando had called Malcolm Midgely late Thursday afternoon requesting a driver and a hearse for Friday morning at nine-thirty, The perpetually cheery —his sister, Phyllis Hathaway preferred slap-happy or goofy — funeral director was over the moon. Here he was actually speaking with the renowned illusionist. He told him that he would not only provide the hearse but he would deliver it himself and would stick around for anything else Rolando needed or desired.

Friday morning, right on schedule, the hearse pulled up to the *Ashby-upon Avon* theater. Malcolm was dressed in his more formal sepulchral attire. By request, he brought along a black suit shiny from too much dry cleaning along with a suitable black tie for Rolando to wear.

Finding the magician near the casket on the stage, he rushed forward, "Mr. Rolando, this is indeed a pleasure. More than a pleasure. I am one of your biggest fans. I remember a show you did at Madison Square Garden and when there was a moment's pause, someone with a distinctive Brooklyn accent shouted out, 'Yo, Magic-man, can you make Yonkers disappear?'" His accent was spot on.

Rolando gazed up at the tall, blimp-shaped man with his round, happy face all abeam. "I do remember that. I believe he stunned me into silence. The truth is I'm ill-equipped for that sort of repartee. As you probably noticed, there's no comedy to my act. I depend on drama and tension."

"I, too, am in a business where humor doesn't show its face a lot. And look at me, even when I frown or try to look serious, I look happy." He tried to produce a somber expression but to no avail. "Anyway, I am here and reporting for duty," he said with a mock salute.

"And you don't mind my being your assistant for the day?" Rolando asked.

"Oh my, no."

"Well, first things first. We need to take the casket out of here and put it in the hearse. Then we need to park it somewhere for a few hours."

"Where would you like me to put it?" he asked.

Rolando thought a moment. "The most important thing is that it's not close to here. Do you have an idea where we can park it until, let's say, three-thirty?"

"The funeral home is too far and traffic could screw up your timeline." He snapped his fingers. "Wait a minute! We can park it at my sister's in Piedmont. I can visit with her until it's time to come back to the theater. She hates it when I drive the hearse. She wonders what the neighbors will think." Like a vaudeville comic, Malcolm moved his head about to see if they were alone. "Any chance you can make Phyllis disappear?"

Rolando laughed and pointed to the casket. "I'm going to be too busy making the man in there disappear."

Malcolm had no problem registering shock at that news. He put his manicured hands to his face and stammered, "You mean, he's... He's already in there?"

Chapter 26

Phineas plays the game of *Gotcha*

For those taking part in putting a halt to Phineas Flanagan's imminent demise, there were two different Fridays on the first of March, 2019. There was the pre-four o'clock and the post-four o'clock. For those minimally involved, which was most of them, the first period was no different than any other day. Most of the Banter Foundation and the actors and crew of the Midsummer Players were in this category. Maggie called them her extras. They had no speaking parts. All they had to do was be present at the wake at the appointed time, express sadness at the passing of Phineas and keep it all a secret. At least for a day or two.

They were few, but those directly involved had a busier day. This was an excited but also fretful group. This latter feeling was brought on by Rolando's secretive ways of handling the most important part of the plan, namely getting Phineas in and out of the casket unseen by the Connor twins. Rolando had only told them he would make Phineas disappear and they must trust him. He did expand on it a bit by assuring them Phineas would go from the casket to a safe environment without anyone knowing.

Maggie was particularly nervous as Rolando insisted they have no further communication with Phineas after twelve noon. So fifteen minutes before the enforced curfew, she phoned him. She was surprised to hear him sounding so chirpy, so upbeat.

"Maggie, hold on. I am just saying adieu to my niece, Quinn. Sometime soon, after my revivification, you'll have to see her put away Belgium waffles," he said. "Where do these children put those calories?"

"They burn them, Phineas. And they can burn them while standing still which is even more hateful. It's called youth," she replied. "Now, let me ask you. Are you still all right with Rolando's plan or would you rather we go back to basics and let Phil sedate you temporarily?"

"We definitely stick with Rolando," he said without hesitation.

"You seem to have a lot of confidence in him."

"I do, my dear Maggie, I do. But I have more confidence in me."

Maggie didn't like that answer. "Phineas, what have you been up to?" she asked suspiciously.

"This quarantine you imposed on me has been extremely beneficial," he told her. "It has given me a good amount of time to think and I did just that. What concerned me most was how can I make all this easier for you. You see, I know you're rattled a bit. Well, just thinking about that sent my mind down all sorts of byways. I soon discovered how to lighten your load and I acted on it. If we flub up somehow now, it won't be catastrophic, only problematic but easily solved. And Magnus will not be called upon for muscle."

Maggie tried to interrupt him. "Phineas..."

"Look, I know I'm rambling, my dear, and I know everything sounds so ambiguous..."

"Phineas," she shouted. "Please, let me speak. I just want to know. Do you still intend to commit pseudocide and do you still want Rolando to help you?"

"Yes to both questions. What on earth is pseudocide?"

"It's faking a death to mislead others. Interestingly, pseudocide itself is not illegal."

"That's good to hear, because that's exactly what I'm doing. I am thrilled to hear I am not breaking any laws."

Maggie's laugh was a sharp snort. "Phineas, everything else you're doing is against the law: fake passport, driver's license, birth certificate, death cert..." She paused to think of more and gave up. "To sum it up, Reggie Pennington will be a living, breathing fraud."

"Maggie, there was a time when I didn't mind breaking a law or two, 'he replied. "I've been dong it all my life. The irony is that I thought Reggie would provide me with a clean slate and those days would be behind me."

"Seems to me it's a bit more complicated. I mean, consider the money that will support you. How clean is that?" she asked, sounding like a prosecutor.

There was a silence. Both waited for the other to speak. Finally, Phineas did.

"I need to do more thinking," he said, his tone serious. "Maggie, can we just leave everything as it is and then deal with these other issues later?"

"Of course, we can." she assured him. "I guess the next time I see you, you will be supine and lifeless. Tell Rolando we are counting on him."

"I will. He's due here any minute as is Amelia and Berra who have my two outfits, he said, taking a deep breath. "And, Maggie, this is all your idea and for that, I am eternally grateful."

"This is no time toss out the word eternally."

***

By three-fifty, everything was set. Duffy Hart and The Redhead had set up a full bar adjacent to a long table full of specially-made tapas that would stay fresh until after the dress rehearsal. Now they were busy pouring white wine into small plastic glasses, the only refreshment during the hour-long wake. Sylvie was helping them while sneaking glances at Samson Webb who was busy with his small production crew that was going to film both the wake and the rehearsal. Magnus was meeting with his cast who were all in costume. Ambrose Dowling stood nearby ready to answer any questions the crew still had about dialogue meaning and interpretation. People were beginning to filter in. Phyllis Hathaway, resplendent in a funereal black Donna Karan dress and matching lightweight trench coat arrived alone as her husband insisted on going to their country club's annual crab feed. The uninvolved members of the Banter Foundation were also early. Only Walt Gillespie was missing because his team were still alive in an elimination bowling tournament in Reno. Invited by The

Redhead, Professor Lauren Ainsworthy arrived just ahead of the hearse. Meantime, miles away in Livermore, her ex-husband, Kenneth Richter, Professor of Economics, media celebrity and amateur extortionist was pulling into the *Going Up? Funeral Home, Memorial Park and Crematorium* parking lot.

RIchter made his way to the main building. As he walked he saw very few people and wondered if he was late and they were all in some chapel mourning Phineas' faux passing. During the boring drive, he entertained himself with dreaming up plans on how to spend the hundred thousand Phineas had promised him for keeping quiet about his pseudocide.

Entering the main office, Richter was struck by how attractive and sexy the young woman behind the desk was given her austere outfit and hairstyle.

"May I help you, sir," she asked as if they were at a church service. Still, she had a hard time disguising a seductive breathiness.

"Yes, I am here to pay my respects," he said, not finishing his answer as he was enchanted by her looks and voice.'

Sweetly, she replied, "That's pretty much why people come here."

"Why's that?" he asked, confounded by her response.

"To pay their respects." She was tempted to add "Duh." but didn't.

"Oh yeah," he laughed. "Sorry, you need more information. I am here for the Phineas Flanagan memorial service."

She looked puzzled. "Do you have the right date? I'm afraid the only memorial service happening today is for ninety-three-year-old Gladys Piper from Pleasanton."

She gave the professor a close, second look. "You don't seem Gladys 'type," she said, trying to suppress a giggle.

"Her type?"

Gladys was married eight times. Six are still alive and here for the service. They all resemble each other," she said, this time with a silly giggle.

"Are you certain there's nothing for Flanagan?"

"Wait a minute," she said excitedly. She looked up at the man standing in front of her desk. "Are you Professor..." She reached into the drawer on the right side of her small desk and took out an envelope. Looking at it, she finished her question. "Are you Professor Richter?"

"I am," he said, his manner boastful. He adjusted his media smile.

"This is for you," she said, handing him the envelope.

He remained where he was. Opening the envelope, he began to read Phineas 'missive.

Dear Professor,

There is a catchy term you Yanks use for situations like this. It is gotcha. And, indeed, I gotcha. Whatever made you think I would want my memorial or wake, as i prefer calling it, to be in a remote country village that I know nothing about? So there you are and here I am resting comfortably in a comfy coffin being mourned by my many friends at the theater in Berkeley. Don't even try to make it back here in time. By the time you arrive, they will be in the midst of a dress rehearsal and will not appreciate you storming in, shouting, "He's alive! The conniving, son-of-s-bitch, thief is alive." Therefore, I suggest you stay in that lovely hamlet. Visit one of their many wineries and have dinner on me. Enclosed is $200. You might even ask that comely assistant sitting in front of you to join you. Mr. Midgely, the funeral *director, has informed me she's single and more robust than that uniform suggests. And yes, you can kiss that $100,000 goodbye. I confess I befriended you so that I might impose on you to help me with a university situation. It was worth fifty thousand. Now that you are out of the picture, it has been recommended I seek out Professor Lauren Ainsworthy. You may or may not know her. I am sure she can use the fifty thousand consulting fee.*

Kindest regards, Phineas Dermot Flanagan

He stood there stone-faced. As bad as the news was, Richter's mind, which was heavily influenced by whatever stirrings were going on below his waist, was on Andrea, the woman to whom Mr. Midgely mentioned, who was just a foot away and still paying attention to him. He issued a soft cough and put the letter and money is his coat pocket. Anger and anything else he might feel could wait.

"Well, it appears to be my mistake," he said, once again producing his media smile. He had decided to take Phineas 'advice. Leaning in toward the desk, in his best broadcast voice, he said, "So, Andrea, I'm here now with nothing to do and all the time in the world to do it. Do you have any suggestions as to how to enjoy the pleasures of Livermore?"

Andrea did and it included her. He did, though, have to wait as she first had to chase Gladys 'six ex-husbands out of the chapel as they started a high volume argument about inheritances and were about to come to blows.

Chapter 27

"For now they kill me
with a living death"

William Shakespeare

It was almost four and Maggie decided to scurry about alerting everybody as to the seriousness of the forthcoming wake. On stage, the cast stood patiently dressed in their costumes for the rehearsal, but looking like they were part of a Humphrey Bogart 1940's gangster movie set. Their instructions were to remain on stage throughout the wake. After Maggie worked her way through the group of invitees. she gave the cast one final pep talk. Magnus then give them the go ahead to have a glass of wine or beer. No sooner had they left the stage than Franny Gaspar who was positioned outside to warn them about the arrival of Phineas Flanagan and his entourage, rushed inside and warned everyone that the hearse had arrived. It was exactly four o'clock. Quinn straddled the cello and began to play. It was a sweet melody, not at all mournful. Whatever conversations there were ceased. The door opened and six dark-suited pallbearers, employees of Malcolm Midgely, carried the casket to the platform at the stage's center edge. Once the casket was situated exactly where Rolando wanted it, they stepped away. Malcolm Midgely would have normally taken control of the event but this time he retreated to the middle of the theater and took a seat on the aisle. This was Rolando's evening. Dressed in the shiny black suit that Midgely had given him, he stepped in front of the casket. Signaling Quinn to stop playing, he introduced himself.

"Good evening, my name is Harold Cunningham from the *Going Up? Funeral Home.* I am Mr. Midgely's assistant funeral director. In that capacity, I welcome you to the wake of Phineas Dermot Flanagan. In the next hour, I invite you to remember this man. Pass stories amongst yourselves. At some point, I will open the casket for viewing Mr Flanagan. I ask only that you keep a respectable distance from the casket and not linger. This is not anything you have to do if it makes you feel uncomfortable. Thank you."

Quinn had given Franny a detailed description of the Conner twins. Usually fastidiously punctual, they arrived thirty minutes late due to heavy traffic on the Bay Bridge. Arriving in a black Uber SUV, they were several more minutes negotiating with the driver as they wanted him to stay and take them back to San Francisco. Tommy finally held up two one-hundred dollar bills, a gesture that was enough to keep the driver around. While they were dickering, Franny, bored from standing outside for so long, high-trailed it back into the theater to warn the others.

Still dressed as the bad guys on an episode of *Miami Vice*, Tommy and Danny strode in as if they were on a very high-horse. They looked laughable but scary. There was an obvious toughness about them. They marched down the center aisle where they encountered Magnus and Maggie. While Magnus appraised them, Maggie greeted them. "Hello, I assume you're here for the Flanagan Wake?" While Danny looked to the ceiling and then around the theater as if a sniper might be positioned if things got out of hand, Tommy answered Maggie. "Yeah, we came from Dublin... Ireland, that is. I understand you have a Dublin somewhere close to here."

"We do," she said. "But it's not as green. More a dull brown. Oh dear, having come so far, I gather you came here thinking Phineas was still alive. How dreadful for you."

Tommy's grimace told her nothing. "Aye, Phineas worked for us and our Da. We were hoping for a meeting." He glanced up at the casket. "So what happened?" As if on cue, Doctor Phil Seton appeared. "Excuse me, Maggie, I, uh, just wanted to leave several death certificates with you. I have to be off. Sorry, I couldn't have gotten to him sooner. However, his heart was really in a bad way."

"Can I see that?" Tommy Conner asked, pointing to the certificates now in Maggie's hand. She handed him one.

He read it top to bottom and muttered, "Damned."

"Yes, it is very sad. He must have meant a lot to you and your brother. I assume that's your brother. You look so much alike."

"How do we know Flanagan's in that wooden onesie," Danny asked menacingly.

Magnus decided to speak up. "And just what do you mean by that?"

"Seeing is believing," he shot back, staring at Magnus who matched him in size.

They ended up having a staring contest. Danny was a little unsettled that he could't intimidate the old man standing in front of him. As he looked away, he asked, "So why not open the casket?"

Magnus turned around and signaled Rolando.

"By the way, what's your name? Maybe I know you from Dublin." he asked the other twin who seemed more civilized.

"I'm Tommy Conner and that is my twin brother, Danny. So you're from Dublin?" asked.

Magnus never had a chance to respond as Rolando, in the guise of the assistant funeral director, approached them. "Yes, is there something you need, Mr. Flaherty?"

Magnus pointed to the two oddly dressed men. "These gentlemen wish to have the casket opened."

"We want to see if the fecking, son-of-a-bitch is dead," Danny snarled in a brogue low enough that most of it went unheard or understood except for Tommy who told him to watch his mouth. "We're at a wake," he reminded him.

Rolando's smile resembled one of a headwater dealing with a complaining diner. "I was just about to open it. Do you two care to join me?" he asked solicitously.

Danny made a face that looked like he had just drunk a glass of milk turned bad. He looked at the short distance — maybe twenty feet — between them and the body of Phineas Flanagan. "No, we don't go to the casket anymore, do we, Tommy."

HIs brother just nodded. "We can see him from here."

"I understand," Rolando said. With that he waved to two of Malcolm Midgely's employees. Dressed in their black suits, they approached the casket and in a well-rehearsed manner opened the front half cover.

The cast and crew that was behind the platform that held Phineas made no move to view him. Others at the wake were too busy with their conversations to even notice that the casket was opened.

Magnus and Maggie glanced at the now opened casket as did the Conner twins. Their reaction was immediate. "He looks at peace," Maggie commented softy.

"He looks dead," Danny huffed, wondering how much money Phineas had screwed them out of.

As it appeared no one was in any rush to view the body more closely. Rolando signaled Midgely's men to seal the casket. They then spoke to him briefly before he returned to where Maggie stood.

"Ms Leyton, I have been informed that traffic is heavy on 580, probably an earlier than usual commute start. We have a fixed time for the cremation. Would you mind if we leave now?"

As the pallbearers approached the casket, a quiet fell over the theater. Quinn Walsh, Phineas 'niece, began to play the achingly sad *Carrickfergus.* Rolando as the assistant funeral director watched as the six men hoisted the casket and prepared to leave. Rolando nodded to them and they began to walk ever so slowly toward the theater exit and the awaiting hearse. Even though everyone except for the Connor twins knew this was a grand hoax, they could not help but get caught up in the solemnity of the ceremony.

The slow march of the pallbearers was halted by a man entering the theater and shuffling down the center aisle. Seeing the men and the caskets, he made a hurried sign of the cross and ducked into a row of chairs to let them pass. As they did, he let out a gentle whimper. The aisle now clear he walked toward Maggie and Magnus.

"Oh thank the Lyft gods, they got me here just in time to at least see Phineas for the final time. He glanced up at the stage. "And I see you haven't started rehearsal yet." The man's voice, while similar to Phineas 'was higher-pitched, more feminine and the accent was that of a person to the manor born.

"You must be Reggie Pennington," Magnus muttered,

Reggie threw out his hands in a ta-da fashion and then did an awkward, teetering model's turn. "Oh lord, I used to be a dashing gay blade, but now I'm afraid the dash is gone. The gay blade is still here, though," he sang out proudly.

Reggie Pennington was close to Phineas 'height but he stooped where Phineas was military erect, and there was a slight but obvious limp. Any other similarity was hard to detect. Reggie's eyes were a tired brown and looked out at the world from atop baggy eyelids. His cheeks were full and flush. He had a chin with an extra fold, a small mouth made to look wider thanks to a pencil-thin mustache. Maggie and Magnus were hard-pressed to see Phineas in any part of him. Phineas moved with grace and agility. Reggie was quite the opposite.

They knew, though, that Phineas resided in that Pennington body because it was clothed in the Forties ' sport coat and grey slacks that Amelia and Berra picked out for him. What perplexed them was how did he suddenly appear while the casket carrying him dressed in another suit was not even out the door. They were clearly astonished as they'd just seem him in the casket not five minutes earlier.

Danny, who was more homophobic than Tommy, tugged at his brother's sleeve. "Let's get the feck out of here, Tommy. Flanagan's dead, We know it. So let's go," he pleaded.

"Yeah, Danny, there's no reason to stay."

While Danny moved further away from Reggie Pennington who was enjoying looking at him like he was a Reese's Peanut Butter Cup, Tommy told Magnus they were leaving.

Before they were able to move toward the door, though, Reggie let out a scream. "Oh my heavens, where is my head these days," He began to pat his sport coat. Feeling what he wanted, he thrust his right hand into the inside coat pocket and pulled out an envelope. His hand shook. He looked at Magnus and said, "Are the Conners anywhere in the room?"

Chapter 28

"What's done can't be undone."

William Shakespeare

Reggie Pennington was the only person in the Ashby-upon-Avon theater to watch with any interest as Tommy Conner opened the envelope he had been given and had begun to read. While he held the paper, his brother, Danny, behaving like a spirited four-year-old, was tugging at Tommy's sleeve and badgering him ceaselessly.

"What? What is it? Come on, Tommy. What's the hell does it say?" Danny begged.

Tommy freed himself from his brother's grasp. "Danny, I'll give it to you after I'm done."

As he continued to read, he began to redden. The more he read, the brighter his face became. It was a coloring brought on by a odd mix of anger and fear. The more he read, the more he understood how helpless he was in rectifying the problem that Phineas had laid out for him. If it were chess, he'd just been checkmated.

Reggie began to think about the power of words. He knew that if you select words with care and put them in an order that produces a cruel context, you have a worthy instrument of torture. And he could see the effectiveness of the words he chose by just observing Tommy Conner's assorted reactions to the contents of the letter he had penned as Phineas Flanagan just a day earlier.

Magnus decided that he should put some distance between the Conner twins and Reggie Pennington. After all, being Reggie was something new to Phineas and he didn't relish the idea of Tommy and Danny taking a closer look at Pennington than they already had.

"Excuse me, Reggie, but the dress rehearsal starts in a matter of minutes and I need you on stage now," he said. His request fell on deaf ears and that annoyed him.

Magnus was annoyed. "Pennington," he shouted like a platoon sergeant reprimanding a new recruit. "Get on stage NOW."

Reggie spun around so fast, he almost fell over. Magnus steadied him. Whispering, he said, "Aye, Reg, you might be overplaying your character. Get away from these two clowns now before they recognize you."

Without speaking, his face set in a pout, he walked toward the stage, remembering his slight limp and bent-over stance.

Maggie was still standing near the twins and was anxious to show them the door. "So, you head back to Dublin, Mr. Conner?" she asked as Tommy put the letter into the inside pocket of his coat.

"Aye, that's the plan," he said in a distracted manner.

"Is there something wrong?" she asked.

"Have you ever wished that you could bring somebody back from the dead so you could kill him yourself?" he asked. "And I mean kill him slowly and painfully over days. Maybe dig up some of the old tortures from Celtic history and use them on him first."

"Mr. Conner, I have no idea what prompted you to ask that ridiculous and, quite frankly, troubling question. However, ff you're looking for a response, allow me to quote Lady MacBeth, 'What's done can't be undone.'" she said, her heart pounding.

"What is it about you people. Everything's all about Shakespeare in this place, 'he huffed "Come on, Danny, let's go find a strip club and get bolloxed."

"Then I will say goodbye as I have work to do. I'm sure you and your brother can see your way out."

And they did. Tommy rushed toward the exit while Danny chased after him desperate to know the letter's contents.

Maggie waited until the door closed behind them and then she clapped her hands to shush everyone. "Excuse me. Can I have your attention for a moment." The conversations faded and she got her requested quietude.

"We did it!" she exclaimed. "The wake was a success. Those two thugs in their silly Tommy Bahama outfits are gone and they are no longer a threat to our friend, Phineas Flanagan. May he rest in peace."

There was a loud cheer; a mix of shouts, applause and whistles. The sound carried out to the street just as the Conner twins were getting into the Uber SUV "What do you think the cheering is all about, Tommy?" Danny asked, looking back at the theater.

"Ah, they have a dress rehearsal going on. Some Shakespeare shit. Sounds like they like what they're watching. You know, Danny, Shakespeare fans are like football fans but way more manic."

Danny was anxious to see what the letter contained. His brother, after warning him he wouldn't take kindly to its contents, handed it to him with a warning not to overreact. He knew Danny was the more emotional of the two and always exploded after hearing bad news or anything for that matter that upset him. Even with his warning, Tommy prepared himself for an outburst.

Danny turned the smartphone flashlight on and began to read. He read slowly, his expressions giving Tommy no hint as to what his brother was feeling or thinking. He held the letter close to his eyes as they were slowly beginning to fail him.

My friends,

Allow me to quote Shakespeare. It is from the Merchant of Venice. "I hold the world, but as the world, Gratiano, a stage where every man must play a part, and mine a sad one.
"

Danny looked at his brother and waved the letter. "Excuse me for speaking ill of the dead, but the feckin' arse is spouting Shakespeare," he griped.

Tommy urged him to keep reading.

That's my clumsy way of saying I am now in the regrettable position of playing the informant. It is my unfortunate duty to warn you of great trouble heading your way. As you probably know, in my capacity as your money manager for your many concerns, I developed relationships with any number of men and women who love to gossip. Yes, even in our tight-lipped criminal world, they can't help themselves. Thus, it has come to my attention that two longtime, loyal associates of your father and now you, Brendon Reilly and Corbin Monaghan, two longtime and loyal associates recently got word that there is a Grand Cayman bank account called FTC Holdings that was opened by the two of you. Evidently, over the last few years you have deposited several million dollars into this secret account. I don't know the exact amount but I'm certain you do. As you know, Reilly and Monaghan have been eager to wrest control of the organization and this information seems to put them one up on you. I must warn you that Dublin will be a dangerous place for you. As if that's not enough, someone who really doesn't like you has been talking to the white collar crime division of the Garda and they, too, are most anxious to chat with you. I know how resilient and clever you are. Perhaps, this might be a good time to build a closer alliance with your friends in Kiev. The Ukrainian syndicate seems more your kind of organization. Let's face it, your father's company, even though it is run by you, is getting a little long in the tooth. Please say hello to your mother., and remember her loving advice: Always say please and thank you.

Phineas Dermot Flanagan

When Danny finished reading, he put the letter back into the envelope and, after tapping it twice on his other hand, he transferred it to Tommy. He was expressionless. Tommy was amazed. Didn't he understand what he was reading?

Danny looked at his brother and broke out in a grim sort of smile. "Tommy, I read somewhere that Ukrainian Colleens are bleedin 'massive," he said with unexpected enthusiasm. "I mean like really beautiful."

Danny sat back and poked his brother. "Besides, I'm fecking tried of Dublin."

Chapter 29

"'Tis true; there's magic in the
web of it."

William Shakespeare

Magnus was hungry and his complaining stomach was largely responsible for his subsequent action. He glanced toward the buffet table that Duffy and The Redhead had laid out and realized it would remain unvisited until the end of the rehearsal. Deciding everybody had already experienced one exhausting performance, he wondered why they should have to wait another ninety minutes before the party begins.

In his booming voice, he got everyone's attention. "I don't know about you, but when you're peckish, one wine or beer in a tiny plastic glass doesn't satisfy. Now I've had a good look at the costumes and they look fabulous. I also know you have the play down pat. By the way, I want to thank Amelia and Berra," he said, pointing to the two women, "for outfitting everyone. That said, I am canceling tonight's rehearsal. Duffy and The Redhead, man your battle stations as the party has just begun."

A festive cheer went up from the cast and crew as they joined the others in the crush to get to the food and drink. Everyone was thrilled with the change of plan. Everyone, that is, except Ashley Porter who was dressed as a Forties-style Portia. She ran off stage and hurried to her sister who was just coming out of her office.

"Syl, can I borrow the car? I'll be back in less than half an hour and I won't eat in the car," she promised. She held up two empty hands. 'See, no food."

"Sure, the keys are on my desk. What's going on?" Sylvie asked.

"Magnus canceled the rehearsal and the party's underway," she replied, not sounding happy about it.

"That's cool. So why are you leaving?"

Ashley did a slow turn, inviting her sister to give her a close examination. "Syl, I look like Betty Crocker in this dress. It's fine for Portia on stage, but I am not about to socialize while wearing it. So I'm going home to change."

***

Maggie sneaked up on her husband and handed him a whiskey that Duffy had brought over from Bar OSA specially for him. She was having a Martini. "Magnus, what a wonderful idea. I'm not tired but I don't think i have the emotional stamina to sit around and watch an entire rehearsal."

Magnus agreed. "Come on, let's see what Duffy is serving."

Halfway to the table, they were stopped by Phyllis Hathaway, dressed in her black designer dress and trench-coat. "Excuse me, Magnus, might I have a word?"

Magnus told Maggie to go on ahead and make a plate for them. Turning toward the woman who for two years had been a bane to his existence, he decided to greet her with a compliment. "You are looking very Emma Peelish this evening."

She stiffened a bit, unsure whether he was complimenting her or insulting her. "Emma Peelish... Is this some Irish personality?"

He laughed. "No, no," he said. "I was referring to Emma Peel who was played by Diana RIgg, Remember The Avengers?"

Phyllis was delighted. She couldn't wait to get home and tell RJ, her husband. "Well, thank you, Magnus. It's the trench-coat."

"So what can I do for you, Mrs. Hathaway?"

"Oh please, it's Phyllis, with two L's and one S."

Magnus thought that was one hell of a first name, but he didn't comment. "So, Phyllis with two L's and one S..."

She made a scolding face. "It's Phyllis. I was just making sure that you knew the correct spelling should you ever correspond with me."

"I've made a mental note. Now you mentioned wanting a word."

"I did. Frankly, Magnus, and I'll be direct, the wake was for the most part... Well, there's no better word than boring. And what little conversation I had with others, that seems to be a general consensus."

Magus folded his arms and smiled at the woman he just said looked like Emma Peel. "Entertainment wasn't our goal, Phyllis. We were trying to save the life of a good friend and an actor in our company."

Shaking her head, Phyllis showed no interest in understanding. "That may be, but, I suppose because it worked, there was no drama. The two thugs looked more comical than menacing. And..."

Magnus put a hand up. "Phyllis, I'm surprised you're not as comforted by it as we are. Let me explain." He pointed to Phineas, disguised as Reggie Pennington, who was chatting up one of the female cast members. "Do you know who that is?"

Phyllis turned and looked at the stooped man in the splashy sport coat. "Yes, that's the man who is replacing Phineas in the play. I hate to say it, but he doesn't look like he has a lot of acting left in him."

"Do you remember him talking to Maggie, the two twins and me while the funeral home people closed the coffin and began taking it out of the theater?"

Phyllis was getting impatient. "Yes, I saw all of you."

"And did you see Phineas in the casket when it was opened?"

"Yes, I did," she said, beginning to sound snippy.

Magnus heard the snippiness and let her know he was coming to a conclusion. "Do you remember seeing Phineas? And do you remember what he was wearing?"

She smiled at the tall man and answered in an even tone. "Yes, I saw him and he was wearing... I don't know. Something dark, for sure. Probably a suit. That's what they bury men in. Actually, when my husband keels over, they'll probably put him in a golf shirt and a country club visor." She tittered at her own joke.

"Phyllis, I'm serious. First off, I am not telling you anything out of school here. Many of us already know that man standing over there flirting with Jeanine is not Reggie Pennington." He leaned in closer to the Emma Peel lookalike. "That, Mrs Hathaway, is Phineas Flanagan underneath all that professionally applied makeup," he told her. "The magic of it is..."

"Oh my God!" she exclaimed, putting her hands to her face. "How... I mean how could he be in the casket and also be standing there with you?" she asked, truly shocked at discovering the trickery. "I saw him!"

"I'm as surprised and confounded by it as you are. ' Magnus took a sip of his scotch and added drolly, "Now, do you think the wake was boring?"

Magnus left a stupefied Mrs. Hathaway and joined Maggie in the food line. Phyllis was more interested in heading home to tell RJ she looked like Diana Rigg.

"Magnus, my dear friend, do you have a moment?" It was Phineas, still acting as if he were Reggie Pennington.

"Reggie, I must eat," Magnus told him. "If you want to chat while I get something, fine."

"I wanted to tell you that I am delighted you called off the rehearsal. This body movement I gave Reggie is killing me. Look, I want to invite you and Maggie to my suite. Let's say in a hour. Rolando will be there. I have asked Samson and Sylvie to join us. Anyone else that's been close to all this?"

"I'd ask Ambrose because he will be there whether you invite him or not. He has this way of always just showing up."

"I'll do that. Now look, don't fill your plate. I plan to have plenty of food and drink. I'm sure you and the others have a lot of questions to ask me."

Magnus laughed loud enough to draw stares. Noticing, he lowered his voice. "Oh, I have many and I'm sure the others do. You may have to have extra beds brought up to your suite because it will be a long evening."

"Rather than a Q and A, I will just tell all," Reggie said, sounding more like Phineas.

"Samson's sister really did well by you."

"She did. And she'll be there to tell you all what she had to do to transform me."

"She must have worked very fast. What I don't understand is how you came to be Reggie while the casket was still in the theater."

"Easy peasy, old chap. I was never in the coffin."

Chapter 30

"Maybe I'll tan myself
in the Seychelles."

Phineas Flanagan

Magnus Flaherty and his wife, Maggie Leyton were the last to arrive at Reggie, nee Phineas 'suite at the Claremont Hotel. Aware that their host always had sumptuous food at the ready, the two were careful not to fill up at the theater. When they left the post-wake party, it was still going full steam and it appeared it would last as long as Duffy and The Redhead wanted it to.

Interestingly, everyone in the theater knew Phineas was now Reggie. What few conversations Magnus had with friends and cast members, he came to learn that most thought Reggie a temporary replacement for Phineas, and they looked forward to the return of the spry, witty Irishman and the disappearance of the limping, stooped Brit. Magnus had wondered why Phineas chose to portray Reggie in that manner as he had planned to remain Reggie til death do them part. It was then that Magnus realized he had a number of questions to ask their host.

"You're here. My favorite couple," Phineas shouted gaily, welcoming the two to his suite with a sweeping wave and blown kisses. The casually but expensively dressed man, who quickly moved aside to let them enter. had the erect posture, the cheery voice and the mischievous smile of Phineas Dermot Flanagan. What remained of Reggie was all on his face that had been magnificently redesigned by Pen, Samson Webb's sister and Hollywood makeup artist. She'd already warned Phineas it would take some doing to finally rid himself of the last vestiges of the highborn English gentleman and reformed money-launderer.

As soon as Magnus greeted his host, he brought up what had been puzzling him since he had left the theater. "All right, Phineas or Reggie, whoever the hell you are at the moment, I have a question. When you left, you informed me blithely that you were never in the casket. Then in typical Flanagan fashion, you left me hanging. So explain yourself."

His Dublin schoolmate put his hand on Magnus' shoulder. "My dear bearded boy, I promise a full accounting. That means I am first going to see that all of you have a drink in hand and food at the ready. Then, like Poirot, who after solving a baffling mystery assembles everybody in the drawing room, I will have my say. Now go on in and make yourself comfortable."

As they walked away, Phineas stopped Maggie. They stood alone "Maggie, my sweet, words can't convey how appreciative I am for all you've done to see that I remain among the living. While those two fools from Dublin look comical and dress funny, Tommy and Danny are true psychopaths. They are violent men who enjoy making people suffer, and they have killed before. Now I'm free of them and that's all because of you." Phineas leaned down and kissed her both her cheeks.

"Thank you, Phineas," she said with a hesitant smile. "But, like my husband, I have lots of questions and I expect answers."

"And I can tell from the funny way you move your mouth, you're slightly irritated with me," he pointed out. "I assure you your questions will be answered before you have to ask them."

Magnus and Maggie walked into the suite which was abuzz with activity. Four servers from the hotel restaurant where busy putting the finishing touches on an array of hors d'oeuvres and assorted small plates. A bartender in a wildly patterned bow tie was arranging a small bar near the food. Phineas had refused the offer from the young man to remain there to make drinks. Instead, he recruited Doctor Phil Seton who had mentioned he had paid his way through Harvard as a barkeep. He agreed if he could wear the young man's bow tie. An arrangement was made.

Once again, Samson and Sylvie laid claim to one end of the suite's lengthy sofa. Ambrose Dowling also made it his home as did the movie director's sister. "Excuse me, Mr. Webb and Ms Blanchard, but I'm not crowding you, am I?" the professor asked with a devilish wink.

Both had blushed. Samson became their spokesperson. "We just wanted to make sure there was plenty of room for you and Pen, Professor. We know how you like to spread out and so does my sister."

As soon as the servers left, Phineas 'guests wasted no time ordering cocktails and filling their plates. The doctor begged everyone to keep their drink orders simple as it had been some time since he had tended bar. Everyone complied except Sylvie who asked for a Cosmo. Seton admitted he didn't remember how to craft the drink that had had its day years earlier.

Ambrose stood at the improvised bar next to Sylvie. "Excuse me, Doctor, check to see if you have vodka, triple sec, a fresh lime, cranberry juice and an orange twist. If you do, I will talk you through the proper measurements," he said. Noticing the questioning stares coming from those around him, the octogenarian explained, "In her later years, Emily enjoyed Cosmopolitans. She hated the magazine but adored the cocktail."

Anxious to explain himself and his actions, Phineas waited while his guests enjoyed the treats he had laid out for them. He noticed they didn't appear to be too eager to have him take the floor as they were all busy tucking into the food and drink he had provided. Phineas was delighted to see all the smiles and occasional bursts of laughter. It's satisfying being a host, he thought, but, damn it all, I'm ready to perform. He laughed at himself, admitting grudgingly that for him It was all about performing. Even when he was working for the Conner mob, it was all about acting. If he had to wait, he decided to have a drink.

"Doctor, I am in need of a gin Martini, and please be generous with the vermouth," he requested.

"Odd that you should order that. I, too, appreciate an overdose," Seton declared. "I wonder where and when the dry phase began?"

"Don't ask that question too loudly or Ambrose there will give us a lengthy dissertation on the history of the Martini," Phineas joked. He took a sip and nodded his approval. Before he could enjoy another taste, he heard Magnus 'booming voice beckoning him to come front and center. It was finally his turn.

Magnus added, "And would you, please, let us know who will be taking the stage. Phineas Flanagan or Reggie Pennington."

With shoulders back, his head up and feeling like he was walking onto the stage of Carnegie Hall, Phineas did a quick dance step toward the middle of the room. What followed was a quick spin and a short bow. Not a drop of his Martini left the glass.

"Reggie Pennington would not have been able to made such an entrance," he told his guests. Phineas held his Martini high. "I toast you all. And I add my deepest thanks and appreciation for all you did to help me. Perhaps, what I ought to do is start from the beginning and tell you how we all came to be here celebrating life after pseudocide."

"I think you can start when you surprised us all by coming to Berkeley," Magnus suggested. "Leave our school days in the past."

"Aye, you just don't want me telling them how you beat up our classmate who went on to become Dublin's premier master criminal," he said. "By the way, if any of you have a question, feel free to interrupt me at any time. Or maybe it's best not to."

"So what brought me here?" he asked aloud and then paused, wondering how to start. He cleared his throat and began, "For many years, I handled the money for an Irish mob. I laundered it and I invested it. While that's all I did for them, I was as much a criminal as the thugs on the street. I don't know why I feel compelled to add this, but the Connors never dealt in sex trafficking or prostitution." He shrugged and looked at his guests. "That was important to me. Anyway, over the years, I had been taking a barely noticeable but healthy cut of the profits of the Dublin crime syndicate. The money which is now in the oodles-and-oodles category is tucked away in a couple of off-shore accounts in the Caymans. When Shamus Conner, the mob boss, the man Magnus beat up in school, died, his two sons took over. The twins are evil incarnate. These two violent, not very bright bullies allied with a gang from Ukraine who are even nastier pieces of work. The twins were increasingly difficult to work for so I began to think about how to free myself from a company that doesn't take kindly to anyone quitting or retiring. After learning there was a master forger in San Francisco, I decided to load myself up with all those legal documents one needs to both perish and exist. My aim was to disappear by simply trading me in for a new me. I decided to become a rakish Brit named Reggie Pennington. My plan was to become Reggie and dash off to the Seychelles and tan myself mahogany. Then who knows where. Thailand was also tempting."

"So we have been helping a gangster get out of trouble so he can sun his ass off in the Seychelles," Samson snorted. He quieted realizing he might have overreacted.

"My ass is the only part I would not tan, dear boy. However, as tempting as sunning in the Seychelles is, Samson, I passed on it as a future. I was about to say those plans changed and for the better."

"You had an epiphany," Ambrose guessed. "It happens quite a bit in your seventies."

Phineas laughed at the professor. "I don't know about that. I do know, though, that I came under the influence of a group of people who are quite unusual for so many reasons and all of them good."

Sylvie put her plate down and looked at Phineas. "If this is a story of redemption. I want credit because it all started with me. Do I count among the influencers?" she asked with a teasing smile.

"You most certainly do. Magnus is fortunate to have you running the theater." Phineas looked at the others. "What happened was, while in San Francisco, I read about Magnus and the Ashby-upon-Avon theater. We had grown up together in Dublin and as young adults acted in many stage plays. When I read about him, I immediately headed to Berkeley and the very first person to welcome me was that young lady. She sent me off to a bar where I not only reunited with my old mate but I met a rather extraordinary group of people. The professor here was kind enough to tell me the story of the Banter Foundation. After witnessing their fondness for one another and learning of their highly unusual charitable endeavors, I was convinced God must have had taken a huge aerosol can of altruism and sprayed it over them."

Maggie spoke up. "I know Magnus offered you the role of Antonio that afternoon. That meant you had to stick around here for three or more months. Weren't you concerned about staying in one place that long?"

"Not at the time, Maggie. I felt comfortable and safe because Danny and Tommy had no idea where I was, and I was confident they didn't know how I had been enriching myself."

"Now it seems you're giving some of it away," Maggie observed.

"Ah yes, those donations," Phineas sighed. "What a satisfying thing to do. As I said, I was inspired by the Banter Foundation's charity work," he answered. "There's one more sizable donation in the works and that's it, I'm afraid. I'll explain in a moment."

"So what happened to suddenly take such a drastic action like faking your death?" Phil Seton asked.

"Word had reached the twins that I was in Berkeley." he replied. "To make matters worse, they also learned of my secret Caribbean stash. Fortunately, their mother who detests them for cheating her out of her share of the Shamus estate, became my confidant. That I was also helping her financially put her solidly in my camp. So it was, I knew when they were arriving in the Bay Area. I figured I had better pack up and leave. Then Maggie suggested they kill me, host a wake, let the twins see me dead and Bob's your uncle."

"Who the heck is Bob? And what's he got to do with anything?" Sylvie asked, turning to Ambrose for an answer.

"It is often thought that the phrase came to be when an English prime minister named Robert Somebody, the Marquess of Salisbury, in the late 1800's, gave his nephew, Andrew Balfour, a high-ranking post in Ireland. Because of the obvious nepotism, he was nicknamed 'Bob's your uncle. 'It has come to mean 'and there you have it,'" the professor explained.

"How do you know weird things like *that?*" asked Samson, in awe of his spread of knowledge.

Magnus joined in. "Before Wikipedia, there was Ambrose Dowling."

Maggie put everybody back on track. "Phineas, you told Magnus you were never in the casket. But I saw you. My husband saw you."

"I think I saw you," Sylvie interjected, looking at Phineas.

Aha," Rolando exclaimed. "Now that is what I wanted to hear."

Chapter 31

"Good name in man
or woman, dear my lord,Is the
immediate
jewel of their souls."

From *Othello*

Rolando popped up like a manic Jack-in-the-Box that hadn't seen daylight for years. The magician had been sitting quietly, arms and legs crossed, listening attentively to Phineas 'tale. That is, until Sylvie's seemingly innocent utterance. He pointed to the young woman who seemed velcro-ed to Samson. "Thank you, Sylvie. That is what I wanted to hear. You said you didn't see Phineas. You *thought* you saw him."

Sylvie beamed. She didn't know what she had said that got such a rise out of the magician but she loved being the one who did. She sat back and grabbed Samson's hand to hold.

Magnus rubbed his beard, a habit he'd developed whenever he was addled. "You mean to tell me Phineas was never in the casket?" he asked Rolando suggesting he didn't believe his old friend when Phineas told him the same thing. "I saw him, Rolando, just like I see you standing there. We all saw him."

With a wider than usual smile, Rolando took a small bow. "Then, ladies and gentlemen, my job is done." Sitting back down, he continued, "Perhaps, I misspoke, though, when you first approached me. My apologies for that. I said I would make Phineas disappear, which probably meant to you that I would get him safely out of the casket and the theater without the twins knowing. That was a thought, of course, but after careful consideration, I decided an illusion would work best. It was just a matter of concocting a way of convincing all of you he was in the coffin. I seem to have accomplished that."

"So how in the blazes do you do something like that? Mass hypnosis?" Samson ventured.

Without speaking. Rolando gave him an indulgent smile and a shrug.

"That's a hell of an answer," Samson mumbled.

Phineas took the stage again. "While you were all thinking you saw me, I was right here being made over by Pen." he explained, pointing to the attractive woman sitting on the other side of Ambrose Dowling. "She turned me into Reggie and then I waited until I got a text from Rolando to come to the theater. I arrived early and that was worrisome, but it worked out fine in the end."

Ambrose turned to look at Samson's sister. "Is there a chance you can make me look like Gregory Peck?" he asked with a devilish wink. "I'd pay handsomely to look like that Cal alumnus."

"Professor, you already have matinee-idol looks," Pen said with an ingratiating smile.

Ambrose turned right to stare at the pretty woman seated on his left side. "Ms Blanchard, please, don't ask who Gregory Peck was," he pleaded.

Samson leaned forward to face him. "She won't, Ambrose. Mr. Peck was one of my all-time favorites and I told her all about him. The Pecks used to have dinner at our house, but I wasn't even an idea back then."

Maggie prodded Phineas to return to center stage. "When you came into the theater, shocking us all, by the way, you handed the twins an envelope. What was that all about?"

His answer was forthright. "During the week prior to the wake, I decided that I might as well play some offense while you so capably handled defense with the wake preparations. It didn't take me long to devise a plan. First, I called my contact at the bank who, for a hefty contribution to his retirement fund, transferred ownership of FTC Holdings to Tommy and Danny Conner and backdated it to when the account was opened. Than it was just a question of letting some senior members of the Conner gang and the Garda's white collar crime division know about it. There's still a considerable amount of money that the twins will have a very hard time explaining," he said with a grim laugh.

"And in the note you told them you'd done that?" Magnus asked.

Phineas laughed. "Good heavens, no. I acted as an informant, someone who just wanted to give them fair warning. I did suggest, though, that they might be better off in Kiev for awhile. I'm sure they're booking tickets as we speak."

Magnus had heard enough. For him, the story had been told. Putting on his director's hat, he had another question for their host who was seated across from him. "Phineas, it appears I have two actors competing for the role of Antonio. One is an escapee from a nursing home who can't stand for longer than one soliloquy and no doubt has already forgotten his lines and the other is this..."

Phineas reached across and put a hand on Magnus ' leg, interrupting him mid-sentence. "I think the words you're looking for are suave, charming, intelligent bloke who possesses a bitingly wry sense of humor."

"No, none of that came into my mind," Magnus said with a bemused look.

Phineas assumed a thinker's pose with finger to his lips. "Um, Ambrose, what's that phrase you coined for me when we were chatting at Bar OSA in what seems like years ago?"

Ambrose, who had sunk into the cushy sofa to the point of almost disappearing, somehow managed to work his way back into view. "I remember our conversation, Mr. Flanagan. It was about aging. You referred to us as fossils and I said, if that's the case, you are certainly a flamboyant one."

"That's it," he exclaimed. "A flamboyant fossil. Boastful and self-deprecating all in a single breath. Of course, it's not anything to put on a marquee."

"I wouldn't think of it," Magnus muttered.

Maggie, returning from the bar after topping off her drink, stopped where Phineas was seated. "Okay, one last question before we get serious about eating all your food and drinking you dry. Just who in the hell are you? Phineas Flanagan or Reggie Pennington."

Phineas rose from his chair. "That's an answer that I'd like everyone to hear. I am Phineas Flanagan and will be until my next wake which I hope is a long time off. That said, I fully intended to become Reggie but began wavering while Pen was applying my makeup. I remembered Iago's spin on names."

"Act 3, scene 3 from *Othello*," Magnus said. "My favorite line is 'who steals my purse, steals trash.' Obviously, Will hadn't asked Maggie about that."

Sylvie joined in. "Or me."

"Will you let me continue, please." There were mumbled apologies and then silence. "Thank you. Anyway, I won't bore you with the whole verse, especially because your purses are so valuable. It's the first sentence that struck me." He cleared his throat. 'Good name in man and woman, dear my lord, is the immediate jewel of their souls.'" Phineas looked around. "It stayed with me like an annoying ear worm. My resolve to create this new and, dare I say, more flamboyant person was now on shaky ground. Then the ground got even shakier the minute I walked into the theater and I spotted the twins and the departing casket. Instantly, I knew the Reggie I wanted to be would never fool the Connors. They'd spot me in a moment. That's when I decided to become a limping, feeble Reggie. It worked but it ruined any chance of my sticking with him as an identity. I suppose that's when I decided I was and will always be Phineas."

It was an answer that seemed to please everyone. Samson, though, had another inquiry. "If you put that off-shore account into the twins names, then all the money in it is theirs. How are you going to support yourself, besides asking me to give you a starring role in my next film?"

"Ah, if only," Phineas sighed. "Actually, Samson, I believe you'll appreciate my answer. When I worked in finance before being recruited by Shamus Conner, I had several other clients who were pure as the driven snow. The money I earned handling their finances, I invested wisely. I'm rather good at that sort of thing. The result is I have a tidy nest egg of money that is so clean you can eat off it."

Magnus, with effort, rose from his chair. "I propose a toast. That last metaphor proved Phineas is tiring. I think we all can pat ourselves on the back for a job well done. Maggie, the wake was one for the ages. It my wish that it's the last one I attend for a very long time. Rolando, a special thank you. You took your well-deserved break from Las Vegas, only to go to work for us."

"Nonsense, if Samson hadn't stopped by my parent's house, I'd be painting bedrooms, and helping my mom redesign her garden. It is I who thanks you." he said, raising his glass.

Maggie popped up. "Okay, it's done. I assume you are sticking around to play Antonio, so we'll have your company for awhile more." She cast him a suspicious eye. "By the way, you don't have any other mobsters who want to knock you off?"

Phineas 'laugh was hearty. "No, Maggie, none that I can think of." He walked toward the hotel phone. "I say, let's make this a real party," he said with gleeful enthusiasm. Pull out your phones and call ... Let me see. Sylvie, call Ashley and have her spread the word amongst the cast. You know the suite number. Magnus, alert Duffy and The Redhead. Oh, and that woman with all the plastic."

"You mean Phyllis Hathaway," Magnus told him.

"Yes, I love watching her try to smile." Phineas picked up the phone. "Dr. Seton, prepare to relinquish that horrible bow tie, we are going to need that young bartender to bring up and man a real bar. And I need more food."

Before he was able to dial, there was a solid knock on the suite's double doors. There were three rapid, loud raps. Phineas put down the phone.

"I'll get it," he told everyone.

Moving past the sofa and noticing the closeness of Samson and Sylvie, he leaned down and whispered, "Do you two want to use the bedroom?"

Sylvie blushed beet red but managed to laugh at his naughty suggestion.

Phineas did not bother to look through the peephole. Instead, with an exaggerated move, he swung open the two doors.

Standing there, unsmiling was Professor Kenneth Richter with one hand behind his back.

"So you are among the living?" he asked the vibrant but cosmetically made-up man in the doorway.

"I am indeed."

"Good, then you'll feel this."

And that's how Phineas Dermot Flanagan got his first black eye.

EPILOGUE

The *Merchant of Venice* was a hit. So much so, the play ran an additional three weeks. Everyone connected to the production knew one of the reasons for the success of the play was the man who played Antonio. Stories about the Flanagan wake began to spread like flu in the wintertime. Of course, every version was more colorfully exaggerated than the next. The result was everyone wanted to see this famous Irishman who, by faking his death, avoided a real one.

Realizing he would be around for awhile, Phineas moved out of the Claremont Hotel into a well-furnished garden cottage in the Berkeley Hills owned by a pot-smoking, elderly hippie named Geranium George. Berkeley and Phineas were a match made in heaven as both were quirky, free-wheeling and delightfully whacky. Phineas decided he might just stick around for a while. At some point it was a forced matter as he, unfortunately, had to add prime suspect to his curricula vitae.

Meantime, his niece, Quinn, went on a three-state, eight-city tour with her trusted cello with a promise to return to Berkeley. A dalliance with a Country/Western bass player named Hickory extended her stay in Seattle which also provided her with a rock solid alibi. Even so, upon return, she too was considered a suspect.

***

Samson Webb and Sylvie's touchy-feely relationship was put to the test in late April. While waiting to check out at the College Avenue Safeway, Sylvie, perusing the glossy magazines, spotted on one of the cheesiest. On the cover was a grainy photograph of a sheepish-looking Samson in a questionable pose with Chelsea Chalmers, an A-list movie star who played the popular action hero, Rubella Rogue. The headline read *Chelsea loses 40lbs on Director's Order.* Samson called Sylvie in a panic from Hollywood and told her the picture was photo-shopped and that he didn't even know Chalmers. He suspected her agent was trying to cover up the star's anorexia. They kissed and made up with a warning from Samson that social media hanky-panty was going to be part of their life. And, you guessed it, both would be branded as suspects.

***

Malcolm Midgely was, perhaps, the one who most missed the adrenaline-flow of the Flanagan wake. The owner and funeral director of *Going Up? A Midgely Funeral Home, Crematorium and Memorial Park* in Livermore had thoroughly enjoyed playing such an important part in the grand hoax. He was delighted to learn Phineas would remain Phineas which meant no laws were broken. Back in Livermore, Malcolm pined for the genial company of the Banter Foundation crew. But his pining would be short-lived as his services would once again be required, and this time for a real death, not pseudocide. Stay tuned.

ACKNOWLEGEMENTS

When I decided to take up writing novels after retiring from broadcasting, my wife, Mary Ann, not only encouraged this unusual hobby but quickly became a partner in the process of self-publishing a book. Her creative input is invaluable. She is someone who can spot a typo at ten paces. Most importantly, though, she has an artist's eye for designing an entertaining cover. She did it again with *The Flamboyant Fossil* and for that I thank her. She is truly my cover girl.

Bar OSA is a fictitious version of Cesar, a tapas bar we proudly call our local. Located on Shattuck Avenue in Berkeley, the popular bar has a number of regulars, some of whom have inspired various characters in the Banter series.

It would not be a proper acknowledgement without mentioning Doctor Phillip Chase, my daughter Amanda's father-in-law, neighbor and close friend. An avid book reader and a medical expert, his counsel was much appreciated.

Finally, an enormous thank you to Brother L. Raphael Patton, FSC, a retired professor of mathematics and astronomy at St. Mary's College in Moraga, California. Space does not allow me the opportunity to adequately describe this railroad-loving, Great Books-tutoring prankster. With the promise of a couple of Martinis, he agreed to proofread my manuscript. I quickly learned he could have also been a highly qualified English Lit professor if he chose to do so. More than just spotting the occasional split infinitive and scolding me for using genitive when it should be plural, Raf, as he is known to many, went the extra mile; supplying me with creative alternatives for dialogue and description. I am hugely grateful to him. God bless you, Raf.

ABOUT THE AUTHOR

Mike Cleary is a longtime Bay Area radio personality who is best known as being the Mike of *Frank and Mike in the Morning*. The highly rated radio show ran for many years on KNBR in San Francisco. In 2007, he was inducted into the Bay Area Radio Hall of Fame.

A proud neatnik, Mike has a fondness for colorful socks, pocket-squares, Martinis and memorizing Shakespeare. To date, no one, not even a family member, has asked him to recite any of the Bard's stuff which he committed to memory. He and his wife, Mary Ann, have retired from long-distance running and now enjoy long-distance walking. Their longest to date is a clockwise stroll around the island of Manhattan. They have no intention of doing it counter-clockwise.

Mike and Mary Ann are blessed with two daughters, two sons-in-law and four feisty grandsons. They reside in Piedmont, California.